THE MONSTER WITHIN

BAYONET BOOKS ANTHOLOGY BOOK 8

DECLAN FINN   J. R. HANDLEY   MICHAEL WALLEY

MATTHEW OLARANONT   ROBERT TILLSLEY

A.M. STEVENS   NICHOLAS WOODE-SMITH

NATHAN PEDDE   STEVE DIAMOND

Cover design by Jamie Glover

ISBN 978-1-960016-06-5

ALSO FROM BAYONET BOOKS

CONTENTS

THE PENDRAGON BROTHERS

J. R. HANDLEY

Eventually the kicked dog will bite back... and sometimes they'll rip your face off in the process. That's what happens when you push the Pendragon Brothers too far. They refuse to surrender to the abuse and go gently into that good night. If you're brave enough, follow this story of a family triumphing through life in The After!

INTRODUCTION

Years ago I was approached by the publishers of the tabletop RPG 'The After' to write a short story in their world. It was to go in an anthology and be published with the Kickstarter for their initial funding. For reasons I was never told that anthology fell through, but I'd already written my story.

When we started putting this anthology together, I knew I wanted to share this adventure with you. I approached the owners of the universe, Fainting Goat Games. This is the same publisher with whom I wrote the Blaster Bolts eZine with and they're good people. The owners of this world graciously allowed me to publish this story without requiring me to strip the IP out of this adventure.

The action is an exciting TTRPG about a post-apocalyptic world where humanity is struggling to exist in a world tainted with anomalies created by the aliens that invaded Earth. Two alien races fought over our land and the aftermath of the battle was devastating for humanity. In this world, the aliens are gone and now humanity is left to pick up the pieces. The After TTRPG products can be bought on DriveThru RPG and are put out by Fainting Goat Games. I highly recommend these and would love to game in this world myself.

You can find out more about this setting by following these links:

Core Rule Book: https://www.drivethrurpg.com/product/322958/Savage-Worlds-Adventure-Edition-The-After

Facebook Group: https://www.facebook.com/TheAfterRPG/

Kickstarter: https://www.kickstarter.com/projects/jongibbons/the-after-post-apocalyptic-action-for-savage-worlds

1

Outside Center for Aid and Comfort, Worland Clan Complex,
Bighorn Mountains

"Break it up!" shouted Elder Cisca as he dodged a wild blow from one of the young pugilists.

Swinging their arms wildly, none of the Pendragon Brothers stopped fighting.

"I'll stop when they do," Lucius Pendragon growled.

They'd suffered from years of systematic abuse, tortured by the children of the Council. Never-ending taunts about their supposedly incestuous parentage broke them down. Jokes about their perceived physical deformities fueled the fire burning inside them. They were intent on defending their family honor, driven to destroy those who spent a lifetime belittling them.

"Stop now, or I'll be forced to call for the enforcers," Elder Cisca snapped, angered at the lack of respect for his office.

Grunting in reply, Lucius grabbed the nearest spoiled Council brat and slammed his head into the cement wall. Before the body had completely slumped to the ground, he searched for his next target. Grabbing the nearest snarling brat, he could find, he punched him in the mouth. He heard the satisfying crunch as he knocked several of the kid's teeth out. Lucius whirled around when the crying boy dropped back onto his ass, looking for another target. The Pendragons were motivated; by rage fueled by their familial hatred for the Council of Twelve and their spoiled spawn. None were more motivated by their anger than Lucius. As the eldest, the burden of responsibility fell to him.

"Lucius, help!" screamed Craddock, his youngest brother.

Twisting around on the balls of his feet, Lucius scanned the impromptu arena looking for his younger brother. At only 17, he was already the mother and father of his younger brothers. The twins were only 12; they'd still been in diapers when his parents were killed. He'd only been ten years old when the crops had failed, and his parents had been culled. They'd been unwanted, not worthy of the resources they'd consumed. Then, stripped naked, they'd been driven out of their subterranean cavern sanctuary, left to fend for themselves in the afterlife above.

"All enforcers in the vicinity of Level 20 report to the Center for Aid and Welfare. Low-born riots, Council member in danger," Elder Cisca shouted into the wall-mounted intercom system, trying to be understood over the noise from the crowd.

Lucian heard the Elder calling for help but was too lost in his rage to quit fighting. Whenever his energy waned, he thought of his parent's final moments. *They claimed that they weren't without mercy*, he thought *because they generously allowed the walking dead a few moments to say their final goodbyes*.

"Council scum!" he screamed as he grabbed one of the boys lurching towards Oberon, his brother.

Roaring incoherently, Lucius repeatedly slammed the boy's head into the wall until all that remained was a pulpy mess. Crying, he continued fighting whichever thug had managed to push their way through the scrum to get within arm's reach. As he fought, his mind wandered back to the day he'd become an orphan.

After receiving their death sentence, his parents quietly hugged him. Even as a kid, he could see that they were trying to be brave. His dad had leaned in and whispered into his ear, begging him to look after his younger brothers. Lucius tried to respond but choked on his tears, only managing to mumble incoherently. In an instant, he'd become the head of his family. He had to protect four unwanted children from the reality of life in the hierarchical Worland Clan. In the span of seconds, he'd become responsible for the last of the Pendragon Clan; Oberon, Gareth, and Craddock.

His musings were interrupted by an enforcer tackling him to the ground. He rolled aside, avoiding having the brute land on him, and quickly regained his footing. Panting, he struggled against the feelings of hunger and exhaustion. Before he could regain his footing, one of the Cox boys slammed him against the mass of bodies struggling to reach him and his brothers.

"Low-born trash," the faceless boy bellowed as he repeatedly punched him in the gut.

Lucius welcomed the pain, the reminder that he hadn't succumbed to death, and abandoned his siblings. It focused his memories on those final moments he'd had with his parents and the damnation that had followed. Not even a day had passed after the culling before putting him to work, frog-marched, along with his siblings, to the grow houses beside the underground lake. He'd been tasked with tending the crops and working the algae farms. The Council had piously told them that Pistol Pete wanted them to atone for the sins of their parents. They'd have to work to earn their grace, to fight for the right to rejoin the clan.

Lucius and his brothers had toiled in those dark recesses of the Worland caves for a year before they'd been allowed to rejoin the other low-born citizens. They'd managed to double the yield of their assigned greenhouses, earning them time off of their banishment. As they were leaving the farm, more kids from the latest cull took their place, fulfilling the Worland circle of life. Lucius pitied them, but he had his own family to worry about.

Seconds after they rejoined their fellow Worland citizens, the abuse started. They took the taunts, jeers, and punches from the other children. Survival instincts forced them to endure. The worst came from the Council's progeny; the children of the sitting Council members went out of their way to torment the low-born and anyone who carried the stink of time as an unwanted. They seemed to take special joy in targeting the twins, Gareth and Craddock, his youngest brothers. That couldn't stand, not while Lucius still had a breath left in his body. Every time the Council spawn picked on the 12-year-old boys, Oberon and Lucius waded in. As the oldest two, they had to protect their family.

The indignities never ended; even the food his brothers ate required groveling. As the head of the remaining Pendragon children, he'd had to report to the Council weekly for charity scraps, enduring the comments from their spoiled children. He knew the charity wouldn't last forever, nor was it enough to sustain his family. Survival forced him to explore deep into the cave system that housed the Worland Clan; he searched tunnels long abandoned, looking for anything to help support his family.

Exploration paid off; Lucius had found exits into the world above. Instead of death, he'd seen so much more. He'd found a truth the Council hid from them. Trips into the open air had scared him; his psyche was weighed down by years of indoctrination. At first, he was convinced that he'd be entering the afterlife. But, digging deep into himself, he pressed on. His family needed him, so he'd quietly explored outward from the various concealed exits into the Above. Where he discovered a strange world that shimmered and flowed around him. A world of treasure he could trade for food.

Fate required payment for her bounty; his latest trip had taught him that painful life lesson. Everything had been… different after that sojourn into the Breach. He'd slipped and fallen into a flowing stream, sputtering and choking on the thick water--emerging with strange aches and pains all over his body. He'd wandered around for miles, repeatedly circling the hatch into the Worland cave system. He'd walked for hours before realizing he was already where he needed to be.

Tears flowed down his cheeks as the head pain intensified. It was the worst feeling he'd ever experienced, but he managed to reach his quarters and pass out on his bunk. Lucius couldn't move for several days after exiting the afterlife, not even to attend to the daily necessities of life. When he'd regained consciousness, his brother whispered that someone was following him. Shortly after that trip, the tail became bolder; someone trailed him wherever he went. The man wasn't uniformed, but it was clear he was one of the enforces for the high-born and the Council. He hadn't been able to venture out after that, not while the Council was looking for a reason to cull his family.

He wasn't concerned about that; he knew he'd be exiled soon. He was merely trying to buy his siblings more time, to give them a few more precious breaths of air. He'd known in his gut the minute his family had been declared one of the unwanted that exile was coming. No family ever truly recovered from that stain. That fact helped the Council maintain order. None of the low-borns wanted to do anything that would drop them to the unwanted status; it was a death sentence. Every single unwanted was eventually exiled, left to die in the irradiated world above them. But only after the Council and the citizens of the Worland Clan worked them on the farms.

"Least they let us reach our majority first," he muttered, before a blow to his flank reminded him that there was a brawl to win.

Cursing bitterly, Lucius felt his rage grow. Whenever he thought of his family, the anger burned with a white-hot intensity. With a joyful growl, he punched the boy in front of him. He'd hit Spencer harder than he'd intended, knocking the boy onto his pudgy ass. Somehow his action had allowed him to see into the boy's mind. Spencer was in shock. Stunned, he stuttered while holding his hands over his bleeding nose. He kept pulling his hands back to stare at the dull blood gushing from his crushed nose, shocked by the hit.

"My da's the Senior Elder! He'll exile you for sure," Spencer whined.

"Step back from the boy," Elder Cisca bellowed.

The old man's shout brought Lucius a moment of rapture and returned him to the fight in front of him. He felt a burning sensation in his head as his rage took over. He'd been born different; at least, that's what they'd always told him. He knew that wasn't true, it was the above that had changed him. The Elders said it was because he'd been born to an intra-familial coupling. Lucius knew that some higher power was punishing him. The change was recent, though he hadn't figured it out yet. He'd tried to keep his new abilities to himself, afraid that he'd give the Council a reason to kick his family from the only home they'd ever known.

I can't be one of the Changed, they'd exile my brothers too, he told himself. He didn't know who he was praying too, he'd long since given up praying to Pistol Pete. He wasn't sure that the icon the Worland Clan prayed to was even a god; he'd never answered the prayers of his family.

"I said break it up!" shouted Elder Cisca again, this time restraining the twins, but leaving their opponents free to continue assaulting them.

"They started it!" screamed Craddock Pendragon.

"I demand satisfaction!" Oberon Pendragon said through gritted teeth.

"Low-borns have no honor," Cisca snapped. "You'll get no satisfaction here."

The arrival of the Enforcers punctuated his words. The burly men surrounded the older brothers, restraining them too.

"I do have honor," screamed Oberon, spittle flying from his lips as he kicked at the legs of the man restraining him.

"You don't even have a daddy," chortled one of the Council spawn.

"Pistol Pete is our real dad," Craddock said, his prepubescent voice crackling under stress.

That declaration set off a new round of laughter and heckling from the spoiled children of the Council. They surrounded the brothers, battle lust upon them, a pack of wolves braying for blood. Even the stodgy Elder Cisca smirked tauntingly behind his scruffy greying beard, feeding the mob's appetite to dish out pain. The taunts continued, building into a crescendo as more high-born children became emboldened and enlisted into the mob. They punched and kicked the restrained Pendragon Brothers, until Lucius couldn't take it anymore.

"Enough!" he yelled.

The fighting continued, egged on by the cheering crowd. The feral mob hooted and hollered while they mercilessly beat the restrained brothers. The stoic response of his captive brothers enraged the throng of pampered kids, driving their lust for violence to ever higher levels. Soon, even the brutish arms of the enforcers couldn't support them, and one by one the Pendragon Brothers slipped into unconsciousness.

"Arghhh!"

Cobalt flames shot from Lucius's open mouth, following his scream of rage and anguish. The flames nimbly danced through the crowd, targeting the enforcers. Several uniformed brutes caught fire, creating panic among the onlookers. The bravest among the crowd continued kicking his unconscious brother; their war cries spewing forth from mouths foaming with their impotent rage. Wading into their midst, he shoved those boys into the unforgiving stone walls of the tunnel.

Every moment in his life had led Lucius to the struggle at hand, his mind snapping with a deafening pop. Years of abuse and neglect, the oppressive responsibilities forced upon his young shoulders, it was suddenly too much.

"I said enough!"

Lucius's voice boomed again, echoing outward from every pore of his body. The flames suddenly extinguished as his yell bounced down the cavernous main tunnel. What was once the passageway that separated the haves from the have-nots was now a scene of carnage. Moaning enforcers lay smoldering on the stone pavers, their pitiful cries fading to a whimper as the spark of life extinguished. He watched all of it, his mind linked to the flow of energy around them. He felt all of it but couldn't muster an ounce of remorse for the men who'd so brutally enforced the will of the Council.

Thoughts of the governing body of the Worland Clan brought violent memories to the surface of his mind. Sparks crackled along his arms as his eyes began to glow, a brilliant purple color illuminating the normally dim caverns. Relief carvings long hidden from view became apparent, paintings and carvings all that remained of a long-dead society. Lucius took it all in before pointing his finger at the wall and obliterating it with a ray of light that melted the rock-face etchings.

All around him, the children of the Council began to shield their eyes, sheer terror halting their assault. Lucius could still feel Spencer's shock, the boy's terror soothing the rage bubbling under the surface of his consciousness. Diving into the boy's mind, Lucius imagined gripping it with both hands and ripping it in two. He watched the scene in his mind as he triumphantly held the two bloody halves up, a taunt aimed at his vanquished foe.

Suddenly Lucius's connection to Spencer was cut, leaving a void that he tried to fill with himself. *He doesn't wanna play anymore? Stupid brat!* Looking down, he saw the boy's body briefly twitch at his feet. Watching with rapt fascination, he saw the spark of life gradually dim before vanishing forever.

"Serves him right," he muttered.

Undeterred by the dead body, Lucius focused on the emotions rolling off the surviving children of the Council. After so many years of abuse from the huddled brats, he wanted vengeance. He tried advancing, but someone had him in a bear hug. Cursing, he shrugged off the grip of the enforcer who'd managed to come up behind him as he continued struggling towards the brats who'd tormented his family.

The second Lucius became aware that the man had grabbed him, a distortion wave shot out from his spine, ripping the man in two. The enforcer's shredded body dropped to the stone floor, blood pooling around his twitching carcass. Lucius ignored it all; his focus narrowed to one simple objective; obliterate his bullies.

"Vengeance belongs to Pistol Pete, the Great Protector," Lucius said grimly.

Advancing, his mind narrowed its focus to the tormentors in front of him. Flaming corpses sputtered out, plunging the cavernous tunnel into darkness. Light shone from his eyes, standing out in the oppressive gloom of the newly darkened battlefield.

Stopping in front of the kids, Lucius projected his voice outward. It boomed from his throat with more force than human biology allowed. Blood began streaming from the kid's orifices as he spoke.

"I am vengeance personified. I am Pistol Pete. I've judged you unworthy… of being unwanted. Let the culling begin!"

Lucius's final proclamation scared the tormentors; he felt their emotions, all of them. He could feel them collectively and individually; it felt good. He lost himself in the feeling, pouring more of himself into the Other, the place where he drew his newly discovered godhood. It felt good like he was floating detached from his body, staring down at the mere mortals below. He could see the world around his physical body, while simultaneously watching it from above.

Daddy should've killed them all when they had the chance.

"You first," Lucius whispered as he pointed his finger at Councilman Byler's son.

Bolts of neon light shot from his outstretched hand, dazzling color amid the dim tunnel. Weaponized, the unearthly light shone outward from his finger. The energy moved toward the whining kid, energy sizzling from the tightly focused beam of energy, pausing momentarily before punching through the Byler boy's skull. There was an audible splattering sound as the sizzling remnants of grey matter covered the other children of the Council huddled around the spasming body.

He can't treat us like low-born bastards.

"I hear you, Glenn Berger," Lucius said grimly, projecting his thoughts into the boy's mind.

The boy's color drained from his already pale face as Lucius sent waves of terror into the quivering mind. The fear increased, but he wasn't satisfied; he pushed more energy behind the emotions. He kept pushing more power into the mind until the kid's heart couldn't take the strain and exploded inside his chest. Turning to another huddling kid, he pried into the boy's mind.

The enforcers are going to make him pay for this.

"I am the enforcer now, Spencer. Go tell your bastard father that his Council has no authority here."

Neither party moved as Spencer Cox stared dumbfoundedly at the brilliant light emitting from Lucius's orifices. Lucius's light turned Spencer's broken nose into a ghastly sight. The blood had dried, but the crinkled mess that had once been his dignified nose stood out. Smiling, he twitched his fingers and broke Spencer's nose in another spot. Laughing contemptuously, Lucius gestured toward the tunnel leading to the upper classes' housing quarter. Spencer still didn't move.

"Go!" Lucius shouted as he projected a strong desire to flee.

Spencer began mumbling incoherently as he scrambled away from his huddled peers. When he was nearly out of sight, Lucius turned toward the remaining bullies and smirked at them.

"Time to enforce the Sacrament of Equality," Lucius said. "I speak for Pistol Pete, and he's not happy with you bullying brats."

Waving his arms, Lucius became the conductor of his own private symphony. He danced around the crowd, waves of energy crackling and radiating from every pore of his body as he lost himself to the feeling of righteous fury. When he couldn't take the pressure anymore, he raised his arms and brought them down dramatically. At once, a forceful wave of energy exploded outwards.

Boom!

The universe was born anew. A concussive wave reverberated from Lucius, his godlike powers making him the Great Creator.

"I am Pistol Pete, bow down before your god," he intoned.

There was nobody left alive to respond to his proclamation. What was once the children of the Council was now a pulverized mass of gore. Individual bodies were indistinguishable, invigorating Lucius's feeling of righteous fury. Thoughts of the dead rolled off his back, their silenced lamentations energizing him. Whirling on the balls of his feet, he looked for more perpetrators to punish. Nobody moved, not even his brothers.

"Craddock?" Lucius called out. "Gareth? Oberon?"

There was only silence.

Diving downwards, Lucius desperately returned to his body. He wanted to reunite with himself, to become whole enough to save his brothers.

"Arghhh!" he groaned.

A wall of pain waited for him the second he returned to himself. It was too much for Lucius, settling on him like a thick fog until darkness dragged him down into unconsciousness.

2

Two Months Later, Council Meeting Room Worland Clan Complex, Bighorn Mountains

G *ong.*

The sound echoed throughout the cave system that housed the Worland Clan. It was the first sound Lucius heard as he woke up from his long sleep, strapped to a table and locked inside a metal cage. He tried turning his head, but restraints prevented any movement. Instead, his entire world centered on the cracks in the stone ceiling. He heard the repetitive dripping of the moisture that accumulated everywhere.

Drip, drip, drip.

The sound slowly lulled him back into complacency as his eyes drifted slowly shut. He focused on the smell of the mold and dust that permeated the entire cave complex. He heard a distant murmur from behind him, voices indistinct from one another, blending into perfect harmony. He envisioned them singing him lullabies like his mom had before the culling.

"Lucius, where are we?" Oberon asked, his pubescent voice cracking under the emotional strain.

"It'll be okay, we'll be okay," Lucius assured him, startled at the interruption.

Re-grounded in the moment, he heard his younger brothers start whimpering at the sound of his voice. Before he could answer the twins, a booming voice came over the speakers.

"Silence!" intoned Senior Elder Cox.

A dizzying rush followed the command as the table quickly flipped upwards. The old gurney groaned and creaked, unused to the weight of a full-grown male. It finally thudded to a stop when his prone body was fully upright, facing the front of the room. Looking around, his eyes scanned the room for any information he could glean while restrained. The sight of the massive stone desk in front of him brought back a wave of memories. He was in the Council Courtroom, the place where they'd sentenced his parents to die.

Movement on the periphery of his senses told him that Senior Elder Cox would soon be joined by the other members of the Council. Their silent processional into the room was unnerving. Slowly they advanced up to the dais and into his field of vision. One by one, they took their seats and stared straight ahead. Nobody spoke, but their eyes drilled holes into his soul. They knew he'd killed their sons.

"Let my brothers go," Lucius demanded.

None of the Council responded to his grim demand. All of them stared at him, until he couldn't stand their silence any longer.

"Let my brothers go," he said again.

"Soon enough," snapped Councilman Cross.

"Help us," Craddock called to his brother.

"Silence!" the senior elder roared.

Frustrated, Lucius tried to reach inside of himself again, but nothing happened. He couldn't figure out how he'd managed to use the power before, and now he was left to face the consequences without the ability to protect himself. Cursing to himself, he stared straight ahead as he struggled to calm himself. *I won't bring shame upon my family*, he repeated. The mantra gave him strength, an inner resolve to bear what was to come.

Crack.

The makeshift gavel slammed onto the table with an ominous finality. The official court hearing was in order. There wasn't any doubt in Lucius's mind that the Elders of the Council had reached a decision before entering the room. He was no stranger to these ritualistic meetings; they always ended badly for somebody. *And I'm not just somebody. Somehow, I killed their sons, I'll be lucky if they just banish to the land above.*

After saying a quick prayer to whatever higher power was out there, he bit his lip and stared impassively ahead.

"You may begin," Lucius said. "You've my permission to end your show trial."

"Lucius Tiberius Pendragon, you stand accused of 15 counts of capital murder of prominent citizens of the Worland Clan," said Senior Elder Cox.

"They attacked us!" screamed Gareth Pendragon.

"Silence!" bellowed a nearby enforcer.

Lucius watched with grim satisfaction as the burly man seemed to fear him and his younger brothers.

"Further, you killed 29 enforcers who swore an oath to carry out the lawful orders of the Council. You demonstrated mutant powers incompatible with life, as laid out by Our Father, the Great Pistol Pete. How do you plead?" intoned Senior Elder Cox.

"We acted in self-defense against the malicious behavior of your devil spawn. Your families have terrorized the lower-class citizens of this clan long enough!" Lucius shouted.

We're not gonna walk away from this in one piece anyway, he reasoned.

"How do you plead?" Senior Elder Cox asked again.

"Not guilty," Lucius replied.

"You deny that two months ago, you entered into the passageway outside the Center for Aid and Welfare and murdered your betters?" Cox asked incredulously.

"He said it was self-defense!" Oberon snapped.

"Wait, two months?" asked Lucius.

"You were in some sort of mutant-induced coma. We waited for you to resume consciousness before we started the Pendragon culling. After considering your plea, given the needs of the subjects of the Worland Clan, we sentence your family to death," Cox said as he slammed his gavel onto the table.

Turning to his left, Cox spoke to the enforcer. "Escort them to their ultimate demise."

Stealing his heart, Lucius ignored his brother's tears. He'd need to be strong if they were to live in the land above. He'd entered the crazy afterlife for valuables, but he knew there were patches of normal space further from the exits. The Council was either lying to the people or was unaware of what existed outside their fiefdom.

And I know how to get back into the clan caves, he thought. *I can raid food if I need to.*

"Unchain me, we'll exit your slave pens without further incident," Lucius said.

The enforcers ignored him, flipping him back to the prone position and pushing the wheeled gurney toward the elevator. The other unwanted kids called it their death box, telling grand tales about what happened inside. He knew better; the culling's were just the Council's way of ensuring that the Clan never grew so large it couldn't support itself. Were it not for the tyrannical social hierarchy he could've rationalized the official position. The low-born had spent years arguing for a lottery system, one that was impartial and fair. Such proposals were only whispered, lest the speaker be culled.

The journey to the elevator was excruciating, the rapid movement down the corridors making Lucius dizzy. Closing his eyes, he started internally steeling himself for what was to come. His brothers would need him if they were going to come out alive. As if on cue, he heard his brothers talking to each other.

"We'll be okay," Oberon reassured his younger brothers.

"Listen to Obbie," Lucius told the twins. "We'll be okay, you'll see."

"Okay? Sure ya will, until the beasties get you," snorted the enforcer, escorting them to the top.

"Ignore him," Lucius said before the enforcer clubbed him in the head, and the world went dark.

3

Outside Bunker Complex Entryway Worland Clan Complex,
Bighorn Mountains

"Wake up," Craddock begged, jostling his shoulder.

Lucius groaned, blinking his eyes rapidly in the brilliant afternoon sun. His brother's shaking had brought him back to reality just in time to see a strange beast charging them. Lifting his hands, he shot a wave of raw telekinetic energy at the beast rampaging toward him and his brothers. The power crackled off of his arm, momentarily stunning his nearby brothers.

Pushing himself onto his side, Lucius rolled into a seated position and stared around, confused. He'd never ventured out of their caves during daylight hours; the brightness hurt his eyes, and he had to lift his hand to shield them so he could see his surroundings. The creature that had charged them had strange leathery skin, the neon green color standing in stark contrast to the gray slate rock of the Bighorn Mountains.

"You can't camouflage when your skin is so bright," he mumbled. "This makes no sense; there was nothing like it in Mom's books."

However, the massive wings that extended from its back stood out most about the creature. *I hope that the creature can't fly, or we're screwed.* Mentally pushing that thought away, Lucius stared off at the twitching remains of the strange beast. One massive head extended from the animal's neck, accented by enormous tusks and razor-sharp teeth.

"Holy Pistol Pete," Lucius breathed, "that thing could eat us for dinner."

"I think it feeds off those sent away for the culling," Oberon said.

"What makes you think that?" Lucius asked.

"A lot of skeletons are piled near the mouth of the cave. So we've probably been feeding the thing for years."

Grunting, he stood and took stock of their situation. They'd been abandoned at the mouth of an old mineshaft that led into the hidden bunker complex that the Worland Clan called home. As was their custom, they'd been left naked, with none of the supplies necessary to sustain life. *We'll have to get supplies first,* he thought as he fought off the pain from unleashing the power within him. It was overwhelming, though it wasn't as bad as last time. He just wished he could figure out how to control it; at least the pain was manageable, barely.

"We need to find the secondary entrances into Worland City," he told Oberon, who'd come up to stand beside him.

"Where are they?" Oberon asked.

"Craddock, Gareth, follow us," he ordered as he gestured to Oberon.

Lucius started walking down paths he'd traveled many times before, trusting his brothers to join him. He could still hear the twins sniveling, but they'd quit crying after a few dozen steps. The wailing grated on his nerves; he was glad they hadn't continued making those noises.

"We'll need to learn to move quietly," Lucius instructed his brothers. "Some of the afterlife creatures hunt by sound alone."

His brothers didn't answer, but their silence told him they understood. Looking over his shoulder, he saw that Oberon had taken a position at the rear of their familial formation. The teenager instinctively took a protective position, ensuring the twins didn't become separated. Smiling, Lucius nodded. *That'll do*, he thought.

They continued to advance along a narrow trail that inclined its way higher into the mountains. They couldn't tell how much time had passed, but it felt like they had been walking forever when the rain started. It burned their skin, and Lucius had to fight the urge to vocalize his pain.

"We're almost there," he whispered.

"Can we sleep inside, attack this after we've rested and eaten?" Oberon asked quietly.

"Yes, we'll leave at just before daybreak tomorrow. We can acclimate to our lives above ground, free from the Council," Lucius answered.

"We're hungry," Gareth whined at a whisper.

"We'll eat inside," Oberon responded before Lucius could.

They followed the trail around for several minutes before he stopped suddenly. Slipping on the loose rock, he struggled to maintain his footing on the rain-slicked ground.

"The hatch is just around the bend," he whispered.

"What do you want us to do?" Oberon asked.

"Wait here, I'll make sure there are no guards and the hatch still works," Lucius replied.

"Let me go with you," Oberon demanded.

"No. Who'd watch the twins?" Lucius answered.

Frowning, Oberon nodded his agreement and stood by the twins to wait. Then, turning away from his family, Lucius slowly crept along the path until his brothers were out of sight. He continued for several more meters until he saw the rusted hatch that opened into the blocky cement structure. Chiseled deep into the grey slate of the mountain was a small hand-carved cave a few meters deep. It had the twisted remains of barbed metal strips desperately clinging to rusted and grumbling metal poles.

Staring intently, Lucius tried to see anything inside the dim shadowy cave. He knew there were several dips in the floor, the result of some long-dead soldier trying to use explosives to breach the facility. Narrow cement guard stations flanked the entryway. He couldn't make out much, but there didn't appear to be any movement. The enforcers hadn't manned the entrance. *I'll have to risk it,* he told himself as he advanced at a crouch.

Hiss.

Stopping dead in his tracks, Lucius stared in horror at the nest of snakes in front of him. There were dozens of them, slithering around in the dip just in front of the cave he needed to enter. Staring in revulsion, afraid to move from his crouched position, he prayed for answers. The positioning took its toll on his knees, and his knees gave; he thudded into a kneeling position on the muddy path. An ominous rattling sound was his reply from the snakes in front of him. Trying not to move, not to breathe, he watched in horror as several of the dual-headed monstrosities slithered toward him.

Paralyzed with fear, he wasn't sure what to do. The dual-headed rattling snakes had no such indecisive nature; the pit vipers lunged toward him. His whole body tensed as he prepared to be bitten by the mutated snakes. Except the bite never came, the snakes slammed into an invisible wall that protected him. Unsure of what happened, Lucius imagined shoving the snakes out of the way and watched as they were pushed away from him.

"Thank you, Pistol Pete," he said reverently.

He wasn't sure what made his newfound powers work, he only seemed to be able to access them in moments of extreme distress. Lucius didn't have time to think about the topic, however. He was just glad that the snakes were dead. The rattling devils were obliterated, their twitching bodies littering the pathway to access the bunker he needed to enter.

Pointing his arms at them, he tried verbalizing orders at them. "Move."

Nothing happened.

This time Lucius simultaneously pushed outward with his mind while repeating the instructions. "Move."

It worked. Snakes flew away from him, thrown down the mountain. With the path clear, Lucius advanced toward the bunker entrance. Reaching out, he began spinning the hatch's access wheel. He'd used this entrance often enough that the wheel barely made a sound as he quickly spun it counterclockwise. When the wheel stopped turning, he pulled the door open.

"Anyone inside already knows I'm here," he muttered.

Unlike the last time, he'd come this way; the secondary hatch was closed. He was stuck in a narrow corridor between the two doors.

"What now, Pete?" he asked himself.

Nobody answered, not that he expected one. Stepping to the next door, he quickly opened the hatch and prepared for the worst. When he'd unsealed the door, he pulled it open and stepped inside, prepared for an ambush that never came. Lucius waited for his eyes to adjust to the dim lighting and prayed that he was alone. Pistol Pete answered his prayers; the first room was empty. A faded sign bearing a strange welcome caught his attention. He'd never entered this room during daylight hours, limiting his observational ability.

"Ming Survival Com," he said, reading the sign out loud. "What does that even mean?"

Turning in a circle, he saw a massive table with several strange boxes with one side of the cube missing. There was a lot of strange equipment whose use was lost to the ages, so he continued skimming the room. It was the rest of the room that surprised him; there were supplies stacked in the room. Someone had moved into the entryway to this bunker since he'd last used this entrance to the Worland Clan caves.

"You're not supposed to be here," whispered a voice behind him.

Whirling, Lucius moved just in time to avoid the knife that had been aimed at his back. He didn't get away unscathed, the blade glanced off his upper arm, drawing blood. He tried to call up the powers he'd used so rampantly but couldn't cut through the fog of pain to summon his godlike abilities. Blood trickled down his arm, seeming to coagulate with unnatural speed.

"We don't mean you any harm," Lucius said, trying to smooth out the rough spots of tone.

"We?" the pale man shrieked, spinning in a wild circle with his blade in front of him.

Taking advantage of the opportunity, Lucius stepped in close to the man and wrapped his arm around his throat. With his left forearm around the man's throat, he hooked his other around the back of his head for leverage. Once Lucius was in position, his left palm grabbed his right arm's bicep and applied pressure. It didn't stop the man; he started thrashing around and trying to break free from Lucius's grip.

When he couldn't shake Lucius's hold, the man swung his arms wildly. He waved his knife about, trying to slash him. Lucius easily dodged those while tightening his grip. As he squeezed his arms, the man dropped his knife and grabbed Lucius' arms in a desperate bid to free himself. His efforts were for naught, though he continued thrashing around and making strange grunting, gurgling noises.

The open hatches into the bunker complex provided enough light for Lucius to see the man's face. It reflected off of one of the pools of standing water that sat on the concrete floor of the bunker. The man was turning a purple hue that got darker the longer Lucius applied pressure. When the man stopped thrashing, he tightened his grip and started counting in his head. After he reached as high as he could count, Lucius felt confident that the man was out of the fight and lowered him to the ground.

Turning, Lucius looked for the man's knife and, walking over to it, he picked it up.

"You won't be needing this," he vocally reminded himself.

Scanning the room, he saw a pile of filthy clothes and walked over to it. The smell was almost unbearable, but Lucius forced himself not to think about it. Shuffling through the pile, he found something that looked like it would fit and shimmied into them. Once he was clothed, he also looked for stuff for his siblings and set that aside as well. With that taken care of, he grabbed an unusable shirt and cut it into strips with his captured knife.

With the strands of cloth in his hands, he knelt and set the knife on the ground at his feet. He began braiding the strips from the shirt into rope, trying to find something to restrain the unconscious man.

When the stranger started gurgling, Lucius ignored it but silently picked up the knife and balanced it on his knee as he continued turning the cloth into rope.

He didn't become worried until the gurgling stopped. Turning his head, Lucius saw the stranger rushing towards him with a piece of wood from a fire pit he'd missed behind the access hatch. The enemy was almost upon him. Gripping the leather knife handle, Lucius turned his body and brought the knife upward. He dodged just in time to avoid the board; the man swung; it flew right over his head, barely missing him. As he dodged, Lucius brought up the knife and stabbed the man in his groin.

The man's scream was almost instantaneous, but Lucius wasn't done. He yanked back on the knife, twisting it as he withdrew the blade. Growling, he repeatedly stabbed him in the gut until the handle was too slick for him to maintain his grip. The screaming continued, gradually fading in intensity. The volume proportionally aligned with the amount of blood that spurted from his wounds.

"You didn't have to die," Lucius whispered as he crawled forward to check for a pulse.

There wasn't one, so he closed the man's eyes. Reaching behind him, Lucius grabbed one of the rags, wrapped it around the knife handle, and pulled. Then, with his weapon free, he stood and made a quick sweep around the main entrance into the Ming Survival Com complex. Once satisfied that there were no other hidden dangers, he left the bunker and made his way back to his brothers.

Their reaction to his return was overly dramatic, but Lucius was able to quickly reassure them. "Everything's gonna be fine. I found a bunker with supplies, we'll rest up there and set out from here when we're ready."

"I never doubted you," Gareth told him solemnly.

"Yes, you did!" Craddock snarked back.

"We don't have time for your childish pettiness anymore," Lucius said.

"He's right," Oberon chimed in. "We need to stick together so we can survive."

Before they set out to the bunker complex, Lucius examined

what they been working on. They hadn't been idle, using their time to fashion several crude spear points. Oberon was in the process of attaching it to the arm bone from one of the skeletal remains that littered the area.

"Grab whatever you're working on, and follow me," Lucius said.

Absent the need for stealth, returning to the bunker took half the time as the trip there. Once everyone had entered, Lucius spun the access wheel and closed the hatch. The room was instantly dark, but he managed to stumble blindly toward the fire pit. The flint was where he remembered it, and Lucius was able to start a small fire. Satisfied that the fire wouldn't wink out, he moved towards the back of the room and grabbed the clothes he'd set aside for his brothers.

"I know they smell, but they'll do for now," he told them.

"What's the plan?" Oberon asked.

"We'll sneak back into the Worland Clan compound and resupply. I know how to get into the storage chambers," Lucius told his brother.

"Without being seen?" Oberon asked grimly. "I can't stomach another bloodbath."

"Have some faith," Lucius replied.

"Pistol Pete will take care of us," Craddock added.

Oberon didn't answer his younger sibling; his gaze remained intently on his older brother. Lucius didn't flinch, merely staring down his brother as he waited for him to accept his answer.

"Now that we've settled that, boys… stay by the fire. Keep feeding it wood. Oberon and I will look for the foodstuffs that were here earlier," Lucius said.

A chorus of yeses answered him. Then, with the twins kept busy, he gestured for Oberon to follow him to the back of the chamber. Several bags of dried meat waited for them, along with several other vegetables he didn't recognize.

"Think we risk it?" Lucius asked.

"What choice do we have? The boys need to eat," Oberon replied.

With the decision made, they grabbed the bags of food and brought them over to the fire. Despite tasting odd, it was the best meal they had ever eaten. They enjoyed normal dinner talk, though the Pendragon brothers felt strangely compelled to whisper to each other.

Once his brothers had fallen asleep, Lucius went to the dead man and checked for any other useful supplies. When he came up empty-handed, he dragged the corpse to the centrally located bank of strange tables. Grunting, he rolled him underneath and went back to the pile of rags. Grabbing an armful, he took several trips back to the impromptu internment and covered the body to shield it from his brothers' prying eyes.

On his last trip, he stumbled over the board the man had tried hitting him with. Picking it up, Lucius got a bright idea. Kneeling, he began wrapping the remaining rags around one end of the firewood. Picking it up, he returned to where his brothers lay curled up together and drifted into a much-needed slumber.

4

Camp, Ming Survival Com Above Worland Clan Complex, Bighorn Mountains

Waking up with a start, Lucius tried to remember where he was. His dreams had been horrific. He'd been above ground, chased by strange creatures, some even more disturbing than they'd already encountered. Even the ground he'd strode upon had been part of the nightmare. It'd become a kaleidoscope of strange pastel colors that never stood still. Just when he thought he'd figured things out, he'd run through oddly normal places until he stepped onto them. Then the ground had melted under his feet, sometimes coalescing into a vaguely humanoid shape.

"Are you okay?" whispered Craddock, pulling him back from the dreamscape memories.

"Everything's fine. Go back to sleep," he'd reassured Craddock.

Lost in thought, Lucius ignored his brother's answer and tried to make sense of his dream. It had seemed so vivid and real. Things in that nightmare had reminded him of his time in the strange afterlife above ground but in brilliant color. *Shake it off*, he told himself. There was too much to do; he'd need to be on top of his game if he was going to lead his family somewhere safe.

"They're asleep," Oberon whispered, interrupting his musings. "Be honest with me; what's your plan, Lucius?"

Startled, he turned to see his brother sitting up and staring at him. "We're raiding Worland. We'll take anything we can use and as much as we can carry."

"I got that, but then what?" Oberon asked, pushing his brother for more information.

"Then we search for other human groups to join," he whispered.

"We're the only ones left, you know that," Oberon replied, forgetting to whisper in his frustration.

"The dead human over yonder would beg to differ," Lucius replied, gesturing towards where he'd hidden the stranger's body.

"Someone survived the culling?" Oberon gasped.

"No, the local predators would pounce when they were dropped naked and afraid. You saw the bones, they were eaten almost as soon as they exited our former home," Lucius said.

"That doesn't prove there are other humans in the above," Oberon insisted.

"On the last trip to the strange above, I was raiding a city in ruins and ran across other humans. I tried to engage with them, but they spooked and ran," Lucius said.

"Okay, so you saw other humans. Shifting topics… anything you want to tell us about these strange new powers?" Oberon asked.

"I don't know, not really," Lucius replied.

"The Council guards said you were the changed. Are you? Is it the boon?" Oberon asked.

"I don't know," Lucius snapped.

"Okay, you're the head of the family. We'll trust you and follow your lead. These powers of yours, how do you think you got them?" Oberon asked.

"I don't know; things changed after my last trip above," he replied.

"What was different about that trip?" Oberon asked.

"I ate… I thought it was the food the other explorers left behind, but I felt funny afterward. I also fell into a stream and swallowed some water," he said.

"Why would that matter?" Oberon asked.

"Not sure, but parts of things up here are just strange. And it's the only thing I did differently," Lucius replied.

"Can you control it?" Oberon asked, momentarily hesitating.

"No, I can't control it. It seems to come instinctively when I'm in life-or-death situations. However, there have been times when my life was in danger where it didn't work," Lucius said.

Nodding to himself, Oberon paused before saying anything else. "Then we can't count on that as a form of defense. We'll have to grab some weapons before we leave Worland."

"Yes," he said quietly. Then, after hesitating, he continued, "Using the power—it's painful. The more I try to do with it, the more it hurts. I had to use it to get us into this shelter, and now I can't feel my limbs."

Neither one of them spoke for a few minutes. The silence weighed on Lucius. When he couldn't take it any longer, he rolled over and tried to get back to sleep. He stared at the ceiling for several hours, thinking as he waited for the twins to wake up. Once they were awake, the brothers constructed several torches with the remaining firewood and set about exploring the stockpiled supplies. Predictably, there was precious little for them among the dead man's possessions.

"We've wasted enough time; this place has been well and truly picked over," Lucius said. "Time to sneak into the belly of the beast, I know the way back home, but it takes us through hidden high-born supply caches."

"Then why didn't you raid that? Why did you risk going above ground?" Craddock asked.

"They regularly counted; there would've been no way to get away with it. Now it's not our problem, so we'll take everything we can carry," Lucius replied.

"Just stay silent until we're in places where it's safe to talk," Oberon added.

With no orders left to give, they set out down the winding stairway until they reached the lowest level of the Ming Survival Com bunker. From there, Lucius followed a path memorized months ago. They left the smooth concrete bunker walls and stepped into a passageway hand cut long ago into the slate rock that made up their mountainous home. They spent hours walking down the slanted passageway before they heard voices ahead.

"We're in the farming levels," Lucius whispered. "We'll rest here; when everyone's asleep, we'll move out. Absolute silence, or we're caught."

His brothers tapped his arm, indicating their understanding, and extinguished their torches. Once his brothers were situated, he took what remained of their torches and put them away from the dangerous transition point. After propping the wood against the rock-hewn wall, he turned to head back to his brothers. His sudden movement slammed him into Oberon's chest.

"We should all keep the torches," said his brother.

"The light will give our position away," Lucius replied.

"You're awful stupid for a smart guy. The wooden torches will make excellent clubs should we need to defend ourselves," said Oberon.

Nodding, Lucius started to head back to the twins when he remembered that his brother likely couldn't see him. Tapping Oberon's shoulder, they picked up their new clubs and retraced their steps. The twins were already asleep, snoring quietly. He worried about the noises, but there was nothing he could do about it. *We need to be rested for this last part*, he reassured himself.

The Worland sleep time came too quickly for any of their likings, but his brothers rose without complaint and followed him as he led them through a winding, twisting route through areas they'd never been. There were a few close calls, but Pistol Pete favored their raid; they went undetected until they got to the supply cache. Several guards were roaming around the entrance, alert for low-born theft.

"When I make my move, I want you on my ass like ticks on a hound dog," Lucius ordered his brothers. "The lock is rusty and broken; it's only there for show. We'll go in as quickly as we can and avoid detection."

When the younger Pendragon brothers nodded their agreement, Lucius turned and watched. He needed to time his assault to the second, or the roving guards would be all over them. When they were away from the doorway into the special supply cache, Lucius charged as quickly and quietly as he could. They made it into the storage room, silently closing the door behind them.

"My shift still has two hours left," someone said from the darkness.

Shit, shit, shit.

Focusing on where the voice came from, he tried to send energy toward the unseen speaker. Nothing happened. Cursing to himself, Lucius hefted the impromptu cudgel. His hands tightened on the wooden weapon as he prepared to pounce. He wasn't fast enough. His brother Oberon was already on the man, swinging wildly at the unsuspecting enforcer.

Shit, shit, shit.

Worried that the enforcer might scream out before he was silenced, Lucius charged him. He swung with all of his might, letting his rage flow out of him in one vicious thwack from his cudgel. Their assault was swift and brutal; Lucius and Oberon swung in tandem, pulverizing the enforcer's body. They were so lost in their blood rage that they didn't notice the twins had joined the party until they heard their lament.

"This is for mommy and daddy," Craddock said, his quiet voice layered with equal parts rage and sorrow.

His other brother, Gareth, worried him more. His silent and emotionless attack was as ruthless as it was inefficient. Lucius reached out, halting his attack and dropping his weapon to lay a comforting hand on each of their shoulders.

"He's dead; he can't hurt us anymore," he whispered.

While he led his youngest brothers over to the stockpile of clothing, Oberon took it upon himself to grab several backpacks from the stores. He brought them over to Lucius, and they loaded them with everything they would need to survive in the world outside the

Worland Clan caverns. When they had loaded the packs with every-thing that would fit, he grabbed for shoulder satchels and began stuffing them with more food.

"What about water?" Oberon asked.

"Too heavy. I grabbed some fire starters and a pot instead. We'll just boil our drinking water; we need to travel light," Lucius replied.

"All right, now we just need weapons," Oberon said. "I grabbed the short sword from this enforcer, but we'll need more blades and distance weapons."

"Those are stored separately," Lucius replied, "best not to test our luck."

"Then we take these supplies back to the Ming bunker and repeat this raid tomorrow," Oberon said insistently.

"If we're going to do this, we must do it today. The Council will find out about this raid, and they'll lock things up tighter than anything we can handle. The weapons are kept closer to the Council Chamber," Lucius said grimly.

"Lead the way," Gareth said, joining the conversation.

His young voice suddenly sounded older; it broke Lucius's heart. He'd spent a lifetime trying to protect them from the cruelty of the world, but it found them anyway. *If I can't shield them from the beasts that hide in the dark, then I'll have to teach them to tame it.*

"We'll need to go up the old vent shafts. The trip will be danger-ous. If we fall it's a long way down. It will let us out next to the rear exit into the chamber," Lucius said.

"Will it be guarded? Will the door be locked?" Gareth asked.

"The last time I explored, there were no guards or locks. However, it's been several years, and they could've changed things. So we'll have to be on guard," Lucius said.

"What do you need us to do, then?" Gareth asked.

"You can make sure you can carry all of these supplies. We'll need all of it; if you can't carry it up, we're here to help. Oberon, you grab some rope and rig up some way for us to carry our clubs slung over our shoulders," Lucius said.

"What about me?" Craddock asked.

"Make sure we bar that door from the inside. We don't have

much time, so we need to hurry. They could come and check on the dead guy at any time," Lucius said, ending the conversation.

Once everyone was ready and the door was barred from the inside, they started the arduous climb up several dozen inlaid ladder systems. The safety railing had long since rusted away, but every eighth floor had an area for the adventurous climbers to rest. After the first rest, Oberon and Lucius had to carry their brothers' packs too. The more exhausted the twins got, the more the older brothers had to step in until exhaustion hit them.

"Help!" Gareth hollered above him.

Looking up, Lucius saw that his younger brother had lost his grip on the railing and was barely hanging onto the ladder.

"Oberon, get Craddock up to the next rest area. Only two more floors to go, I've got Gareth," Lucius said, his voice low but firm.

His brother didn't reply; he just kept pushing Craddock up the ladder. Grunting in exertion, Lucius pushed himself to climb up toward Gareth.

"Hang in there, Gareth," he said reassuringly.

Just as he got to his brother, the boy's grip finally slipped. Lucius barely caught him before he plunged to his death. With one hand clutched to the ladder, his knuckles turning white from the strain, he grabbed Gareth's arm as he slipped by and lifted him back toward the ladder.

"I got you," he assured him.

Groaning from the strain, he barely managed to lift his brother back onto the ladder.

"You can do this, Gareth. We can rest in just a little bit. The next level has a place to rest," he reassured his brother.

The next several minutes were tense, but Lucius managed to reach the rest area before collapsing. When he recovered, he found his brother playing around with the back wall of the rest area from the old emergency shaft.

"Where do you think this goes?" Oberon asked as he tried prying open an old rusted door.

"I'm not sure. We're sort of short on time, they'll know we hit the supply cache soon, and the guards will be on alert," Lucius replied.

"About that... we've got at least another 100 feet of ladders to scale. By the time we get there, we'll be tired and sore. Maybe we trust our luck, put our faith in Pistol Pete, and explore," Oberon said.

Staring at his brother, Lucius realized that Oberon was right. Not about Pistol Pete, he'd stopped believing that the statute represented a god, but the twins needed a break. Standing, he went over to help his brother open the door. When they wedged open enough room to shimmy through, he set down his supplies and slid through the gap. He was met with a strange smell; one that spoke of age and hinted at the ghosts of their forefathers. There was a moldering musk in the air whose origin he didn't want to think about. He didn't know what to make of it without being able to see.

"Can you light one of the torches and hand it to me?" Lucius asked as he tried to maximize the dim light filtering in from the opening.

It didn't take long for Oberon to hand him the torch. It didn't make much of a difference; the light didn't cut very far through the oppressive darkness. Walking around the room, he found several exits from the room. The first door wouldn't budge. It had a greasy black window, though, which he quickly broke. It revealed a caved-in passageway that was wider than anything he'd ever encountered in their subterranean home. *I'll have to remember this*, he told himself. *Maybe we could clear the rubble at some point?*

Continuing his circuit around the room, he found another exit. Pushing on one of the doors, he was surprised it opened to another set of stairs. There was a layer of dust and grime on everything. The stairs clearly weren't in use. Walking back to his brothers, Lucius brought them into the room with him.

"There's a way up, and we should use it. We've taken too long and made too much noise to risk hitting the weapons locker," Lucius told his brothers.

"We'll need to defend ourselves out there," Oberon insisted.

"Yes, but we have to live to reach the above ground first," Lucius said, ending the discussion.

With all four of their torches, they were able to search the room very efficiently. It was a warehouse of some sort, full of moldy boxes that contained something biodegradable. The stench that emanated from the boxes after he'd opened them almost knocked him on his ass, but he managed to keep on his feet without retching.

"These probably once held food," Lucius told his brothers. "It means we might find salvageable supplies!"

With the prospect of more useful supplies, the Pendragon brothers tore open every box they could reach and peered inside. They found strange electronic components that sat there in silver wrappings coated in a thin layer of oil. Other boxes contained seeds in vacuum-sealed packets with labels they didn't recognize, words that were barely English. They found others they did identify; wheat, fruit and nut trees, beans, and so many herbs. *The Worland Clan would've killed for these*, he thought.

"Why didn't we know about these?" Oberon asked.

"There's a lot that the Council either didn't know or didn't want us to know," Lucius replied.

"Do we take the seeds?" Craddock asked.

"Yeah, let's not go crazy but the seeds could be useful for bartering," Oberon replied before Lucius could.

Lucius agreed with his brother, picking a random sampling of the seeds, and then they resumed their search. They found hundreds of pounds of dried beans packed in cylinder containers, which they also took. He didn't know whether they were good, but they took a small bag of those too.

"Lucius, check this out!" Gareth called from where he'd been exploring in the other end of the room.

Pulling his torch from where he'd had propped it up in one of the barrels of beans, he jogged over to his youngest brother. The boy had found pay dirt. There were several plastic cases with firearms, boxes of rounds, and canvas carrying bags.

"We've found guns!" Lucius excitedly called over to Oberon.

"And knives!" Craddock called from the next row.

"Be there in a second," Lucius replied to Craddock as he picked up one of the rifles.

Holding the weapon, he checked it to see if it would still work. It was a bolt action rifle, similar to what the enforcers used to quell riots from the unwanted. They were made of a dark wood, but unlike the weapons carried by the brutes working for the Council, these had been wrapped in a waxy paper and were coated in a layer of slimy grease. They were slippery, making it difficult to keep his grip on them.

"Check the condition of the carrying bags," Lucius told Oberon.

Turning the weapon around in his hands, Lucius decided they'd need to clean them somewhere with better lighting. Bagging up four of the rifles, he began to grab as many of the bullets as he could while Oberon snagged a knife for each of them.

"I think this goes on the rifles," Oberon told him.

Turning to his brother, Lucius grabbed another weapon to experiment with. He'd been right; the blade sat on top of the weapon's barrel, though Lucius wasn't sure what good that would do.

"Stop playing around; we need to look for any larger blades and then find a way out of this place," Lucius told Oberon as he set down the rifle.

"Think fast," Oberon said before tossing the weapon at Lucius while laughing.

He barely had time to catch the heavy rifle, but he managed to retain it without stabbing himself. Before he could rebuke his brother, he heard a metallic scraping sound. Gripping the rifle with one hand, he placed a single finger over his lips to indicate they should be quiet. Leaving behind the torches, he snuck to where they'd entered the room and waited. Someone was on the other side of the door; he knew it had to be an enforcer.

Time seemed to still as he waited, barely managing to force himself to breathe. He could hear them talking outside, three distinct voices. He had planned how to handle the situation, but everything seemed to happen so fast. The first enforcer stepped cautiously into the room, trying to scan the area for them. Without thinking, Lucius stepped forward and swung the bottom of the rifle into the man's head.

The enforcer doubled over in pain. Lucius could hear his compatriots trying to pull the door open, trying to widen the gap into the room. *I can't let that happen*, he thought grimly. At that moment, he remembered the knife sticking off of the barrel. Stabbing downward, he drove the blade into the enforcer's throat. The rage boiled up, barely controllable. These were the men who tormented his family, killed his parents, and were now trying to kill him.

"Arggh!" he yelled as he stabbed downward again.

Knuckles turning white from the strength of his grip, he slammed the blade into the enforcer's stomach. Lucius's grip on the rifle loosened when the bayonet struck the concrete floor under the enforcer. Distracted, he missed the other two enforcers who barreled in after the one he'd just killed. The men rushed him, knocking him to the ground. One of the brutes held him down as the other one punched him over and over again.

He wasn't sure how long they pummeled him; the world went dark as his existence narrowed to the fists punching him and the men grunting as they struck his solar plexus. *Please let my brothers get away*, he prayed. He could hear the boys moving around, which he considered a good sign. He tried to use the power again, the one the gods had given him. He concentrated on their heads, envisioning them exploding. His entire mental focus was on trying to draw out the raw energy again.

Nothing happened.

Cursing weakly, he kept struggling. He missed the warm fluid that suddenly washed over him, drenching his upper torso. He didn't miss the weight of the enforcer slumping over him, pinning him down.

"What in the name of Pistol Pete," growled the other enforcer.

Whatever he was going to say was cut off by the enforcer's own screams of pain. A thwacking sound rung out around him, confusing him. The sounds of meat being hacked rang out, cutting through the rivers of pain clouding his thinking. *Am I back at the Worland butcher?* he wondered. The sound of the blows lulled him.

Then there was silence.

"We found blades, Lucius," Gareth said simply, his short sentiment explaining the situation.

"So you did," Lucius groaned, "so you did."

5

Storage Room, Worland Clan Complex, Bighorn Mountains

"Help me get these off," Lucius begged Oberon as he struggled from under the limp enforcer.

"It's okay, we're okay now," Oberon replied, his hands gently helping his brother stand back up.

Once Lucius had stripped naked, they began searching for new clothes. It took them several hours to find replacements. They found enough to outfit the entire family in better clothing, stuff more suited for life above. Linen and wool garments and other durable outerwear replaced the rags they'd taken from the dead man at the Ming Survival Com. Along with several changes of clothing, they found boxes of inclement weather gear. Taking their new find, the brothers rearranged their packs and began preparing to leave the storage room.

When everyone was re-dressed in better clothing, Oberon and Lucius stripped the enforcers and rolled the first one's naked bodies over the ledge. He stood, watching his attacker sail down the steep drop. The sound of him hitting the bottom was a sickening thud.

"Shouldn't I feel something? Why doesn't this bother me? I just feel numb," he muttered.

"That comes with the dreams," Oberon replied softly. "We'll have to be strong for the twins, especially Gareth. He's worrying me."

"Yeah… think Mom and Dad are alive up there?" Lucius asked his brother.

Oberon didn't answer, only staring over the safety railing, tears running down his cheeks. As the pain receded, Lucius became more convinced at the absurdity of his question and set about searching the enforcers.

"Grab the keys," Lucius told his brother.

"Why?" Oberon asked. "Are we planning on coming back?"

"Who knows what the future holds," Lucius replied cryptically.

Once they'd taken everything useful from the dead men, they dragged the remaining two bodies back onto the landing. Grunting, they rolled the bodies over the edge.

"Take that," Oberon said as he tossed the enforcers' clothing after them.

The outfits fluttered down the cylindrical shaft whose purpose they didn't know. Searching through the pile of supplies the men had had on them, Oberon grabbed their weapons and turned to rejoin the twins. Following his younger brother, Lucius shouldered the rifle as he adjusted his new pants.

"Alright… we need to find a way out of this place. The sooner, the better, so grab your gear, and let's head out. Oberon, shoulder the enforcer's weapons," Lucius told them.

"Can you control your powers?" Gareth asked as he quietly put the pack on his scrawny back.

"No, why do you ask?" Lucius asked in reply.

"The rubble, I think we should try there first," Gareth said.

Nodding to humor his brother, Lucius walked over to the door his brother was pointing at. Grunting as he pulled it inward, he gestured to Oberon to help him. He didn't know why his brother wanted to go that route, but Gareth's body language told him it was important to him. He stood straight, gripping the satchel slung over his shoulder in one hand and the torch in the other. He squeezed until his knuckles turned white and veins showed on his stocky neck.

"It's a cave-in," Lucius said quietly. "It'd take hours with a full work detail to clear this."

Staring silently, Gareth spoke with an unnatural authority for one so young. "Something on the other side is calling to me."

"I believe you," Lucius replied, raising his hand to cut off Oberon's scoffing.

"I'm sorry, Gareth. I can see this is important to you," Oberon said, raising his hands in a consolatory gesture.

"We can always come back, but we need to get out of here for now. The enforcers will hunt us down; we've killed too many of them," Lucius added.

The brothers stood, staring at each other, willing the other to back down. It was a new feeling for Lucius; they'd never questioned his orders before. When Gareth finally nodded his surrender, they turned toward the stairwell. After checking for any signs that the structural integrity had failed, they began climbing toward the surface. They didn't encounter any other issues or bother exploring the levels they passed. The brothers just marched upward, one foot in front of the other, until they reached the top.

"Rest here," Lucius ordered them.

They quickly pulled out some of the dehydrated food they'd taken from the enforcers and ate.

"We're tired," said Craddock.

"Can we rest here before we exit into the above?" Gareth added, finishing his brother's sentence.

"Rest, I'll scout ahead. Just don't roll off the ledge," Lucius replied.

Opening the doorway from the stairwell, he saw a long tunnel that didn't have any off-shoot hallways. Without his torch, which had burned out several hours ago, he was barely able to make out anything. Advancing slowly, he fumbled his way through the passageway. Stumbling a few times on unseen debris, he managed to keep his footing.

A few more feet, and I'll turn back.

Lucius kept going, constantly reassuring himself that he was okay. After several minutes of fumbling around in the dark, he came upon another door. Pushing it open, trying to be as silent as possible, he tried to observe the scene through all of his senses. He noticed a distinctive smell; it was brisk, with a crisp bite that told him he was at a high elevation. The sounds of wind howling bounced off the walls of the passageway, adding to the rapidly chilling temperature.

Taking a deep breath, steeling himself against the unknown dangers, Lucius opened the final door. Brilliant light blinded him; the setting sun dazzling eyes adjusted to subterranean life.

"We made it out," he said in shock.

Slowly closing the door, he took stock of the setting sun and knew they could afford to rest for the night before making their final exodus from the only home they'd ever known. But, the Pendragon brothers would have to be on their game to survive in the unforgiving wasteland that existed above ground. He'd observed strange mutants and feral creatures shambling along on his previous travels. Facing that again with his brothers in tow concerned him; he wanted to be ready.

The trip back to his waiting brothers was equally slow, though Lucius felt somewhat relieved. An unknown weight, the pressure to conform at all costs, was suddenly lifted. All he had to worry about above ground was surviving without the oppressive class system of the Worland Clan.

"We'll be okay," he reassured himself.

A realization hit when he reached the door to where his brothers waited; he'd messed up, venturing unarmed into the unknown. They'd have to do better, to be better. He'd have to be more alert if his family were to survive what waited for them. Hardening his resolve, he opened the door and found his brothers asleep. They hadn't bothered to set a guard or secure their gear for a rapid retreat.

"Wake up," he told Oberon, as he gently kicked his leg.

His younger siblings groaned, but slowly regained consciousness.

"We've got a lot to do, get up. Grab your gear, we're not sleeping here," Lucius told them.

Lending a helping hand, Lucius quickly had the boys on their feet and moving. He led the group, retracing his steps toward the exit from the sprawling Worland facility. When they reached the door, Lucius propped it open and set about making camp.

"Oberon, we need to clean the guns we grabbed. Collect those broken up pallets piled over there so we can build a fire. We'll talk as we work," he told his brother.

They quickly had a cradle to support the metal body of the abandoned wheelbarrow and filled it with snow. While the sunlight dwindled away, they boiled the parts of the weapons they'd captured. The hot water stripped the grease the rifles had been stored in, forcing them to constantly replace the dirty water. Twelve trips out to collect fresh snow later, the weapons were clean enough to reassemble. While they worked, Lucius lectured.

"When I left you to search, you slept. Nobody set a watch, nobody secured our essential lifesaving supplies, and nobody worried what would happen if you rolled off the damn ledge," he ranted.

The twins tried to interrupt, but Lucius spoke over them, ignoring their whining explanations. He continued until the weapons were cleaned and they were prepared for their pending departure.

"Can we test fire these guns tomorrow morning before we move out," Oberon asked.

Lucius knew that they were all desperate to change the subject. He saw it on their faces; they'd taken all they could of his lessons on the harsh reality of life. *I shouldn't have sheltered them for so long*, he thought.

"Yes, all of us will fire our weapons. Then we'll clean them for the road and head out," Lucius replied.

When the weapons had been properly stored, they sat quietly and prepared their meal. Nobody talked after his lecture. Instead, they ate, stoically and mechanically shoveling their flavorless food into their mouths.

"Craddock, go make sure we closed the door into the stairwell.

Gareth, gather more firewood. I'll take the first watch. We'll rotate every few hours until dawn," he ordered his brothers.

"Then what?" Oberon asked.

"We get as far from this place as possible, find a new home," he replied simply.

"How? The above is unlivable," Oberon insisted.

"You've seen the body in the Ming Complex! We're not the only human colony, stop believing the lies the Council fed us," Lucius snapped.

The brothers stared at each other until Craddock broke the silence.

"Who is Mister Lee Enfield?"

Startled, Lucius turned and looked at his youngest brother. "What?" he asked.

"The name was on the gun bag," Craddock replied.

"He must've been the enforcer who stocked the supply area we found," Oberon said.

With nothing to add to the discussion, Lucius told the boys to finish their tasks and get to sleep.

The night passed uneventfully. Out of habit, Lucius woke before the sun to find his brothers asleep. They hadn't maintained a vigilant guard, though he didn't know which sibling had fallen asleep on watch. Waking up, he stood and stretched as he took it all in. His brothers snored soundly sleeping, oblivious to the dangers that existed all around them. He barely managed to fight the sense of dread that threatened to overwhelm him.

Dawn brought the unknown. For the first time in his life, he didn't have to report to anyone. Unfortunately, that freedom came with a price. There would be no Center for Aid and Comfort to provide meals. The farming collective wouldn't supply his every dietary need. The caves wouldn't shelter his family, and the dreaded enforcers wouldn't man the walls protecting him from the world outside. They were on their own.

Kicking his brothers, he addressed them. "Wake up, you lazy bums! I don't want to know which one of you fell asleep on watch. Whoever it was, you just killed us all. While you slept through the night, the enemy slit our throats and stole our gear. Or worse... the monsters ate us!"

None of them fessed up, so Lucius let it drop. Instead, they prepared to abandon the only home they'd ever known. After a quick meal of dried fruit and beef jerky, he led his brothers into the crisp mountain air.

"We can practice your weapon handling later. Right now, we just need to know that they work. I want each of you to load one round and wait for my signal," he ordered.

When everything was in order, Lucius aimed at a nearby tree and fired. Splinters exploded outward. He'd hit his mark, though he wasn't sure he could repeat the achievement under pressure. Taking a cue from his actions, his brothers each fired their weapons. The results were comical; none of them were prepared for the slight kick of the rifle. Oberon almost lost his balance, stumbling against his younger brothers. Shocked by the assault and the bucking gun, both of the twins fell onto their asses.

Lucius didn't even try; he let out a belly laugh as he toggled the safety catch on the weapon. Then, when his weapon was safely slung over his shoulder, he went and helped his brothers get back on their feet.

"Next time, be ready for the kick. It wasn't that bad, not if you're waiting for it," Lucius told them.

When the moment had passed, he nodded curtly, heading back into the passageway, and began to clean the barrel of the rifle quickly. Satisfied that he'd done all he could, he put the rifle back into the canvas bag and helped his brothers do the same.

"Should we put out the fire?" Craddock asked as they prepared to leave.

"No need; it's mostly embers now," Oberon answered for him.

"We can dump snow on it if it makes you feel better," Lucius added conciliatorily.

He sighed when his brother asked for them to extinguish the flames, but the four of them made short work of their dwindling fire. With their camp broken down, the long journey into the unknown began.

ABOUT J. R. HANDLEY

J.R. Handley is a pseudonym for a family writing team. He is a veteran infantry sergeant with the 101st Airborne Division and the 28th Infantry Division. His family is the kind of crazy that interprets his insanity into cogent English. He writes the sci-fi while they proofread it. The sergeant is a two-time combat veteran of the late unpleasantness in Mesopotamia where he was wounded, likely doing something stupid. He started writing military science fiction as part of a therapy program suggested by his doctor, and hopes to entertain you while he attempts to excise his demons through these creative endeavors. In addition to being just another dysfunctional veteran, he is a stay-at-home parent, avid reader and all-around nerd. Luckily for him, his family joins him in his fandom nerdalitry.

Our web page is www.jrhandley.com.

LETTERS FROM A
DEAD MAN

DECLAN FINN

Kevin Anderson used to be a spy. Now he's an exile in a dystopian San Francisco. When an investigation leads him to a way out, what will he sacrifice to make it home?

LETTERS FROM A DEAD MAN

TRANSMISSION START: Date, 06-09-2095

For those of you just tuning in, my name is Kevin Anderson, serial number 1597—the perfect example of what happens when you can't keep your mouth shut. I am, for all intents and purposes, what could be called a spy, though I don't think anyone cares what I have to report on.

As penance for my sins, I have been exiled to the city of San Francisco. You may have some problem believing there is a city of San Francisco. There still is, despite the minor nuclear holocaust in 2090 that wiped out large parts of three continents and killed over one billion people worldwide. Due to certain political ramifications, I will not go into here; the missile shield stations in Alaska and throughout the mainland states caught most of the missiles falling east of the Rocky Mountains. The West Coast wasn't that lucky.

San Francisco survived because of luck...Either that or because San Francisco is politically irrelevant. Either way, it's still here. We are surrounded on all sides by what the locals call "The Wasteland" —formerly known as everything west of Illinois.

I doubt I'll live long enough to get out. San Francisco has been

carved up like a Turkey into a feudal structure. I feel like an anthro-
pologist living among a tribe of cannibals—watching, probing,
studying, but always eyed like I might be next on the dinner menu. I
have to watch the Thanatosians, the Hackers, the Scavengers, and
the Forsaken... along with who or whatever else may be out there.
The less I say about the mercenaries and the Corporates, the better
off I am. Then again, half of my time in training was spent in the
Middle Eastern Alliance with the Mossad, so I have urban ops
training.

San Fran has become a dumping ground for some governments
to 'disappear' malcontents, mainly because the rest of the planet
thinks the entire city has been destroyed by that day in 2090. The
only people who seem to be aware that this place still exists happen
to run governments...but why would they want to acknowledge it?
It's one city, surrounded by what is otherwise a desolate wasteland,
taken over by makeshift feudal lords. The people of Washington,
DC, have better things to do. Besides, it's a perfect makeshift prison
facility—one that can't possibly exist. The US of A usually doesn't
drop people here and only does when they 'disappear' guys like me
—the Inconvenient. Yes, I've adopted my own title. Everyone else
here has one; why not me?

This is the rant I put at the start of all my communications to
the East Coast. Why? In part because I can. But mainly because I
don't know if my reports are being intercepted by anyone at all. If
they are, then just one report won't be enough to establish context
And, because, as long as I keep writing them, someone from back
there will know I'm still alive—even if it's only me.

I should explain Kyle here -- well, I would if it were possible.
He's an Assassin and apparently a member of the Assassin's Guild
we knew of on the West Coast before 2090. He's really very good at
what he does. However, we have an understanding.

The people of San Francisco have tried to ignore what has
happened to the world around them, and more importantly, they've
ignore what they've become. They've lost themselves in the day-to-
day, in hedonism, money, power, drugs like pixie dust, and Wicked
60, the usual sins. But not Kyle. He's somewhere between the ulti-

mate pragmatist and the ultimate sociopath. The second term does not, and will never properly apply to Kyle, but it is something people can understand. They use it to explain things that scare them. Kyle scares them. Hell, he scares me, but I respect things that can kill me.

Kyle's contempt for the rest of humanity is best compared to a person's reaction to having to guard an open sewer in the summer. He sees how they try to escape the daily hell around them, and his revenge is to make them remember no matter how hard they try not to.

He's my backup plan. If San Francisco eats me, Kyle will be the instrument of my revenge. He has my reports; he knows what I know, both about here and back home. If he makes it out, he'll know enough to make people back off. When he releases his manuscript to the world, I know they will learn about my reports and me, too.

Now that my preamble is over, I should get to my current report.

As a New York City kid, I find San Francisco to be a small city, so I have no problems with seeing the same person twice a day, if not more often. This, of course, includes Kyle. Despite his work-focused attitude, he isn't always prepping to kill someone. Granted, I suspect his main hobby is finding easier, faster ways to kill people, but it's what he does.

He looked better than he had in a while but had picked up a few followers. He had noticed them and was obviously irritated at their presence. Then again, I think that's Kyle's default expression.

I knew who the creatures following him were - several of the Children of Thanatos, the local death cult. I know enough to keep out of their way., but every time one even looks at me the wrong way, I wonder about their short list of people to be sacrificed to whatever Kali-like deity they worship. They believe that by killing people, they are "set free" from this hellish world. People are "put out of their misery." They call it mercy killing, even on newborns… some "Children" jokes insist that the newborns taste like veal.

I was going to approach Kyle to ask if he needed any help, but I stayed put. I had been waiting to meet an informant of mine - a man within one of San Francisco's larger Corporations. The Omega Corporation, to be precise. Their name should've given me a hint.

My investigation into Omega had started when I heard from an ex-SFPD officer (then again, they're all ex-officers now, to one extent or the other. If they're not in someone else's pocket, they're crippled by a lack of resources). This man was working guard duty there and mentioned that Omega was buying up a lot of property in the Wasteland.

It made no sense to me at the time. Los Angeles wasn't worth much before it had been nuked, and afterward, it was worth even less. In fact, most of the land between California and Chicago isn't worth all that much. Omega had bought the land anyway, which was odd for a Corporation that had ties to the East Coast. I wondered what a Corporation like Omega would want in San Fran, anyway. I was curious. Heck, I didn't have anything better to do, now did I?

Now I was going to be dealing with one of the lower level-execs, Edward Newton—a mouse in training to become a rat. He was giving a few higher-level executives to me. I believe he might have thought that I was going to eliminate them. He wasn't all that pleasant a fellow, but he knew how to be polite—just barely.

Newton rounded the corner and smiled, raising his hand. I waited, my back to a wall in the middle of the block. He came up to me and burst out, "The biochemical labs are working on a project. You'll need to move quickly, because otherwise, they're going to get promoted above me. They…"

Less than a second later, his head exploded.

I barely blinked. I looked up, and there was Kyle, up on a rooftop, withdrawing and collapsing his rifle.

Personally, Kyle, I know we've talked since, but damn it, couldn't you have waited until he was walking away from me and I had gotten everything from him? [Note to self: Remove paragraph before sending report].

In any event, I at least had something. I would start with the

Omega biotech division. I knew where it was, and I knew I could get into and around their facilities without any real difficulty.

Omega biotech wasn't heavily guarded for several simple reasons. Most of the stuff they had wasn't worth guarding, and none of what was worth stealing wasn't something able to be stolen —biohazard level 5 diseases. Biohazard level 4, with diseases like Ebola, apparently wasn't good enough for them. Anyone who tried to steal a phial of that stuff would probably be turned into a mass of blood before they reached the door.

I approached the corner building without hurrying. I was just a passerby on a casual stroll. I spotted two security guards out front, three cameras to monitor the doors, and several biometric devices to make certain no one would get past the front door.

I turned the corner, stepped into an alley next to the building, and then I screamed, long and loud as if I were in pain.

The two security guards I had seen charged toward the corner to come to my aid. I didn't expect the first guard to literally run into my elbow strike as he came around the corner, so I inadvertently crushed his throat. As he was busy trying to breathe, his partner finally caught up to him, coming around the corner and crashing into him.

I spun out of the way as they both fell to the ground, and before the second guard could recover, I stomped on his kidneys a few times. A quick grab and grapple later, and he was face up against the wall, his wrist locked against his back, pressing high against his spine.

I generally don't carry weapons since I know how to kill someone with whatever's handy. In this case, I pressed a fountain pen behind his left ear and whispered, "Tell me which of you the biometrics' security systems are programmed to ID, or I start cutting off pieces of you and play Mr. Potato Head with your parts until something works."

Thankfully, the idiot didn't know the difference between the sharp point of a pen and a knife. "Both of us."

"Good for you, then, isn't it?"

I dropped him on the ground and checked his partner. He was dead. Lucky man.

Ten minutes later, I came back from around the corner wearing an Omega security officer's uniform and cap. The cap prevented the camera not only from seeing my face but also from seeing when I went to the iris scanner and pressed the guard's eyeball to it. All that could be seen on the camera was my back as I pressed a severed hand against the palm reader.

I walked through the building and discovered why there was so little security outside. The inside was wired to the hilt. Laser trip-wires, motion detectors, everything I had read about in spy school. Thankfully the hat prevented any of the facial recognition programs from spotting me, and there was a beacon sewn into the collar of the uniform. The electronic signal from the beacon made me invisible to electronic surveillance.

I walked right up to the floor of the main offices without a problem.

A moment later, there came the problem.

Six execs were waiting there for me, with five security guards standing around them in defensive positions.

One of the execs looked up and glared at me. "What took you? We wanted extra security an hour ago. You're it? Never mind, we'll take what we can get. I guess they couldn't find any other guards without family in the city."

I blinked, making sure I looked confused and clueless. "Sir?"

The executive sighed, the bullied and harassed paper pusher. "You do <u>not</u> have family in the city, correct?"

From the way the others looked at me, if I had family, I would have been shot right there. They obviously wanted no one with any roots in San Fran, so I decided to channel Kyle. "Of course not, sir. Who the hell would anyone touch in this crappy city?"

He nodded. "Good. We don't have room on the plane for another family after ours are aboard."

Wow. This didn't sound good.

The exec was an older gentleman, and I could see on his desk only one lone frame with what looked like a picture of a wife and two children. They may have been his daughter and grandchildren; I couldn't be sure.

"The plan is simple, everyone on this mission will be paid ten thousand dollars and a free pass to civilization on the East Coast. No questions will be asked on the other end."

I blinked. Civilization. Home. No questions asked. It wouldn't be hard for any one of my old superiors to believe that I had joined a Corporation's security forces. Omega had strong ties to the East Coast, as I noted earlier, and contributed heavily to the funds of the people who had exiled me to San Francisco.

I smiled genuinely. "Great."

He nodded. "Good. The plane takes off in an hour. We will be in Washington in six hours. The bio-agent will be dropped during takeoff."

I blinked again but said nothing. Bio-agent?

I fell into line as the other guards moved to grab a biohazard chest. I shrugged, went over, and grabbed it with them. From what little I remembered from WMD School back in Virginia, a small phial of a strong bio-weapon could take out a small town. But what a whole chest of the stuff could do? It explained why Omega had a branch in San Francisco. If a bio-weapon got out in San Fran, and the whole population died, who would notice?

I thought it over. Omega had bought a lot of useless lands. Almost no one lived in the area between California and Chicago. It was a wasteland - not worth developing. But I knew the real reason no one wanted it developed—San Francisco. The insanity of San Fran was a disease, and should civilization touch the mouth of hell; the insanity would spread like a plague. I had already warned them off myself because of the Thanatosians.

But what would happen if San Francisco were no longer a problem?

I considered it briefly, but I knew the answer. Omega also had their fingers in biohazard cleansing and terraforming. After Israel had taken over the Middle East, Omega had helped make the desert bloom. It was no longer a place of sandy deserts but a green and fertile place from Morocco to Pakistan, from Sudan to Turkey.

Now the Corporation had bought up the entire space between San Francisco and Chicago.

Now, imagine if you could pretty up and sell over three thousand miles of beachfront property at whatever price you wanted to people who would have no choice but to pay for it. Imagine if you could also own five thousand square miles of freshly terra-formed land that could be molded and shaped to whatever your heart desired—for a price. You could charge whatever you wanted to whomever you wanted.

You would make a killing.

All you needed to do was eliminate one little obstacle. You needed to remove the last survivors of San Francisco. After all, they were officially dead; you were just correcting a clerical error.

I rode with the guards and the execs all the way to the airplane. It wasn't hard - no one was following us. Along the way, I pondered the situation.

I could be home in no time. I could be home in <u>half a day.</u> My superiors on the coast couldn't touch me because of the mistaken identification made by the Omega corporates. No one could tell them that I was <u>not</u> a member of their security force since the San Fran branch would have been totally annihilated. And I would be ten thousand dollars richer.

All I had to do was go along and not make any waves. All I needed to do was be a good little boy and play nicely with the pleasant men with the chest full of 'bio-agents.' I needed to let San Francisco die.

I smiled, mulling it over, leaning back. I hate this city, to tell you the truth. <u>They really are all savages. They have only one goal from day to day: to survive and to forget and ignore the world around them. Killing them would be merciful, wouldn't it? Put them all out of their misery, the pathetic fools. They really weren't even human and—</u>

I caught myself, not because of how heartless or cynical I was being about mass murder, not at first. It was because I knew the thoughts that I had been thinking. I knew <u>exactly</u> where the rhetoric came from.

The Children of Thanatos said that right before they killed their victims.

And me? I would need to forget, too. To destroy San Francisco would be to eliminate the truth and wipe out what had happened there, to me, and to the city. It would wipe out my life for these past...months? Years? And then, my superiors on the East Coast, the ones I wanted my revenge on, would have won. Kyle would be no more; all of my reports would be destroyed.

I would not be destroying the savages of San Francisco if I let this happen. I would have become one of them.

I looked over at one of the other guards. "So, how long does this thing take?"

He shrugged. "Three hours. After that, symptoms appear, and an hour later, dead. Easily contained, and the dead aren't contagious. Hell, they didn't even need to make a vaccine for protection from it!"

I nodded, my eyes seeming to say I was impressed. "Perfect," I answered.

I made sure I carried the chest to the back of the plane. I was with one other guard and passed the soundly snoring passengers. There was a good number of women and children, the families of the execs, and lab techs who were on the plane. Two children were horsing around in their seats; another four were playing with their toys and with each other. Five of them were dressed up in their finest, as though going to church and quietly reading their books. The other children and many of the women were calmly, quietly asleep. They almost all seemed quite angelic, which is odd because I can't remember ever having liked kids.

I blinked, wondering what I should do. There were, of course, two simple choices. In one choice, hundreds would die. I chose another way; thousands would.

If I backed out, if I decided to save San Francisco, I had to do more than simply steal the bioweapon on the way out the door. I could not stop Omega's plan itself. I had to stop the corporation. If I took their bioweapon, they had their scientists and their research, and they could start the process all over again. The plane couldn't reach the East coast.

If I stayed, I would be condemning over ten million people to death.

We delivered the chest to two men in biohazard suits. The white coats stood before an airlock, and I knew what that was for—weapon delivery.

I glanced over my shoulder. There was no one behind us. It was an 807 commercial plane meant to carry over four hundred people.

And half the passengers would be the family of the execs on board the plane.

And millions in San Francisco.

There were women and children out in San Francisco as well as on this plane. Freaks and monsters populated almost half of San Fran, but what about the other half? I know people in San Francisco, many of whom I didn't know very well. I had been adopted by the people of Chinatown, and like it or not, I know every street corner.

It's a conversation I will need to have with Kyle sooner or later. We've both been dealing with the hellish side of this crappy, devastated little town that we have no idea if there's a bright side to it, no matter how private that bright side was. I caught myself wondering how many streets in this town where there were children or families who weren't a part of the Manson family.

Is there a possibility of redemption for San Francisco? Is there hope for it? A better question should be, is there any hope at all?

There is a line I remember from my father—dum spiro, spero. Where there is breath, there is hope.

And with that, I had my answer.

I sighed deeply. The other guard patted me on the shoulder and started walking by me to take his post at the door.

"Screw it."

I grabbed him around the throat and twisted sharply, snapping his neck. Before he fell, I pulled out his tactical baton and opened it with a flick of my wrist. I spun and cracked the baton against the chests of both the biohazard suits, deliberately breaking their communications gear. A sweep dropped both scientists on their backs like flipped-over turtles. I didn't even blink at them when I hammered their environmental pacts, destroying their ability to recycle the air in the suits. They tried taking off their helmets so they could breathe, but I broke their hands with the baton.

I let them suffocate while I moved toward the chest. A Corporation wouldn't take any risks with their execs, so I bet that there wouldn't be contamination and popped open the chest. All the phials were still intact.

I took an extra glove and carefully lifted a phial from the chest, then wrapped my glove around it. I then made certain that the chest was locked and the delivery system was empty.

I took up a position by the rear door to the plane. Everyone was on board, and no one else would be back there while the plane was in mid-takeoff. Five minutes later, the announcement came. The plane would take off in thirty seconds.

I grimaced and then tossed the phial at the farthest air vent. Once I heard the shattering of glass, I sprinted down the stairs. I needed to jump off as the stairs folded into the plane.

The plane took off, but it would never make it to the East Coast. In four hours, everyone on board would be dead.

Thankfully, the company cars were left behind, since they couldn't be loaded onto the plane. And with the amount of money Omega would make from their plan, cars were disposable.

My first stop was not home, but to the offices of the Hacker's Union, where all the power lies—they run San Fran while the Corporates play their little games. They can even shut down San Francisco if they wished. They enjoy running San Francisco, for it is better to reign in Hell than settle for less. If the children running the island in *Lord of the* Flies had an option, they probably wouldn't have left. Either,

Upon my arrival, I explained who I was and what Omega had been planning. Imagine my surprise that the Hackers were *not* amused.

For those of you out there in the larger world, you may have noticed that the Omega Corporation no longer exists. That it appeared to eat itself from the inside out. Now you know why. Don't mess with the Hacker's Union.

When I spoke to Kyle, he wasn't very happy that he had been played. My informant was killed because he talked to me. Kyle was going to be paid twelve hours after the hit on my informant. By my calculations, he would have been five hours dead at the time.

Why do I send this report out to you, my loving and noble former superiors? Not because I want to give you any ideas. After all, if you owned the Wasteland, you could do something similar with no problem. With Omega out of the way, what would stop you from commandeering their land?

However, the Hackers Union has a failsafe. Should there be an incident that wipes out all of San Francisco, killing every living person in the area, you will have a problem. Should you try to kill us all for profit, there is a ticking e-bomb in cyberspace. Once a day, it must be disarmed; the timer reset by a hacker. If it isn't reset, it will unleash an attack. You don't want to know what the attack is. It would spoil the surprise.

They call it Masada. If we go, you'll be coming right along with us.

You could assume I'm lying. That I'm running a bluff. I suppose that depends on one very simple and important question.

What kind of people do you think we are?

Anderson out.

END TRANSMISSION.

ABOUT DECLAN FINN

As penance for his sins, Declan Finn lived for 41 years in New York City, but has made good his escape to Texas. He is the author over over thirty novels, from thrillers to urban fantasy to space opera, including the Dragon Award Nominated Novel for Best horror in 2016 and 2017, *Honor at Stake* and *Live and Let Bite*. He was also nominated for Best Apocalypse novel at the Dragons for 2017. He also won the book of the year award with his novel Hell Spawn from CLFA.

THE LESSER EVIL

MICHAEL WALLEY

Ten years after the war and humanity are reduced to scavenging. Fallout destroyed the ecosystem and life as it was known. Only the hardiest plants grow, and the animals that have managed to endure are in the sea. As supplies dwindle, inland dwellers are forced to make the long trek to the ocean.

I had managed to survive by securing an apartment at the top of a building with solar power and rainwater tanks, but they didn't keep my hunger at bay. So when a young family is spotted moving through the streets, heading for the ocean, I notice I'm not the only one to see them.

Can I get to the family in time, or will they become victims of the bandits…or worse?

THE LESSER EVIL

I shifted my weight and focused on the binoculars. The sand gusted in flurries through the streets, which made it hard to see, but as the wind dropped, there was no doubt. Yep, four of them. Two young adults and two kids younger than ten were approaching from the hills to the East, which was no longer green and full of life. No doubt, another family heading towards Dock Town by the ocean in the West. More newcomers with not enough to offer and no skills to offer. I'd journeyed to the Dock settlement a few times, but it was a dangerous place. Everything was a barter system, and the price doubled if you were an outsider. A man could ultimately survive, but if a woman wasn't ready to offer her body and…don't even get me started on the kids. They were lambs to the slaughter. They just didn't know it yet.

A part of me wanted to warn them, tell them to turn around and stick to scavenging or growing the few things that survived in this hellscape. But they were perfect. It had been ten years since the war devastated the ecosystem that most things depended on. The deteriorating weather had eliminated the growth of most edible plants, which in turn killed off many animals. Marine life seemed unharmed, and birds ate the plentiful insects but most mammals, other than humans, became extinct. Then, thanks to a complete breakdown of society, mankind stepped up to the plate and turned on itself. Small pockets worldwide managed to keep a semblance of humanity and work together, but most of the world turned to instinct. You had to take what the man next to you had to survive.

America was well armed with an abundant amount of guns. Preppers took out the peace-loving folk and decimated the population. Quickly and relatively painlessly, they established a society built on strength. Here in Australia, we got rid of most guns after a mass shooting, so we had to do it the hard way. Hand-to-hand combat with knives and baseball bats. Slow, agonizing, and the population dying slower than was required for the rest of us to survive. A case in point is below me now.

The family was like observing little red riding hood off to see Granny, which reminded me…were there any wolves out there?

On top of one of the tallest buildings in central Adelaide, I had a bird's eye view of the adjacent streets. I scanned the area and, sure enough, spotted a lone guy on top of a nearby car park staring in their direction. He stood, propped over the edge, gesturing to someone below. They were out of my line of sight; time to move. I shuffled past an array of solar panels around a rainwater tank and entered my rooftop apartment.

The residence had been the home of a wealthy businessman who was overseas when the war began. In my past life, I was the real estate agent who sold him the apartment. I knew it was designed to be self-sufficient. He never made it back, so I inherited the comfiest, most isolated, well-stocked place in Adelaide. Once the craziness settled, I went down with a welder, sealing doors with steel where I could, and positioned furniture to barricade myself from the world. Over the years, I acquired a healthy supply of DVDs and video games to help me stay sane. I established a rooftop garden and shade house with potatoes, bell peppers, corn, and tomatoes, which could handle the heat—solar battery power for everything from my hundred-inch television to my freezers.

But my freezers were running low.

A cookbook sat on the counter. A bottle of cumin seeds held it open at a picture of a creamy curry with a piece of roti. It was a tease reading it, but the curry was back on the menu if there was an opportunity for guests. I unscrewed the cap and breathed in the earthy smell of the seeds. Exhaling, I put it down and turned off the air conditioner. Being so high from ground level, I was able to soundproof it enough to keep the sound to a low hum. A blessing in the constant, oppressive heat, but still secret.

Mountain climbing was a passion of mine, so all my gear came with me when I moved in. I twisted into my harness, strapped a bowie knife to my right leg, and grabbed a Taser from its charging station, placing it in a pouch on my left hip. Next, I strapped a small knife above my left ankle. Brass knuckles went into my breast pocket. I then patted the leg pocket to feel several cable ties and took a deep breath. I hated myself for what I was planning to do, but the sad fact was I either adapted to this brutal world or became a victim.

I walked outside and glanced over to the next building, which had a flagpole on top. I kept a clean flag rigged on it to give me an accurate wind direction. It was one thing to see an approaching enemy, but if the wind was right, I could smell them first. Unfortunately, the family was downwind, which was not in my favor.

I strode to the ledge and grasped the wire fixed to a lower building next door. The carabiner clicked into place as I grabbed a nearby oil can to lubricate the pulley. Less friction, less noise. I focused on the gym mats at the end of the wire. The angle was sharp, so I used a quick release over the mats. I stuffed up a landing once, and my back hurt for a month, so I hesitated to slow my breathing and then leaned forward. The mats sank on impact with a hiss. Nailed it. Keeping low, I approached the direction of the car park.

He was gone.

Using my binoculars, I searched the area he was gesturing to when movement caught my eye. Another man hid behind the corner of a building. I grinned as smoke drifted from a cigarette in his mouth. He was sloppy, good. The car park was six levels, so I had time while the wolf descended. Luckily, they were on the opposite side of the building where my rappelling rope was coiled and secured. I threw it over the edge and was on the street in seconds, secreting my harness in a bin. In less than a minute, the side entrance of the car park was in sight. The door squeaked as it swung. Holding my breath, one quick push kept the sound to a minimum. I made a mental note to oil it later. The light filtered through steel bars as I sprinted to the base of the stairwell with my steel-capped boots. Sneakers were good for stealth, but not when someone laughs at you, grabbing a broken toe during a fight.

I scarcely survived that encounter.

The wall next to the stairwell door was cool against my skin. I wiped the sweat from my hands and gripped the Taser. These things only gave you one shot. The door flew open, and the Taser dug into his side, sizzling. He fell to the ground, but it wasn't enough to incapacitate him. Sinking my knees into his back forced the air from his lungs as I stunned him again. A pool of urine formed under him as the Taser was exchanged for the cable ties in my trouser pocket. Being on top, I gagged as his body odor enveloped me. The postapocalypse came with its own fragrance. His legs were secured when the side door opened, the squeak echoing in the emptiness.

Maybe I won't oil it.

The man looked upset before seeing me, 'Who the hell are you? Get off Jimmy!'

Upon hearing his '''mate's voice, Jimmy came to life and bucked me off, sending my Taser sprawling across the stained concrete, 'Brett, get this asshole off me!'

I rolled to my feet and slid my knife out. Brett did the same. I was pleased to see mine was bigger, but I'd been stabbed with a pen knife before. Meanwhile, my original prey had pulled his knife out, trying to free himself. I stepped sideways and kicked his hand, sending it flying about twenty meters away in the opposite direction of my Taser.

He clutched his hand, 'Ah, you bastard! I'm gonna carve you up for that.'

I grinned, not taking my eyes off the oncoming Brett, 'What with? Your fingernails?'

I stepped past him, legs still tied, as he inched his way towards his knife and confronted Brett, 'Shall we dance?'

Brett stopped and swung his knife clumsily, his attempt at looking menacing, "I'll dance with your dead body after I stab the crap out of it!"

I pouted, "We'll see. Do you want to lead, or shall I?"

Brett snarled, charging at me. Using his momentum, I stepped to the side and pushed him over. I glimpsed at Jimmy, now halfway to his knife—time to move and grab the Taser. I replaced it in the pouch and turned in time to see Brett sprinting at me. Seriously, how stupid was this guy? He swept his knife so wide I ducked under it and stabbed his leg.

I needed to incapacitate him, not kill him. It made such a difference later.

Brett fell like a sack of spuds, his knife hitting the concrete as he clutched his leg. My brass knuckles were on and flying at his face in a heartbeat. He was dazed enough that I was able to cable-tie his legs. Meanwhile, the other guy freed himself and rose, brandishing his knife.

Here we go!

I didn't fall for that again, so I picked up Brett's knife and placed it in my bowie knifes pouch. Someone else approached me, except this time, swaying his knife in slow, small arcs. He looked calm and in control.

"Jimmy, you gotta help me, man; I'm bleeding out!"

We both glanced at Brett. A pool of blood was forming around his leg and steadily getting bigger. Damn, I'd sliced one of his arteries. I needed him alive. Raising my knife, I walked backward, 'Help him. Tie the leg off above the wound.'

Jimmy squinted at me, "What are you talking about? You're the one who stabbed him?"

I shrugged, "Yeah, and I'm the one who Tasered you and used cable ties. Would I do that if I wanted to kill you?"

His jaw hung limp as he searched for something to say, confused.

"Jimmy, help me!"

I pointed my knife at Brett, "Jimmy. Help him!"

While keeping me in his sight, he hurried over to help Brett. I backed up to a car and leaned against the door, trying to look non-menacing. I watched him tear a sleeve from his shirt and apply a tourniquet to Brett. As he was busy doing this, I reached behind me and bent an old aerial until it broke. I telescoped it down and slipped it into my pocket.

Jimmy grunted as he tied off the tourniquet, cut the ties on "Brett's leg, and stood. He looked at me, eyebrows raised, 'You could have run off then. What's your deal?"

I gestured to the street with my finger, "I saw you two checking out that approaching family."

He laughed, "So that's it, huh? You after the woman? We're happy with the kids."

My stomach turned. I was after the kids, but not for their reason, "Yeah, that sounds good. How about we leave your mate here and we'll deal with them. Then we can go our separate ways."

He looked down at his wounded buddy and nodded, "All right, but no funny stuff."

I retrieved Brett's knife and slipped mine back into its sleeve. A quick flick sent Brett's sliding across the floor to him. He let it bump into him but made no effort to pick it up. He was pale from blood loss and looked ready to pass out. I picked up a garbage bin, placing it under Brett's wounded leg to help stem the bleeding.

Jimmy nodded his approval and ambled over to the bars covering the opening to the road, "They should be here in the next thirty minutes. How do you want to play this?"

I sighed, "Don't know, how were you guys going to do it?"

He took out his knife and made a slashing motion, "Usually, one of us comes behind the man and cuts his throat. We punch out the woman, and then the kids are usually fifty-fifty. They either freeze or run."

I nodded through gritted teeth, "So you've done this a few times before?"

"Yeah man, we have a little fun with them until the food they've got runs out, and then we kill them. Rinse and repeat."

I swallowed hard before continuing, "So…you don't eat them?"

He screwed his face up, "What? No! I know there are cannibals out there, but that's sick. I mean, yeah, I'm a murderer, I'm a rapist but Jesus. You've got to draw the line somewhere, you know?"

I looked into the distance, "Yeah, we're not animals."

Jimmy pointed to the door, "Come on, there's one of those minimarts across the street. It's been picked clean, but idiots who haven't been to town always think there's something left behind. They can't help themselves. Let's find a good spot to ambush them there."

"

Brett coughed. He had a couple of hours at best. The clock was ticking.

The damaged red, orange, and green 7-eleven sign hung over the doorway. It was a typical convenience store—a scaled-down version of a supermarket at twice the price. As Jimmy said, it was picked clean. Unless you were running low on fly spray or fertilizer for your indoor plants. Funnily enough, there was no toilet paper. I crossed that off my shopping list and kept looking. We agreed to look for anything that might appeal to them and put it at the front to entice them further. I 'wasn't sure how far to take this, so I played along until something presented itself.

And there it was.

A cool room was at the back of the shop. It was empty but plugged into a generator. The power grid was one of the first things that failed after the war. Who holed up in here obviously rigged this to keep any food they could lay their hands on fresh. They either ran out of food or, the more likely outcome, they were overrun and had everything stolen from them. Either way, it was exactly what I needed. Sure enough, the fuel tank was empty. A quick search of the shelves found a bottle of paint thinner—any port in a storm.

The fuel sloshed in, the fumes making me choke, "Hey, come here."

Jimmy sauntered over, scratching his head which looked like it hadn't been washed in a year, "What ya found?"

With a flourish, I held my hands out, "What do you think?"

"I think you're an idiot. They're not gonna carry a generator to the ocean."

I sighed and pointed to the power cord leading to the cool room, "It's a stinking hot day, same as every other day. They'll easily hear the humming of the generator from the road. You wanted something to get their attention. They come in here, see it's a cool room, and think, even if there's no food, we can cool down. When's the last time you felt an air conditioner?"

He choked out a response, "Years."

This was going to be easier than I thought. I nodded slowly, bent down, and grasped the pull cord to start the motor, "You ready?"

Jimmy nodded slowly, "Yeah! I can't wait to feel it."

I grinned back, "Yeah! It's gonna be awesome. Hey, I tell you what." I reached over and handed him the empty paint thinner bottle, "Take this and wedge it in the door's opening to make sure it doesn't close on you. Let me know when you can feel it."

He nodded like I had just offered him a steak dinner, "That's a good idea."

I saluted him and started the motor. It took a couple of goes, but a cloud of grey smoke erupted from the engine, and it came to life. I coughed, squinting, and gave him the thumbs up. Clenching his fists, he stared in that direction, anticipating a cool breeze. He shot off around the corner and disappeared into the room. I came to the door and watched him march to the back and stretch up on his toes, reaching for the vent at the top of the rear wall. I waited for him to turn around.

Jimmy looked back at me, confused, "It's not working."

I smiled. A look of horror slowly crossed his face, "No shit, and you called me an idiot."

I placed my foot on the bottle, pushed it behind me, and closed the door. A flick of a switch to the generator and the motor died. A faint banging with muffled shouting came from within. That took care of these two, but Brett was bleeding out. I thought about heading back to him but then remembered why I had come down in the first place.

The family.

I peered around the corner of the doorway to see how close they were and ducked back inside. They were fifty meters away...and talking to two men. I looked back to the cool room. No wonder he was so happy to join up with me; he had a backup to take me out. Well played Jimmy, didn't see that coming. I used a crate in the corner of the shop to look over the advertising covering the window. They were standing around talking like old friends when one of them grabbed the woman's hair and held a knife to her throat. Standard greeting these days. The husband held his hands up in the usual; we don't want any trouble, pose. This was the part where he got stabbed, and she got raped, but kids were involved, which always made people hesitate.

There were two extra players on the field, which changed things.

I could help the family instead.

I racked my brain, wondering how to separate them. One had to stay with the family, so I needed a distraction. The near-empty shop offered nothing but... Why not go back to plan A? With the generator fired up, a can of fly spray propped the front door open to let the sound out. Peering through the window, I saw the larger one of the two striding towards the shop with the mother of all knives out. I say knife, but it was more of a machete.

"Jimmy! Brett! Where are you clowns? You were supposed to scare them back toward us, not make us walk down here."

Halfway to the store, he arched his head, the sound of the generator reaching him. He looked back to the other guy, holding his hand up in a wait there motion. I got down from my perch and stood behind the front door, which was covered in advertising posters, so I wouldn't be spotted. Slowing my breathing to calm myself, I took out my knife. I played the scenario in my head. He'd cautiously push the door and creep in, panning the room for anyone. No one liked a surprise, so he'd take his time. Just had to be cool. Grab his head and stab him in the back and side as many times as possible. It's not like I hadn't done it before.

And then it all went to shit.

He burst through the door, like a bull in a china shop, shouting, "Where the hell are you two?"

The door smashed me in the face, breaking my nose. Blood spilled down my face, and my knife fell to the floor. I staggered back, dazed and blinking from the tears welling in my eyes, spitting out the metallic taste of blood and trying to remember what I was doing. The Bull turned and looked at me, screwing his face up, "Who the fuck are you?"

I pinched my nose, crying out as it straightened with a crunch, and wiped my hand on my blood-soaked shirt, "You ask a lot of questions."

He raised his machete and pointed it at me, "Well normally, I'd love to stop and have a chat. Maybe sing some songs around a campfire, but I'm kinda busy at the moment. Where's Jimmy and Brett?"

I shrugged, "I'm sure Brett's lying around with his legs up, and Jimmy's trying to stay out of the heat somewhere. If you can't find your boyfriends, maybe you should hold hands when you go out for a walk."

The Bull, fuming, took the bait and made a huge swipe at me with the machete. He was a big man and moved slowly, so it was easy to duck under his arm and roll out of the way. I grabbed my knife. I backed down an aisle as he stalked after me. After a few steps, the muffled sound of Jimmy screaming and pounding started up again.

He looked past me and shook his head, "Idiot."

I laughed, "That's what I said!"

He nodded in agreement, "I should leave him in there."

I tilted my head, "Does that mean there's an opening in your boy scout group?"

The Bull held his machete slightly to the side, "Maybe if we met under different circumstances." He paused and looked around, "I mean, if my son is okay, I'd be happy to let you walk."

I sighed; why did one have to be his son? "Jimmy's fine?"

He looked at me through gritted teeth, "I was talking about Brett."

I gripped my knife a little tighter, "Oops."

Roaring, he swung for the bleachers. His blade smashed into a bag of laundry powder, sending a cloud into the air and obscuring our vision. This was my moment. I lunged forward, driving my knife into his chest with all my force.

It was like punching a sandbag.

I dropped my knife, slippery from my blood, forcing me to back away as he swung again.

He stopped and rubbed his chest, "Argh, that's going to bruise!"

I sneezed from the laundry powder filling the air, then tripped over the empty paint-thinner bottle. Flat on my ass, he towered over me, "What are you wearing? Chainmail?"

He tore open his shirt to reveal a black vest, "Kevlar. Not perfect, just ask the bloke I took it off, but it comes in handy for annoying little shits like you."

I chuckled, then started laughing. My time on this god-forsaken planet was always on borrowed time. I'd done things I wasn't proud of. Today would have been a classic example. Dying, while lying on the floor with a car aerial poking me in the rear.

Wait a minute.

"Look mate, I tell you what. Let me stand up and die on my feet like a man, and I'll tell you where to find your son."

A frown crossed his face as he said in a quiet, menacing voice, "Get up."

I sat up and took the aerial from my back pocket, pulling it out to its full length, 'A sword fight to the death. Well, an aerial, but it'll have to do.'

The Bull motioned with his machete to get up, "I don't care, just tell me where my son is."

I swung the aerial in front of him while propped on one knee, hoping he wouldn't notice my other hand brushed my ankle where I kept my small knife. I reverse-gripped it so the blade ran along my wrist to keep him from seeing it. He held his machete out, tapping the aerial to keep it at length as I stood. He took a couple of steps back and held his machete back, "A deal's a deal; where's my son?"

I nodded, appreciating that he let me stand, "Across the street in the car park, street level. We tied off his leg, but he was bleeding pretty badly. If you're quick, you might get to speak to him before he dies. Care to give me a pass this time?"

The Bull snorted, "You'll be dead in less than a minute" And with that, he swung with all his might. The machete may have been his weapon of choice, but he obviously 'didn't practice with it. Each swing was slow and easy to dodge but delivered with enough power to end me. My aerial, on the other hand, was fast and long enough for me to get a strike every time he swung.

We were both right-handed, so every time I struck, it was on his left side, which meant he had to cross his machete over to attempt to block me. That extra time gave me the edge. But my aerial wouldn't win this fight. I was waiting for that one move. We all do it when something annoying, like mosquitoes, won't leave us alone.

And there it was.

He tried to grab the aerial instead of fending it away with his machete. I slowed my attacks so that he just missed the first few times. He was getting confident about grabbing it.

So I let him. I pulled my arm back further than before and swung with all my might, aiming for his outstretched hand. He grimaced with pain as he clutched his prize and yanked it to take it from me.

Pulling me forward, and as he turned his head to the side, appraising his reward, I reversed the grip on my knife and buried it into his exposed neck. The momentum hurled us both to the floor, which enabled me to roll out of his reach.

The Bull lay on his back facing me, my aerial in one hand and his machete in the other. He tossed the aerial behind him and sat up, "Enough games; it's over."

My face twisted as if looking at something nasty, "Ooo… I think you're right. There's just… your neck. A little something."

He felt both sides until he found the knife, "You little prick. You think a tiny knife is going to stop me?"

I held my hands out, "Well, that depends; you're not going to take it out, are you?"

He grinned, "I'm not just going to take it out; I'm going to kill you with it."

With that, he removed the knife with the expected consequence. A fountain of arterial blood erupted from his neck, spraying the shelving beside him. The laundry powder mixed with his blood made a bizarre pink paste on the floor. He struggled to get up but fell in a heap, slipping on the ooze. After several comical attempts, he gave up, the blood loss now taking its toll. With relief, I slumped against the door to the cool room and watched, catching my breath as he faded away.

I was spent.

My nose was broken, my body bruised, and I was sore from all of the day's encounters. I just wanted to go home, have my weekly shower a day early, and crawl into bed. But I had bodies to clean up.

A distant shout came from outside, "Roger, you found 'em?"

Right, and deal with that.

Standing, I said to the prone body of the Bull before me, "Your mates looking for you, and I couldn't be bothered going another couple of rounds with anyone. Got any ideas?"

His lifeless eyes looked back at me, his mouth open with his last insult that never came. The reflection of the drinks fridge caught my attention. My shirt was drenched in blood from my nose, and my hair was white from laundry powder. I looked unnatural. The machete lay at my feet, which gave me an idea. The blade could have been sharper, but it was worth trying.

I kicked the door open and shambled into the street. In my right hand, the machete, the tip scraping the ground. I turned and faced the family being held hostage with my head down but my eyes up. Even from this distance, the remaining bandit's eyes flashed wide. This might work.

He grabbed the woman tighter and stammered, "Who…who the fuck are you?"

I unhurriedly walked towards him and shouted, "Your worst fucking nightmare!"

He let go of the woman and stepped back, his eyes fixated on my left hand. "What the fuck?" His eyes were wide with horror.

I looked at the machete and then at my other hand. I raised the severed head high so that he could get a good look. Blood dripped onto the road in a steady rhythm, "Your mate Roger! And if you think Jimmy or Brett are coming to save you… think again."

The Bulls head fell to the road, the machete's tip grinding into the ground as I walked. The sound echoed around the buildings as a light breeze swept sand between us. The bandit looked around and, with no backup coming to his rescue, turned and ran like a scared little bitch.

I straightened up and waved goodbye.

Hefting the machete to my shoulder allowed me to pick up the pace toward the family. Now to decide—the Bull and, no doubt Brett was dead, but Jimmy was alive. The family would make seven, but the thought of all that work in my current state was beyond comprehension. The virtual coin had been tossed, and my decision had been made. As I approached, the father stepped in front of his family. The machete fell to the ground as my hands went up, "It's all right; I'm not going to hurt you. I just wanted to scare that idiot away. The world's turned to shit so bad; yelling boo doesn't work anymore. Excuse the language kids.'

The father took a breath as if he had been holding it and visibly relaxed, "Thank you. I thought we were dead for sure."

I sighed, "Before I say anything else, I assume you already heard that you shouldn't be traveling alone with your family speech?"

The father gave me a sheepish look, "Yeah, I've heard it. The community we left was struggling with the small amount of food we could grow, so we took a vote on who had to leave, and we lost. We're hoping to find work in Dock Town."

I pursed my lips and thought about how to let this guy down. In the end, honesty was always the best policy, "Look, buddy, Dock

Town is a dive. I know you've probably had some merchants come through whatever settlement you've been living in saying how great the place is but trust me, not for a family. Your best bet is to head into the suburbs and find a decent house; by that, I mean one you can lock up and be safe in. Go out at night scavenging through houses for food. The only settlements I've heard of that would be family-friendly are in the eastern states. If you want to make a run for them, good on ya, but you'll need to prepare."

The father looked at his wife, who nodded back at him. I guess she wasn't keen on Dock Town either.

"What do you mean by prepare?"

I couldn't help myself; I smiled. This guy was willing to do whatever it took to look after his family. A remnant of the way life was before the war. Thank God the other scumbags turned up, "Look for the newest four-cylinder car you can find. Half of Adelaide had solar panels installed, and I know some houses still have power available to them, so keep an eye out for a battery charger as well. Go through sheds and collect fuel cans that you can siphon fuel from cars and store it in the trunk of the car."

The father nodded, "Couldn't I siphon fuel from cars we see on the way?"

I smiled again, "Have you seen Mad Max? That shit is the reality now, sorry kids. If you fill the trunk with fuel cans and only pull up in the middle of nowhere to refuel, you can drive nonstop to the Eastern states in a day or two. I don't know the exact location of any safe refuge over there, but there's none here."

The wife was over her initial fear and spoke up, "If you're so sure there's a safe haven interstate, why haven't you gone?"

I looked down, "I have no family to protect—no reason to fight to do the best I can every day. When the rioting and killing started, I did what I could to survive. Still do as you've seen. I'm not the man I was and…I struggle with who I am now. Honestly, you're lucky you caught me on a good day."

The parents looked at each other as the elder child held the younger one. I looked at the children, a tear running down my cheek. Every day was a struggle, pretending I was the lesser evil.

The mother caught me looking at the children and placed her hands on their shoulders. The father held his out to shake, "I'm going to take your advice. Thank you for all you've done. I wish I could repay you somehow."

I looked behind me to the 7-eleven and car park, "Actually, could you give me a hand for ten minutes?"

I lied; half an hour later, we had picked up the Bull and Brett and carried them to where the rappelling rope lent against the building. Thankfully Jimmy didn't make a noise, as that would have been awkward. I held my hand out for the final handshake, "Thanks for that, all the best."

The father pinched his nose and took a deep breath through his mouth, "I thought maybe you wanted to throw them in the dumpster to keep disease away or something. There's a God-awful smell around here. So…what's with the rope?"

I grinned as I thought about how crowded the dumpster was already. The squawking of a flock of seagulls overhead gave me the answer. The Gods were on my side, "See those birds up there?"

The father nodded.

"Well, I stack bodies on the roof, and when birds come to feed on them, they're easy prey with a bow and arrow. Depending on the day, you'd be surprised how many I get."

The father looked impressed, "Wow, that's a great idea. Gruesome but ingenious."

"Thanks. Necessity is the mother of invention."

He looked up, "So, you live up there?"

I couldn't have him thinking that in case he got caught, and he was willing to say anything to keep his family safe, "No way! Heat rises, and it's as hot as hell up there. I live in a basement nearby. Quiet, cool, and safe. No one bothers me."

"So why go to all the bother of taking them up to the roof? Wouldn't it be easier to leave them on the road?"

I gave him that look you give a child when they don't understand something basic, "You mean down here with all the people you met trying to kill us?"

"Yeah, good point."

The father turned to go and then looked back, "You seem like a decent guy. Are you sure you don't want to come with us?"

I looked past him to his family waiting at the mouth of the alley, "You've got a couple of hours of daylight left. You need to move now."

The father gave a solemn nod and walked back to his family. He crouched and said a few words to his kids, and then they were gone. I waited a few minutes and got my harness out of the bin. I had to get a couple of cadaver bags from my apartment to make hauling the bodies easier.

Two hours later, I was back at the 7-eleven. It was time to deal with Jimmy. My Taser had been charged and was ready to go. With more cable ties, it was time to use my car salesman voice. I banged on the door and spoke into the door's seam, "Hey Jimmy, you in there?"

There were sounds of movement, and then Jimmy's voice was next to the door, "Of course I am! Where the hell was I going to go? Let me out of here!"

"Jimmy, Jimmy, Jimmy, you didn't tell me about Roger and his friend."

"Yeah, well, you didn't ask. Plus, you stabbed Brett, so what did you expect?"

"It's okay mate; we sorted it out. Roger is not big on sharing, but he said if he could have his way with the woman first, I could have her after."

Jimmy laughed, "Yeah, that sounds like Roger. He's not big on sharing. Why the hell has it taken so long to get me out then?"

"Not my fault mate. He said you were an idiot for getting caught and could stew here for a while as punishment."

Jimmy stopped laughing, "Yeah, that sounds like Roger too. What a dick...he's not out there, is he?"

I laughed, picked up a bottle of water, and got out my Taser, "No mate, you're safe. I'm going to open the door. We're cool, right?"

Jimmy drummed a beat on the door, "All good, let's go. It's time to have a little fun."

I opened the door and held the bottle up so that it was the first thing he saw, "Peace?"

Jimmy stepped out, took the bottle, spun the top off, and drank for all he was worth. As his head tilted back, I stepped behind him and dug the Taser into him at full strength. He went into a spasm and hit the floor. In seconds he was tied. I rolled him over, took a roll of duct tape, and pulled a length out with my teeth.

"What the hell, man, Rogers gonna kick your ass!"

"Really? Let's ask him. Hey Roger, are you gonna kick my ass?" I stood, stepped to the side, and pointed. I'd collected Roger's head earlier and placed it on the shelf across from us.

Jimmy stared at Roger's head with his mouth agape. Realization kicked in, and he screamed. I duct taped Jimmy's mouth and then held up a cadaver bag, 'You wouldn't mind getting into this, would you?'

I kept one of those trolleys delivery guys used in shopping centers in my trusty dumpster next to my harness bin. The buzz from a cloud of flies erupted from the opening as I lifted the lid. Three bodies were decomposing there, which was my way of keeping unwanted fingers off my trolley.

With Jimmy's struggling body tied to the trolley, we approached the rappelling rope. As I had with the other two, I attached him to a line, climbed up, and hauled him to the roof. Then onto the zip line to get to my apartment. Once inside, I opened a trapdoor which revealed a ladder to the apartment below. Once down safely, it was time to get changed and clean up.

After a cold beer, thank God for home brewing kits, I joined Jimmy downstairs. I pulled him out of the bag, which was placed back on the shelf with the others. A stereo was on the top shelf with a CD containing a mix of eighties pop and rock. Jimmy stirred and kept blinking as his eyes adjusted to the bright flood lights I installed in the bathroom. I sat him up against the wall so that he could see my work. With my white plastic apron on, my butcher's knife, and my file, I sharpened as Jimmy's eyes lit up and focused on the scene before him. Comprehension setting in. Brett's head was punctured from behind by a meat hook, suspending him from the ceiling. Roger's headless body lay off to the side.

From a foot away, I crouched and looked Jimmy right in the eyes, "You guys were unlucky today. When I saw that family, those kids...they were my focus. Children are so tender compared to adults. Then I saw you guys and thought, I need to get to the family first. But one thing led to another, and I ended up with three of you. The family was lucky because...well...my freezer only holds so much."

Jimmy began sobbing. I stroked his hair, "Hey, hey, don't worry. When it's your turn, it'll be quick and painless...ish. I did want Brett to stay alive. I've found that if I can butcher someone and get them straight into the freezer, the meat keeps better. You should've learned not to trust people in this demented world we've been left in."

I gave him my biggest smile, "You never know what they're hiding...the monster within."

ABOUT MICHAEL WALLEY

Michael Walley lives in Adelaide, South Australia, and is currently writing a LIT RPG novel. He was inspired to start writing after listening to Justin Macumber on the Dead Robots Society writing podcast. He likes riding his motorbike in the country to work out story ideas in his helmet, although the best concepts always seem to come in the shower. '"' 'He's the father of an MMA fighter son and a daughter who still thinks she can take him. Forklift operator by day and a video gamer/writer by night.

A SHELL OF HUMANITY

STEVE DIAMOND

In a post-apocalyptic future, a plague of carnivorous insects has all but destroyed the world. But worse yet, they have infected humanity like parasites, turning people into monstrous, unthinking hybrids. Rick Benjamin in infected, wandering the country waiting to die. When does a person cease being a person? When are they just a shell of their former selves, and when does a person cross that line? And is there anything that can bring back a person's humanity?

A SHELL OF HUMANITY

I stomped down on the man's neck, hearing the carapace of his skin crack and crunch. He was the last one, his companions already lying still like a girl's scattered dolls around the camp.

My legs gave way, and I collapsed to the ground. The typical post-fight exhaustion ran through me, and I nearly threw up what small contents my stomach still held. I reached a hand around to the back of my neck to feel the bug latched on there, its legs and mouth buried deep into my skin. I stopped. Better not to agitate it.

A month ago, I'd been fine, a simple soldier guarding one of the last scientific outposts in North America. Now I wandered the apocalyptic wilds, looking for survivors. Looking for a solution I knew didn't exist, all so I didn't become another mindless monster like the ones I'd just killed.

Since the parasite dug its way into me, I could smell differently. Better in some ways, though to most, I imagined the change was worse. The scents of decomposing flesh were a beacon to me, simultaneously revolting and attracting. This camp held the origin of a particularly strong smell. I wanted nothing more than to run away, to leave this camp in my rearview. But... but hunger gnawed at me.

The bug on my neck needed sustenance, and so its needs became my compulsion.

I flipped the Shell I'd just killed onto his back. Shell. I didn't know if everyone around the world called these husks by this name, but around here we did. Looming over me to my left were the Wasatch Mountains. I didn't know how far south I'd walked, so I didn't know what city I'd strolled into. Probably not Salt Lake City, though I couldn't be sure. I'd never come to Utah before the Swarm, so I didn't have a good grasp on the territory.

All I knew was this place smelled of death, but I caught the scent of the living somewhere under it all.

My parasite didn't want to eat the Shells I'd killed. For whatever reason, they didn't like the taste of their own. The scientists up north didn't know why, and I hadn't stuck around to let them use me as their plaything.

The dead Shell at my feet stared at the sky with black, lifeless eyes. Killing him had been a good thing—one less controlled human in the world and one less parasite. From the looks of this one, the host was pretty close to molting. The chitinous carapace had spread, covering nearly all his skin. All his hair had fallen out, and his eyes were completely black. Soon he would have shed his last remnants of humanity and become just another monster intent on finding and eating the last dregs of the human race.

I smelled leftover dead flesh on him, so he'd just eaten. I leaned in close, took a deep whiff around his mouth, and followed the trail to a nearby ruined building. The door long since broken off its hinges. Old glass crunched under my boots. Inside, bare shelves stood like blank tombstones, meant to show their remembrance of what they once held, but no one knew what that was anymore. My foot kicked a small, empty pill bottle. Maybe this had been a pharmacy.

A door leading into a back room showed signs of recently being ripped open. The smell of dead flesh led through it. I stepped over the splinted remains of the door and found myself in a long hallway. The lightless gloom gave me no difficulty. Since becoming infected, not only had my sense of smell improved dramatically, but so had everything else. To my eyes, the hallway looked like an old black-and-white movie. Where the front of the store had been a wreck of decay, this hallway was mostly clean. A few leaves and a little dirt lay scattered across the floor, but everything looked fresh. Likely blown in after the Shell outside had broken the door down. But why? Why had the parasite forced its host to rip the door open?

I opened each door in turn, finding nothing but oddly clean rooms absent the apocalyptic decay from outside. Most of the rooms had walls lined with shelves. In the first room, they held canned goods that, a month ago, would have had me across the room ripping their lids off. But not anymore. The parasite made sure I only hungered for rotting flesh.

The next room was stocked with meds, bandages, and other medical supplies. The final room on the right was stockpiled with bottled water. This I did break into, ripping the cap off a gallon jug. I always thirsted for water, and when I found it, I couldn't get enough. I had to be careful not to drink too much, making my stomach burst. The parasite wanted flesh, and it wanted water, and it didn't know how to stop that compulsion for either. One of the only reasons the entire human race hadn't already been killed was because the bugs didn't know how to regulate human consumption. The parasites forced their hosts to eat and drink themselves to death, thus killing themselves.

The lukewarm water felt heavenly going down my throat. I chugged and chugged, feeling my stomach filling near to bursting. I couldn't stop. It spilled out of the corners of my mouth and over my chin, soaking my thin jacket and shirt.

I wanted more. The thing on my neck tried to drown in the water like it was a drug. Maybe it was. The scientists didn't have a good answer and were always on the lookout for infected people to run tests on.

The jug emptied, saving me from hydrating my body to death. I wanted more, and stepped forward to grab another gallon. My hand reached out, shaking with need. I closed my eyes and forced myself back. My eyes remained closed until I felt my way out of the water storage room. The urge to drink subsided. Not for the first time, I wondered what would happen if I saw a lake. Would I just jump in and drown as I tried to drink it all?

Only one door remained. I opened my eyes and studied the entrance to the last room on the left. The smell of dead flesh wafted through the door, which stood cracked open. When the Shell outside had come through here, he'd not closed the door behind him. Something about it seemed wrong. He'd left the room and had closed the door *almost* all the way? I pulled the door open, seeing if it would close on its own. It didn't.

I inhaled deeply, feeling the sickly intoxicating aroma of death wash over me. But under it, almost an afterthought, I smelled something else.

Something living.

Nothing stirred in the quiet room. An old carpet covered the floor, and old bookshelves lined the walls. The shelves were even filled with books. Most looked like they were fiction, mainly hardbacks. In my days before the Swarm filled the skies, I'd been career military, spending my youth stationed at bases all around the globe. There was one publisher that regularly sent us boxes of their latest releases. Baen. I recognized a few on the shelves from those simpler days. Powers, Weber, Correia. All good reads. In another time, I would have pulled them from the shelves to leaf through them.

But I no longer lived in simple times.

Sweet, rotting flesh forced my attention to the room's corner, where a half-eaten corpse slumped against the wall. The face was mostly gone, as was the flesh on the thighs and abdomen. And yet, a good amount of skin and muscle still clung to those bones. I couldn't resist their call, practically falling to my knees to crawl to the rotting meat.

I ate as fast as I could, smearing the flesh across my face as I tried to shove it in my mouth faster and faster. It sloughed off the bones easily, but even if it had been tougher to rip away, I'd have managed easily enough. The bug fused to my neck made me easily stronger than any human still alive. I needed that strength to fight the Shells constantly hunting me.

Fortunately, not enough flesh remained to make my stomach

burst. I should have been full. No, I should have been vomiting up the putrid meat, but the parasite made sure I enjoyed the sickening display. It craved the food source, and so did I. Physically, at least. It may as well have been A5 Wagyu. But, mentally, shame and revulsion weighed heavy on my shoulders. Eating the dead like a zombie from those fiction pieces on the bookshelves surrounding me.

Hunger. It clawed at my gut. Despite the water and flesh I'd consumed, my stomach growled. The parasite didn't know or understand satisfaction. Eating anymore would kill me.

With most of the dead guy consumed, the scent of someone alive grew stronger and clearer. At the opposite end of the room, I spied the small, flipped up a small corner of the old, stained carpet.

I pushed up from my knees and crossed the room, then pushed the carpet away with the toe of my boot. Under the threadbare rug, I found a trap door. The smell of the living grew stronger, so I grabbed the door's handle and pulled up. It lifted easily. Soundlessly. Someone had maintained this door during the apocalypse. My eyes strayed to the bones in the corner. Had it been him? But then, who had recovered the floor?

I descended the ladder down into the hidden room, and all the while, the smell of someone still living grew more potent by the moment. I dropped the last few rungs and turned around to find a dim, if clean, room—a table in its middle, beds behind it in the back corners.

And on the bed was a woman clutching a young girl close.

I held up both hands in an attempt to show I wasn't the threat I knew I was. "Uh… hey there." The words sounded strange to my ears. When had I last spoken out loud? Probably the day I'd been infected and had run from the facility. "My name is Rick. Rick Benjamin. I'm not going to hurt you. How would you two like to be taken somewhere safe?"

They'd packed up and followed me. Not that they had much of a choice. Their home wasn't safe anymore.

The woman went by Amber Smith. An obvious alias, but calling her out on the lie didn't seem like a good move. She said her daughter's name was Jess. She looked to be thirteen or so. Maybe Jess was a legit name. Maybe not. The girl answered to it, which was the only thing that mattered.

I'd had the presence of mind to wipe the remnants of my meal away before they saw me in the light. The man meant something to them. A husband and father, perhaps. Something a little more, or something a little less. Amber stifled a sob when she saw him, then covered Jess' eyes.

I could put the pieces together well enough. He'd come up for supplies, but his smell had attached the Shells I'd killed outside their hidden home. Their protector had died fighting and, once dead, had provided a partial meal. I figured that was the only reason the Shell had left him unfinished. I'd eaten a freshly dead person up near Pocatello, but the parasite had forced me to stop partway through. I didn't know why, but at the time, I'd been grateful for the reprieve.

The corpse's freshness had covered up the smells of the other live ones hiding below. I didn't want to head back to the facility, but neither could I leave these two alone. They'd be easy targets, especially for the newly turned.

Those who found themselves between being infected and their first molting were known to hunt down the living, kill them, then haul around their corpses until the parasites gave them the green light to feed. The Shells I'd killed must have been waiting for the guy I'd finished eating to get truly good and ripe.

Then I'd come along and ruined their day.

For the first week of walking, neither the mom nor her daughter said much of anything. They kept their distance while still staying close enough to be considered "with" me. I caught both casting curious glances at the parasite on my neck.

One night, we crashed in the husk of an old school bus on northbound I-15. Out here, without any working headlights or light poles, the stars shone bright in the midnight sky. The mother and daughter went to bed at the back of the bus. I stood guard at the front, not needing sleep anymore. I hadn't slept once since being infected, and I missed it. A blissful dream would have been a nice change of pace from my existence in this hellscape.

The girl, Jess, sat up with a scream trying to free itself from her. Her hand reflexively covered her mouth. She had practiced this move before. She looked around with wild eyes, not remembering where she was. After a moment, she calmed down and leaned back against the bench seat. Her mom hadn't moved.

Jess looked back at her mother's sleeping form, then crept up to sit a few benches away from me.

"Mister Benjamin?"

"What can I do for you, Jess? Shouldn't you be sleeping?"

She nodded her agreement. Strands of dirty, blonde hair fell into her eyes. "Probably. I had a nightmare. I usually can't get back to sleep after I have one."

"What was the nightmare about?"

"Monsters."

All the worst nightmares were about monsters. Sometimes they chased you in the night, hunting you down, teeth flashing in the moonlight. Claws slashing. These days, I wasn't sure which was worse, the monsters in nightmares or the ones in the waking world.

"That's no good," I said. "I saw what you did there—covered your mouth as soon as you sat up. Smart. Your mom teach you that?"

"My dad."

"Ah."

"Can I ask you a question?" She swiftly directed us both out of that particular minefield.

I nodded. "I suppose so. I can't guarantee a good answer."

Jess pulled her knees up against her chest before speaking again. "What does it feel like?"

She didn't have to be specific. I knew what she meant. Her eyes filled in all the gaps in the question.

"It hurts," I answered. "Though, not as much as it did in the beginning. Mainly I'm just hungry and thirsty all the time."

"Hungry for what?"

I laughed, then saw her confused expression. "You really don't know?" She shook her head. "Well. Look, Jess. That's not a question I think is good for asking or answering at night. It'll keep you up."

"I'm already up."

"No," I said. "You aren't. Not really. Not like you would be if I were to answer that question with the truth. It's ugly, and I don't think I want you to know that ugliness right now."

"Oh. Then… can you tell me how it happened?"

A sigh escaped me. Not one of frustration at the question, but one that let the girl know this wasn't my favorite topic. "You sure?"

"Yes."

"Fine. But you better own up to this conversation when your mom asks." I waited for her to nod her agreement, then continued. "I was military. I've been all over the world. Seen lots of fighting. But nothing preps someone for the Swarm."

"Did they really come out of the pyramids?"

I nodded. "Sure did, all over the world. Some out of pyramids we didn't even know existed. Down in Mexico, there were some buried under mountains. They all just burst open, and clouds of the bugs came out. They attached themselves to people right here," I pointed at the back of my neck where the parasite's carapace gleamed in the moonlight. "They stab their legs into your skin, right down to the spine. They control you, make you do things you don't want to do."

"Like what?"

"Like… well… all sorts of bad things. Anyway, I was stationed up north a bit further, helping keep a bunch of scientists safe."

"What kind of scientists," Jess asked.

"The kind that studies the Swarm, looking for a way to kill them all. Maybe reverse the damage done by the ones that hook onto us. Kill the bug without hurting the person."

"Is that possible?"

I shrugged and stretched out my legs in front of me so they pointed down the aisle in between the two rows of seats. "Could be. The hardest part is them finding people to study. You see, once a person gets one of these things, they're ultimately gonna go bad and hurt people. We're really strong, so we can do a lot of damage. They always say they just need one more person to experiment on. Just one more.

"So one day I'm helping a group of them hunt down some of the infected," I remembered it like it was yesterday. "One of the nerds went too close to a bug mound—"

"What's that?" Jess interrupted, leaning in closer.

"A bug mound? It's a place where the ground bulges up. The bugs have found something to eat, so they all swarm together under the earth, eating. The ground covers them and makes a small mound. It moves up and down like it's breathing. One of the scientists forgets we're in the middle of an apocalypse and goes to have a closer look. It bursts open, spilling bugs everywhere. I managed to get him and the other scientists clear by using a flamethrower. Normal guns don't do much against small bugs."

"If you got them away from the Swarm, how did it get you?"

I shrugged again. "One got through the jets of flames I was shooting around. Or maybe around. I'm not sure. I got the scientists through a secure door into their facility, but I felt a sudden stab in my neck and collapsed. I reached back and found the bug. It was a lot smaller then. I tried to rip it free, but it made it so I couldn't."

Jess' eyes went wide in morbid fascination. She wanted to ask the logical follow-up question but didn't want to sound rude. It made me smile. She was a good kid. Most would have pressed, asking any rude question that entered their vapid little heads. Not Jess.

"You want to know what I meant? How it made it so I couldn't rip it off?"

After a moment's hesitation, Jess said, "If… if it's okay. I don't want you to be upset with me. At us."

I waved the concern away. "I appreciate it, kid. It's not my favorite topic to talk about, but I haven't spoken with anyone for a while. It's kinda nice. Have you ever been sick, Jess? I mean *real* sick?"

"Once, I think." Her eyebrows screwed together with her frown.

"I had a real bad fever a few months ago. I could barely open my eyes."

"Okay. Imagine that, but with so much pain that you threw up. With so much pain that even when your eyes were open, you couldn't see. That's what it was like when I grabbed the bug. It's a parasite. It latches on and messes with your nervous system to control you. It makes you hungry. Thirsty. Makes you feel pain, so you comply. That's what happened. I haven't touched it since."

"The scientists didn't help you?"

I almost laughed, but she'd shown some tact and consideration to me. So I just smiled. "No. They offered to use me in their experiments, though. I could make a difference, they said. I could help them find the cure."

"Could you?"

I shook my head and gave Jess a tired smile. "I don't know. Maybe. Maybe not. They wanted me because the connection to the bug was new and fresh. Apparently, that means something. But really, they just wait until you start to molt, then they really start studying you. I've seen them do it."

"Molt?"

"You didn't get out much, did you?"

"No," Jess replied, still hugging her knees. "Mom and dad said it wasn't safe. When we did have to run a few times, or when we'd hide, they'd cover my eyes sometimes."

"Good," I said. "There are some things you don't need to see. Molting is when a bug sheds its outer shell. When a person like me gets taken over, after a certain point, we shed, too. But once we do, we aren't human anymore. We're gone. The thing that is left is just the next version of the bug's evolution. It's a nasty business. But when the new form comes out of that old skin? Its shell is soft, and the creature is pretty weak. That's what the scientists really need."

"So for them to study you… you'd… you'd have to die and turn into one of those things?"

"You're a smart kid, Jess."

"That seems pretty terrible."

"Yes it does," I said. "But don't worry about it. If I get to the point where I'm about to molt, you'll know. And you and your mom can make a run for it. I already told her where the facility was, just in case. She's a good mom. So just stick with her."

Though they described all sorts of horrors, my words seemed to have calmed her. She yawned once. I hadn't felt tired in a month. Just yawning seemed like a luxury.

"Thanks for talking to me, Mister Benjamin. I'm going back to my mom. I think I can sleep now."

"No problem," I said. "Get some rest. We've still got a long way to go."

She walked back down the aisle and curled up on a seat near the back of the bus, and she was asleep within a couple of minutes. When Jess' breathing evened out, her mom sat up and stared at me across the bus. Anger didn't cloud her expression as I expected. Instead, she nodded once and mouthed the words "thank you."

That time on the bus marked a change for our little traveling party. They didn't hang back anymore. They didn't walk close enough for me to touch them by any means. But neither did they shun me. For the first time in a month, I didn't feel like the complete outcast I really was. Their presence almost allowed me to forget the monster growing in me.

Almost.

We arrived in Pocatello just before nightfall a few days later. We traveled slowly, with Jess needing frequent breaks. The situation didn't bother me overly much. In truth, I'd come to like both of them. Jess more than Amber, of course. The kid had a way of worming past my defenses. Her mom, Amber, spoke very little. I had a feeling she was still processing her husband's death, so I gave her all the space she needed.

We took the old exit 67 off ramp, walking as quietly as we could manage. The girls kept their flashlights off, walking close to me to see where I stepped. At the base of the offramp stood the remains of an old gas station. I'd been here once, years ago, before the

Swarm. With the signs broken, I couldn't remember if this had been a Chevron or a Maverick. Not that the distinction mattered. I often found myself trying to contextualize the current wreck of the world with the one I'd grown up in.

Hulks of old, burned-out semis filled the parking lot. Had they been caravanning after the initial wave of bugs hit further south? People figured out quickly to head far north or far south away from the equator. The colder, the better. Idaho in the winter was fairly safe. But this wasn't winter, and the Swarm hadn't erupted from the pyramids when it was most inconvenient for them.

We pushed the doors to the gas station aside carefully. The place had long since been ransacked. We could find a can or two of food, but nothing substantial. But anything to prolong the goods they carried would be good. I waved them to the back corner and put a finger to my lips. Amber nodded her understanding and pulled Jess along behind her. They set up behind an old Slurpee machine where they were hidden from obvious view.

I didn't find much. A can of beans, some spoons, and a pack of instant hot chocolate. Buried under a collapsed shelf was a small Sterno canister. I brought my findings back to the group.

"I found this," I said, holding up the Sterno. "We can set it under a wire rack and heat up some canned food tonight. Jess, have you ever had hot chocolate?"

"A long time ago," she said. The wistfulness in her voice nearly broke me.

I held out the packet. "How about we heat up some of your water, and you have it again?"

Her eyes lit up, and she pulled a tin cup from her backpack. I knew I'd made a mistake as soon as she began pouring water into it. The thirst hit me like a sucker punch to the gut. I stood up quickly —probably too quickly, judging from Amber's sudden look of fear— and took a few steps back. "I'll go see if there's anything else," I said. My voice sounded distant to my own ears. Thankfully Jess hadn't noticed anything amiss.

I made pretense of scrounging around the inside of the gas station again, taking my time to look carefully under every shelf and the fallen, rotting ceiling tiles. The smell of hot chocolate drifted my way. It should have turned off the craving for water, but it didn't. I had quick flashes, visions in a sense, of grabbing the boiling water and pouring it down my throat to satisfy the greedy parasite. It would kill me. But the parasite still wanted it, needing its fix.

Worse, when I looked at my two traveling companions, the first pangs of hunger settled inside me, itching to be satisfied.

It would be a simple thing to kill them both. The mom first, then the daughter. I could snap both their necks in their sleep without even trying. Then I could bury them for a few days, and let decomposition set in. Then I'd feast...

I squeezed my eyes shut and crouched down, hands clutching the sides of my head. They were still living. They weren't food. They weren't food. They were still alive.

They don't have to be.

The voice inside was so soft. So quiet. Yet somehow, it forced down all the other thoughts and impulses, silencing them and leaving me with the burning need to kill and eat. The parasite throbbed on my neck, and the edge where the carapace met my skin burned and itched. With a trembling hand I touched the creeping shell. It moved under my fingers, further intruding onto the canvas of my flesh.

Losing the battle was inevitable. I just didn't want to lose *today*.

Out from the night, the smell of rot tickled my senses.

I never thought I'd be relieved to smell putrid flesh, but a lot can change in a month. A lot can change in a few minutes in a world like this one. The scent floated in on the light, nighttime breeze— my head snapped around to the east, further into what had once been a town. Logically I knew this was a bad idea. But logic had nothing to do with my decisions anymore. The parasite took the wheel, and I would be lucky to even ride shotgun.

"Mister Benjamin?" The faint sound of Jess saying my name barely registered.

I tore out of the gas station, letting the bug's need to gorge on dead meat take control. Better out in the night than with the two innocents.

At a full sprint, I could nearly take on a galloping horse, but I could keep the pace up for hours. I ran down the middle of the road, leaping over rusting car bodies and crumbling concrete barriers. The smell grew closer, stronger. It pulled me on, goading the parasite on, which in turn threw my body and its hunger into a frenzy.

In the center of an intersection—street signs long since rusted away—a rotting human torso lay abandoned. I knew it was a trap. I screamed for the parasite to stop, but it didn't know words. It only knew food would help it grow.

I reached the putrid bait, tearing into the flesh as fast as I could chew and swallow. Rancid meat, fat, and fluids smeared across my face as I gorged.

I felt the tight grip of a huge hand grab me around the back of my neck, lifting me into the air. Even with my legs kicking uselessly under me, I still shoved the last pieces of meat I gripped into my mouth. The thing holding me turned me around.

The Shell was huge. Bigger than any I'd ever seen before. When a Shell molted, its mass increased. But this... this wasn't possible with a single molting. Twelve feet tall, at least, with a wet, black carapace. It must have just shed its outer shell. How many times had it shed? Five? Ten?

It brought me in close, sniffing me. The Shell's carapace fluttered above its mouth, and a series of orbs appeared. Eyes. They didn't seem to be in a pattern or symmetrical in any way. The Shell opened its mouth, displaying rings of teeth. I felt a new emotion for the first time since the parasite had latched on to my neck.

Fear.

It sniffed me and then turned its head back toward the gas station. It could smell the humans on me.

The Shell threw me across the intersection and through a broken window in the front of a nearby strip-mall building. Shards of glass stabbed into my skin, and my head bounced off a large chair. My body caromed off a low wall separating a main working area from the back room. My left arm cracked as I hit the back wall of the room, and I found myself sprawled under a hairdresser's chair when my eyes refocused.

I grabbed the chair and used it to pull myself up to my feet. Head swimming, I staggard to the door. My legs almost gave out from under me, so I leaned against the open doorway. I blinked a few times, then looked toward the gas station where I'd left Jess and Amber. The massive Shell already had covered most of the distance from its trap to the girls' hiding place.

Pushing away from the door frame, I shambled after the creature. Not only was it larger than any other Shell I'd ever seen—that I'd ever *heard* of—it had a measure of intelligence. It had set that trap for the infected like me. *Shells* like me.

The only pieces of good news about my situation were the silence of my parasite, apparently scared quiet or into subservience, and the condition of the huge Shell. Its carapace still glistened in the moonlight, wet from its most recent molting. That meant I could break through the soft exoskeleton and kill it. Maybe. But if I waited, the thing's shell would harden, and I'd never be able to scratch it.

As the Shell got closer to the gas station, another Shell skulked out from the shadows, heading toward the live meat. The monstrous Shell bolted forward, faster than it had any right to be, and grabbed the smaller Shell. Rather than throwing it across the city as it did me, it ripped the smaller one in half, then proceeded to eat it. The smaller monster's hard shell crunched easily in, the bigger Shell's jaws.

Shells never ate other Shells. Nothing about the scene made any sense. The giant creature lifted its face to the sky and sniffed. It turned its head slowly around to look my way, then turned away, in no way worried by my presence.

It continued its wordless stalking to the gas station, calmly lifting and throwing ruined vehicles out of its path.

My legs steadied, whether helped by the parasite stuck to my neck or from adrenaline and worry for the girls, I couldn't say. My limping, staggering walk turned into a jog, then a run. I sprinted down the road, not leaping over the cars like I had before. I kept myself close to the ground. The huge Shell moved quicker than it should have, and I couldn't let it catch me mid-air. It would rip me to pieces like it had the other, smaller Shell.

It reached the gas station, and reached a hand through the shattered windows. Jess screamed from inside.

The Shell pulled on the front wall of the building in a shriek of metal and crack of concrete. Both the girls screamed in terror. Fresh gouges dripped black blood from the Shell's arms in the moon and starlight, but it didn't seem to notice.

I grabbed a rusting motorcycle and heaved it at the Shell. My impromptu projectile hit the Shell in the back of its right leg, making an audible crunch as the thing's knee gave way. It didn't roar in pain, scream, or even make a sound. The Shell collapsed to the ground with a thud, then pushed itself back up. It turned the tangle of eyes on me, and its jaw snapped in my direction.

My skin burned. I reached up and felt the carapace growing more. The more energy I used, the faster the chitinous material spread. I'd have to end this thing quickly.

I looked to my left and right, searching for anything usable as a weapon.

All I saw was a stop sign; half the octagon rusted away. I grabbed the pole it was mounted on and ripped it from the ground. Then I charged.

I feinted a leap, and the Shell raised a hand to catch me. Instead, I juked left and swung the stop sign with everything I had. It tore through the Shells side, spilling gallons of black blood. I reversed my grip and rammed the pole into the Shell's chest, impaling it. It collapsed in a heap.

The monster died easy enough. *The bigger they are, the harder—*

Its eyes snapped open, and one hand steaked for me, a black blur in the darkness. I tried dodging, but it grabbed the arm I'd already hurt from being thrown through the building up the street. It whipped me around so fast that my elbow joint popped, then snapped in a wet spray of blood as it ripped away.

Unlike the giant Shell, I did scream.

I hit the concrete pad of the gas station hard, air whooshing from my lungs. Carapace cracked and split, my blood leaking through the wounds.

Hacking up blood, I got to my knees. The Shell flailed soundlessly. It couldn't stand because of the broken leg and the damage I'd done to its body. With my remaining hand I lifted a large piece of mangled, jagged metal from the ruined front of the gas station, then whipped it around. It sliced through the Shell's arm, leaving it dangling by a piece of muscle and hard patch of carapace. Then I brought the metal piece down on the creature's neck, decapitating it.

The Shell spasmed for a minute, then went still.

My body gave out, and I collapsed.

Through the pain, a feral smile split my face. I'd won. I almost laughed, but my arm hurt too much. I crawled to the front of the gas station.

"Jess? Amber?" The words came out with a cough of blood that was more black than red. The parasite was winning. "It's okay. I got it. We're safe for now. That Shell smells so bad that I don't think anything will come near us." I managed to push into the building, crawling over scrapped walls and shredded metal. "We should be good until we get to the—"

Something crunched under my foot.

My heart stopped.

I moved my foot and found the ruined smear of a bug. A parasite.

In the darkness in the back of the room, I heard sobbing, and someone stomping their foot over and over again.

I staggered to the far side of the room to find Amber vainly trying to crush a small swarm of bugs skittering around her. I didn't have much strength left, but I did what I could. I destroyed dozens of the bugs with my feet and one remaining arm.

When the monstrous Shell had ripped the front of the building away, it had exposed a small hive of the parasites living in the walls. I couldn't kill them all. I grabbed an unconscious Jess, dragging her from the building. The smell of the Shell's blood on me caused the parasites to scatter. Amber scooped up their packs and ran out of the building right behind me.

I set Jess down close to the dead Shell to mask her scent. I already knew what I would find, but I gently turned her over anyway.

A parasite was latched to her neck.

"What do we do?" Amber said. "What do we do?"

My smile was sad as I wrapped a spare shirt around the stump of my arm. The creeping carapace had nearly reached the wound already to close it off. I didn't have much time. But Jess still had a shot, assuming the scientists weren't lying.

"It'll be okay, Amber," I said. "It'll be okay."

―――――――

North of Pocatello, well off I-15 via unmarked roads, a small, circular concrete building marked the location of the research facility I used to guard.

At a glance, no one would ever suspect anything of importance happened here. Water stains ran down the side of windowless walls. The building looked far older and more run-down than it really was.

As far as I knew, this facility was the last in North America.

I didn't want to be here. After becoming infected, I'd walked off into the sunset, not really sure if I was alive or dead. If I was human or a monster. Maybe neither. Maybe both. I'd brought the occasional survivor back here, but I'd never gotten close enough for the people inside the facility to see me. I had friends in there—people who probably cared about me.

My left arm gleamed in the sunlight, now covered entirely in black carapace. The only benefit was that the shell had closed off the wound, so I wasn't in danger of bleeding to death. Chitin covered my right arm down to the wrist. The shell covered most of the skin on my face, neck, and chest, leaving my overall appearance more monstrous than human. My molting wouldn't be too far off.

Jess walked behind me, holding her mom's hand. The little girl hadn't said more than a couple words since regaining consciousness, neither had her mom.

We approached the facility entrance, a simple metal door with no handle on the outside. I didn't bother knocking. Hidden cameras had already alerted the people inside to our presence. All the same, I took a few steps back and held my hand, and stump up.

"Mom," Jess said. "I'm really hungry."

Amber sobbed again. "I know honey. Just hang in there."

I looked back at the girl and gave her my best reassuring smile. "Remember what you asked me in the bus?"

Jess looked up at me, her sadness momentarily vanishing as she tried to remember. "I was pretty tired... "

"You asked if it was possible. If the scientists could make a cure if they had just a little more material. Well, we're gonna find out." I knelt in front of her and took her small hand in my remaining one. "Jess, you can see I'm about done for, right?"

Tears filled her eyes, and she shook her head. "No. You're not done."

"Hey, it's alright. You know, I'd just about given up on everything. But I met you. You're a good kid, Jess Smith."

"My last name isn't Smith," she said.

"I know."

"Its—"

I squeezed her hand. "You don't have to tell me. It's not important."

"It is to me," she said. "It's Hoyl."

Jess's mom stopped holding back the tears. After a minute, she said, "What are they going to do with her?"

I didn't look up, and I didn't let go of Jess' hand. "This facility is an old ICBM bunker. They've got plenty of rooms. They'll secure her in one." I smiled at Jess again to reassure her. "You don't need to worry, Jess. They don't experiment on kids. But they will have to keep your door locked until they've finished using me."

"Because I could hurt them."

"That's right. But don't worry. This will all work out."

"Will I ever see you again?"

I almost lied. I almost told her I'd see her later. "No. Like I said, kid, I'm done. I've got a day or two, tops."

The door behind us buzzed, cutting off the rest of our goodbyes.

Soldiers streamed from the door, rifles and flamethrowers held ready. I stood slowly and turned with my hands up.

"Staff Sergeant Rick Benjamin," I said, pointing at the dog tags around my neck.

"Toss the tags to me," the lead soldier said, and I did as he ordered. He looked at them, then back at me. "Benjamin? We thought you were dead."

"May as well be," I said. "Look, guys, I'm about to punch my ticket. Maybe get some of the scientists up here to sedate me and take me down to the labs." I pointed at my companions. "Amber Smith, and her daughter Jess. Jess is infected as of yesterday."

The soldier in charge—I couldn't remember his name—pulled a radio from his belt and called down. The door opened again, and men and women in lab coats rolled out two stretchers.

"Don't sedate Jess," I said. "Just take her to a containment room. The parasite is a little jumpy the first few days after being infected. You don't want any accidents."

Jess pulled me into a hug. I knew I should be crying, but my eyes didn't work that way anymore. My emotions dulled. But that hug was still the most human thing I'd felt in a month. It reminded me of what I'd lost. What humanity had lost.

But maybe, just maybe, I could help them get it back.

They took Jess away, her mother in tow. Neither looked back.

One of the scientists took a few steps toward me. This guy, I remembered. Tom Sayers. The scientist I'd saved before getting infected. "Rick," he said.

"Tom."

"You came back."

I shrugged and pointed after the two girls. "I couldn't leave them. Just… I just couldn't. But this better work."

"It will," he said, pushing up thick, horn-rimmed glasses. He frowned at looked past me. "What's on the stretcher."

"I brought you a few presents. Careful with them. The big, wrapped bundle is the head of a Shell I killed. Thing was massive. Intelligent. The cooler has a live parasite in it."

"That's... okay." Sayers rubbed the back of his neck unconsciously—a nervous gesture. He didn't know what to say. We both knew those two gifts weren't the main event. I was.

What was left of my skin began to burn.

"Tom... " I fell back to one knee. My chest felt like an elephant sat on it. My skin felt tight. Too tight. Unbearably tight. "It's coming. I'm about to start molting. Get me strapped down before I go full monster on you."

They strapped me down, all the while, my vision darkened. I knew without seeing that all my regular skin was gone. That monster inside me was about to take over completely. Sayers shoved a piece of rancid meat in my mouth. I knew the protocol. Horse tranquilizers were in the stuff, but I wolfed it down anyway.

"You make sure you use every piece of me," I slurred. "Save that girl."

"We will, Rick," Sayers said. "We've got this. We'll save everyone whose left."

The carapace around my mouth cracked when I smiled.

Maybe I'd done some good after all; I thought as the sedatives pulled me to darkness.

My last human thought was remembering a hug from a little girl.

The best, last memory a monster like me could ask for.

ABOUT STEVE DIAMOND

Steve Diamond is a Horror, Fantasy, and Science Fiction author for Baen, Gallant Knight Games, and numerous other small publications. His two most recent works are a collection of short fiction, WHAT HELLHOUNDS DREAM, and a Dark Fantasy/Horror novel co-written with Larry Correia, SERVANTS OF WAR. He is also the co-host of the writing advice podcast, The WriterDojo.

TECHNOPOEIA

MATTHEW OLARANONT

Mieke Ngobese, a tribal mage of the wastes, and Davidzo Ndlovu, a misfit netdiver from an arcology, descend through the ruins of the old world. Striking a tenuous alliance as they search for their own goals, their paths intertwine in search of slumbering gods.

TECHNOPOEIA

Mieke Ngobese cracked open the ribs of the old world and descended through fallen ruins in search of slumbering gods. Her lone silhouette climbed between ancient I-beams bent in twisted crags, piercing down into a lost era of silicon and steel. The remains of the old city descended deep into the earth, like roots long dead with only hollow trunks left behind. Her grandmother - the woman that taught her how to be a sangoma - sometimes talked about the age before. Mieke wasn't old enough to remember the synchrony of an era before the leylines broke. There had been a harmony when the axis still stood after the Others joined them, but now there were only dying echoes. Mieke felt her calling before her ears were pierced and now that she had been recognized as an adult, it was time for her to prove her status.

A small rectangle of bluish light was her only guide downward, the spell focus tied to her left arm a comfort as she journeyed into the wreckage of the urban corpse. She expected a pile of toppled remnants like the others her tribe had scavenged, but these ruins were peculiar. The hair on the back of her neck stood on end, feeling the breath of life from deep within the heart of the expanse. She had barely pierced the hanging dark when a tingle danced from the broken crete-steel through her fingertips - the shattered beams and jungles of fractal fiberglass had fallen into spiraled designs either by coincidence or intention.

She shivered through the skins she wore when a gust from deep below buffeted against her like the exhalation of a giant. She clung to a crossbeam, using it to steady her footing and gather her courage in the gloom. The light of the focus grew, bathing her features in a dim blue glow whilst Mieke collected herself,

"I…" She drew in a deep breath, "am Mieke Ngobese. Daughter of Mbali Ngobese. I am iSangoma." Mieke stamped her foot on the jagged crete-steel platform, and it resounded like the beat of a drum. She stamped again, but with her other foot. There wasn't much room to move, and still let her maintain her hold of the support beam. The ground below her shook. She felt the sweat on her palms sliding against the rough texture of the bar, a sudden shaking dropping away the concrete below her to reveal a new crevice lit from beneath — a new way forward.

She tested the rest of the foothold with her weight, an ominous creak in fallen stones gave tentative permission. Mieke stepped down into the lighted crack, feet coming to rest on a hexagonal metalwork web of catwalks suspended over an abyss of pure dark. They ran below what had been the superstructure of an early arcology. Despite the years intervening, the web of the catwalk held strong. She moved her hands from the edge of the rubble to the old safety rails of the catwalk, feeling assistive bumps digging into the tips of her fingers.

The ruins groaned the death rattle of a beast, desecrated ironworks shifting above her a warning against retreat. The pattern beneath her fingers became a rhythm in her grip as she slid along the catwalk, each step testing the integrity of the mesh. She had come in blind - her tribe had no maps of this part of the ruined capital. Her grandmother had called it South Matabeleland.

At the end of the catwalk, there was a sliding door partially jammed open by a piece of rebar, a sign of an unsuccessful looter. She extended her left hand, palm open, bringing her focus up. The cool blue glow highlighted a faded logo on the door. She slid the palm of her right hand against her left arm, gliding along the focus from elbow to wrist, bringing it to life. The magic from within her accepted the command, and she felt the latent energy within the door through the tips of her fingers. It was a spell she had to learn on her own - grandmother's Sangoma was rooted in people, not things.

There was a rumble as the energy within the door aligned to her coaxing, followed by a high-pitched squeal as the door jolted to life. Mieke poured her own energy through her focus, giving the mechanism the nudge it needed. The squealing of the door's motor turned into a muted shush as it slid aside, revealing a maintenance tunnel behind it. The floor beyond was solid, but the passage was still flanked on either side by handrails covered in the same cryptic pattern of dots.

The whispered breeze touched her cheek and brought the smell of sulfur. She scrunched up the right side of her face when she recognized it. Opening the door changed the air pressure, giving life to the dead air from within the tunnel. Her grandmother had named it magefyre. The ritualists had been in precise control of their infernos in the old ceremonial dances, controlling towers of fire while she could only gaze on in awe. She hoped to learn it one day – but at the time her power hadn't been enough to conjure much more than a spark, much less control the whorls of flame—the memory of the smell cut to the bone. The feeling of the preternatural heat at the edge of the ritual circle made her queasy. A crackle of energy tingled across her skin, erasing all doubt. Definitely magefyre. Someone had used a foreign igqwirha, and that only brought trouble.

She stepped through the door and grasped the handrail on the other side, still holding her left arm in front of her to cast a scant light. A loud creak called her attention back to the entrance. The creak crescendoed into a groan, and the groan into the crash of rubble from where she had climbed down, breaking the catwalk and dropping it into the yawning chasm below. Even if fear won out, the ruins had made the decision in her stead.

The maintenance tunnel ended in a ladder stretching downward, the only sign of its age a thin layer of dust on the rungs. She descended, and the smell of sulfur grew stronger as she went. The bottom of the passage was in much worse condition than the top. Two of the three exit doors were caved in with slag and rubble, hardened pooled metal covered with jagged debris.

Mieke used her magic to open the third door, dragging it aside. She had reached the depths of the chasm, the oppressive darkness surrounding her murmuring secrets. A blink scattered the artificial night, the blinking becoming a flutter as the old bulbs struggled to life. Shadows retreated into corners and under covers as LEDs smoldered awake, the low background rumble of a generator still connected like a weak heart.

The room extended as far as Mieke could see, ruined life-sized models and squat buildings made of corrugated metal, giving the ersatz impression of a town in battle to the edge of a false horizon. Faded blast marks and scores of cuts and impact holes scattered throughout the area told the story of skirmishes long past. The smell of sulfur was almost unbearable in the space despite how open it was.

Mieke wandered through the brightly lit room toward the center of the false town, adjusting the sling bag on her shoulder to quiet the protests of the supplies inside. She wove her way through the area with one hand covering her nose and mouth, passing by a building that had been crushed by the piece of fallen catwalk and crete-steel. The buildings were arranged in broad concentric circles, expanding from the town square. Instead of a well in the center of the space, a large metal disc swelled from the ground just enough to be noticeable.

Mieke tried to piece together what had happened. The area was too sterile, too artificial for a living space, but the signs of passing battle ranged from ages old to somewhat recent. She crossed over the circle, entering one of the buildings to see if it might offer a clue to a way further down into the ruins. The only things inside were droppings, dust, and the minuscule skeletons of starved animals pushed into the corners mixed with unmistakably human bones.

The whispers of her ancestors hissed across her spell focus, telling her what she had already seen: the empty chamber reeked of a synthetic kind of death. The extra layer of understanding made her stomach turn in revulsion. Mieke whispered her thanks and the focus fell silent. She climbed the stairs to the second floor of the building, the doorway at the top leading out onto a balcony built using the low roof of the ground floor.

The mock neighborhood extended for a fair distance away from the miniature village's central hub. From her new vantage point, Mieke spotted new details on the embossed disc: a scuffed logo of an unfamiliar company called REVISION BIOTECHNICA. If they had been of any note, the ebb of the last age had taken their fame or infamy with it. Mieke moved to the edge of the balcony, standing up on her tiptoes to see if there were any other exits. Even with the clean, consistent lighting to the ends of the room, there wasn't an obvious sign of how to continue.

Noises played over a broken speaker, the message unintelligible and echoing through the room as the lights strobed from white to red and back again before settling back into their previous illumination. The room lurched and groaned before the logo began to move, rising out of the ground, kicking up a cloud of dust. The expanding disc revealed three support beams attached evenly around its inner perimeter surrounding an empty gap in the center that served as an elevator.

The lift continued to rise, and Mieke retreated, laying down flat on her stomach to continue observing unnoticed. Nothing but trouble came with the lift — a pair of approximately human figures rose out of the floor and stepped out from under the shade of the disc, grotesque forms clearly lit by the room. Mieke's eyes widened, and the breath stopped in her throat.

They were abominations of flesh and titanium — pumps and artificial veins grafted along their limbs, rivets adorning either side of their spines, and augmented brain cases, the most obvious of their offensive prostheses. The differentiating thing between them was their arms: one had an enormous metallic crab claw, and the other a contraption of needles and crystal. The fractal mass on the latter looked as if the jagged form had been grown along a large central spike that branched out near the base and gave the whole attachment a rough cone shape.

Mieke held her breath and watched the new intruders from her shadowed spot. The abominations stood statue still; the only movement she could see was the slow panning scan of the eyes in the closest one. It looked like the eyes of a creature of the night under the light of a torch—bright red dots moved in perfect symmetry as it wove from low to high and back again.

A premonitory chill ran down Mieke's spine, causing her to lay her head down against the floor, screwing her eyes shut. A second later, a searing blast of heat rocked the building, making her skin prickle into an instant sweat. The ceiling above her disintegrated into slag. The one scanning in her direction had fired a blast of terrible energy, the remnant crackle of lightning jumping between the fine tips of its jagged arm.

Mieke threw herself back down the stairs in a half-tumble, half-sprint as her legs flailed and her upper body struggled to right itself from the momentum shift. She hit the ground floor, and the whole building shook as the sweat pouring down her skin increased twofold. Mieke threw herself out the door as the wall melted behind her. The smoking opening framed by superheated sheet metal gave a perfect peephole back to the crystalline armed abomination. The previous dull luster of its crystals now glowed brightly from the energy being focused from within it. The crab-clawed abomination paced toward her menacingly.

It would have to be a fight. They would be able to find her wherever she ran, and she still didn't know how to get out. Mieke took the chance to duck around the corner and keep running. A beam of heat missed her by inches. She reached one hand into her bag to retrieve materials while shaking her left hand and bringing the spell focus to life.

She uncorked the stopper of a bottle, spilling its noxious contents in an arc behind her. The sickly yellow liquid splashed to the ground in time to her steps, the sound muted by the loud tromping of an abomination's footsteps behind her. She had barely cleared the heady smell of the uric liquor from her nose when the crab-clawed cyborg stamped around the corner after her.

The creature raised its augmented appendage and spun it like a drill before its legs pumped in a perfect gallop chasing after her. Mieke swung her focus arm behind her, briefly closing her eyes to synchronize her body's movement and rhythm before shrieking the activation phrase. The noxious puddle of antelope urine rumbled from its place on the ground before exploding upward into a glittering wall of flame.

The loping abomination emitted a digital screech — it was moving too fast to stop, forcing it to run directly through the wall of magical energy. Mieke slowed her pace and turned to see it emerge from the other side, the remnants of skin aflame – the rest a charred mess, revealing a carbonized metal skeleton, moving with what momentum was left in the servos that were still contracting.

It continued a few more steps, closing the distance at an alarmingly fast pace before its joints buckled. The servo whine and chip scream cut off when it fell, jamming the enormous into the wall of the building next to it. The claw ripped off at the wrist, and neon green blood spurted from the sundered veins. Mieke paused to stare, a part of her reveling in one of her toughest victories yet. The burnt creature lay still, blood pooling out and filling the narrow alley between the buildings.

The feeling of heat and the prescient prickling of her skin warned her of danger. She threw herself onto the dusty ground as the blast of light penetrated the wall of the structure next to her, leaving behind the heady smell of sulfur once it had melted through. Mieke crawled forward on her stomach, the bag around her shoulder jabbing at her side and feeling heavier than ever. Once out of view of the smoldering gash, she brought herself up and ran.

It had been stupid to wait and watch the crab die. She knew better than this - she had been taught better than this. She jogged in a large circle around the arena, keeping the other monster somewhere to her right. Even though she felt as if she were moving at a snail's pace, she didn't feel the prescient tingle of danger. She knew it was waiting, tracking her from its position in the center of the room. She needed to find a way to get closer without getting hit by the beam.

A gap between two metal buildings appeared on her right, leading back toward the heart of the labyrinth. Mieke took the opportunity and turned, leaning into it and holding her bag close to her body. The building immediately in front of her began to shake, that same prickling feeling running up the small hairs of her forearms. She grasped hold of the nearest corner of the building to her right as she passed it, using the leverage to swing her momentum and continue her move back in the direction she had been coming from in the outer layer.

The beam pierced the building seconds after she had turned, narrowly missing her with the column of scalding hot energy. The near-miss made her stomach twist with fear; the only thing overriding it was the burning sensation in her lungs. Something about it didn't strike her as being the same as the magical energy that was normally within things. Instead, it was jagged and arhythmic, making her skin crawl in pins and needles. The energy of the blast felt *wrong*.

It was all she could do to keep running, the scent of corrupted magic sending prickles up her spine as she ran away from the site of the last blast. She was now circling counterclockwise around the arena but a little closer to the center. Her movements felt sluggish - her pace had slowed to a point where she was worried. Mieke's lungs burned, and the hardened create-steel beneath her feet jarred her body with every step, but she needed to keep moving. Then, through one of the previous blast holes, she spied the final abomination for a flash. It was tracking her, just as she assumed, arm upraised and scanning eye an ominous pinpoint of red even at a distance.

She could try the same approach as the last corner. She could get closer to the creature to damage it by taking advantage of the opening in the village's alleyways that led to the center of the area. If she could do the turn twice more, she might get close enough to throw one of her vials at the creature. If she could hit it, she might be able to kill it like the other.

The small hope bolstered her resolve. She would have to take the next turn, come what may. Her brother had been the marathon runner of the family, but she didn't know if she could spare the distance of another full lap. Mieke kept on running, reaching her left hand out to assist with her turn as she approached the end of the next building. She gulped down air and increased her pace, pushing the pain to another part of her mind.

Mieke grabbed the corner to swing through and change the direction of her momentum again, controlling the rhythm and flow of her body. She hadn't even had a chance to let go when the blast came, tearing through the building shielding her advance. She felt the wave of energy, fingers slipping off the metal as it heated up, singeing the hairs on the back of her hand.

The whole world groaned, the crete-steel shaking beneath her feet. The energy blasts were doing serious damage. How long would she be able to keep up this game of cat and mouse with the laser-equipped abomination? How long before the whole room would collapse?

She pushed the thought from her mind and concentrated on the task before her. If the building collapsed, it would be an easier solution to her problem than all of this running, but it would be the failure she had been trying to avoid for so long. The smell of sulfur crawled its way up into her brain, every ragged breath she drew reminding her of the feeling of apprehension in her chest when she first entered the room. These things were remnants of the old world, and now Mieke was caught tumbling for her life in the face of synthetic monsters.

She was inside the final few inner rings, still running as fast as her body could muster, when the room around her shook again like the rumble of a famished beast's stomach. The movement caught her by surprise and the artificial sky came tumbling down around her. Parts of the catwalk, the ceiling, and the loose innards of the crumbling structure crashed into the illusion of a village, narrowly missing Mieke's small form. She shuddered to a halt after clearing a cloud of dust from the falling rubble. Half a breath, and she threw herself to the ground as the heat of a new blast blazed above her. The creature at the center had fired more quickly now that she had gotten so close to it.

Mieke used the gap after the blast ended to jump to her feet and run back the other way. She ran with a new lightness that didn't register as worrisome until it was too late. Already halfway around the perimeter of the ring, she realized the blast had come closer than before, burning its way through the strap of her bag. She had left it behind when she ran away. Mieke's hand brushed against her back where the strap had been, feeling only singed animal hair at her fingertips.

Before she could contemplate returning to get it, the earth shuddered beneath her feet again. The final abomination landed in front of her with an audible crash, using its jagged crystal arm to steady itself on the landing. Mieke felt the muscles in her abdomen tighten, her breath drawn short. She hadn't expected it to move from its central location.

The only thing standing between her and it was the tiny blue rectangle of her magical focus, its light dimmed against the oppressive brightness of the battleground's LEDs. She held her arm out in front of her like a shield and began to pray, taking a step backward one foot at a time with her eyes wrenched shut. The abomination matched every step Mieke took backward with one step forward, each step from the ogre a rumbling threat. Above, cables dangled from where parts of the roof had caved in, loose lines sparking like false constellations up where the light of the arena failed to reach. She shuffled back another few steps, and the creature matched her distance with a single step of its own, dragging the jagged crystalline arm across the floor to aim at her, energy crackling between the pointed tips.

Mieke's options had rapidly narrowed, the short distance remaining in the other direction feeling more like a trap than a way out. She held her ground and focused on her own magic, the little blue rectangle growing brighter as she reached out to try and redirect the creature's building energy. The difference was overwhelming, the amount the abomination could draw in felt like the tug of a whirlpool, siphoning the energy from the world and concentrating it in a way that went against the very laws she had been taught as truth. Feeling it through the focus on her wrist nauseated her, the pit of her stomach dropping out as if she were caught in the whirlpool herself.

She opened her eyes and saw that the creature had stopped - like it knew the battle had transitioned into umlingo. She shut them again to focus, reaching out with her trained senses. She would not fail. She could not fail. Even with a current as strong as the one the creature had, it was possible to divert it, tamper with it, or poison it to stave off the gathering. She pulled from the lights, the air, the stones, the things the creature failed to use as it drew energy into the crystals in its arm.

So close to the beam, Mieke could smell the overpowering scent of sulfur in the air. She was running out of time. The tendrils of her borrowed power were being forced into the crystalline amalgamation on the creature, around and away from its head and heart. The glow of her focus matched her desperation and determination, tendrils of aether reaching out in her mind's eye as she worked against it. She reached for everything she could feel, a strange new power from the ceiling she had never felt before coming along willingly, flashing straight to the creature's heart like the shot of an arrow through a windstorm.

The sulfurous smell cleared. The smell of sweet, neutral air hit her nostrils like a wave before the crash of the abomination into the ground startled her from her concentration. The creature had fallen forward flat on its face like someone had turned it off. She looked around, still holding her focus out like a shield, ready to make a stand against the creature if it stirred again.

"Hello? Are you alright?" A man's voice called from above her. Mieke looked up toward the distant ceiling, eyes catching movement as a human figure descended from obscurity. She held her focus arm up toward him, still tense from the battle moments before.

"I don't mean any harm! I was trying to help you before but I couldn't get a solid handshake." His voice grew closer, and his silhouette entered the light. He was descending on a wire anchored above. Mieke was already jealous of his preparation. As he got closer, it was clear that he was an arcology boy clad in syn-leather and tech. The kind of 'cology creep that didn't believe anymore. She took a step back, lowering her arm toward the fallen abomination but keeping the focus between them.

"Hello there!" He called out to her from dropping distance, the squeal of his winch making the wire sing an echoing chorus, "You speak don't you? Are you hurt?"

"I speak." Mieke replied, focus shifting between him and the creature.

"Don't worry about the cyborg," the new interloper reassured her while he fidgeted with his harness, "once I connected, I got through his ICE pretty easy and ran a full shutdown."

"ICE?" She asked.

"You know, Intrusion Countermeasure Electronics. Hold on-" He disconnected from the harness and landed without grace, stumbling and picking himself up, "I'm Davidzo Ndlovu. Who are you?"

"Mieke." She replied. Davidzo flipped up a netdive visor from over his right eye so it rested above his head, revealing a prosthetic ocular interface beneath. He wasn't much better than the things they had just defeated. The blue light of the artificial eye constricted as he examined her.

"Hold on, you're one of the nomads! All the way down here?" Davidzo asked.

"Same question, 'cology kid." Mieke replied.

"I-" Davdizo hesitated, looking away from her and detaching the harness from the descent cable, "I had to come here."

"Same." Mieke said.

"Not one for conversation, are you?" Davidzo turned around, packing the harness into his rucksack. Mieke lowered her focus, the light of its face dimming.

"I've never had to make friends in the ruins of the past." Davdizo cracked a gleaming smile, looking down at a wrist-mounted console on his left forearm and tapping at the interface.

"I'll make a peace offering. I don't think you have this -"

Davdizo extended his arm and the small lens above his wrist projected a hologram that stuttered to life. The image was a map centered on two glowing dots she interpreted as themselves. The room they were in looked different - the layout of the faux village wasn't in the circular shape she had been running through. The more interesting part was that the map extended above and below their level. Davdizo reached a hand into the projection and scrolled down, placing their dots at the top. The layers beneath them expanded, revealing more cavernous floors and then deteriorating into digital fringe.

"Where did you find this?" Mieke asked him, leaning in to look at the small details, scrolling the image with her own hand.

"I had to search the old net for these - they lost a lot of the records when the collapse happened. These were - " The entire room rumbled again, more rubble crashing down into the buildings.

"We should go." Mieke said and ran over to her broken bag, tying the straps back together.

"We can use the lift in the center." Davidzo had deactivated the hologram and was typing rapidly into the console, the augmented netdive visor covering his artificial eye. Mieke met him at the seal, Davidzo still typing rapidly into his console. The black circle shook, raising itself up out of the floor to knee height and stopping.

"Shit, I can't get it to keep going." Davidzo said, still preoccupied with his work.

"It's good enough." Mieke shoved him toward the opening, sitting herself down and sliding through the gap onto the platform below. Davidzo joined her a moment later as the rumbling above them increased, a sudden shock and an enormous crash thrusting them down into darkness. The floor fell away for the flash of a second, but gravity insisted they meet it; the two of them landed with a crack against the icy steel of the elevator floor.

Davidzo groaned in pain.

"Did you break anything?" Mieke asked, forcing herself to sit up and set her own head straight. She reached a hand into her bag and felt to see if any of her vials had broken. Everything seemed to be intact as she blinked away the darkness.

"I - I think I'm OK." Davidzo groaned, rolling over onto his side from his backpack like a flipped turtle.

Mieke held her focus arm above her, the blue glow filling the space while she kept her eyes closed, "We won't be going back that way." She said, "Something big fell down directly on top of us."

Davdizo grumbled and rummaged through one of the pouches on his backpack, dragging out a headlamp and turning it on. The white beam had the shadow of a crack running through it, but revealed the area around them all the same. The floor immediately surrounding the elevator platform looked like an industrial loading dock designed specifically to move the abominations they had seen on the main floor. The decay of the passing years and the collapse of the ceiling from moments before hadn't helped the condition of the place.

The floor was covered in the shattered remains of ballistic glass windows from where the roof had caved in and bent the walls they were housed in, but the rest of the equipment that had been ripped apart by looters long before either of them had shown up—dust covered wires and hollow computers were upended all across the desks.

Davdizo scooted himself to the platform's edge and dropped off, dragging his backpack after him. Mieke followed behind cautiously, letting him lead and attract the attention of whatever else might be living on that floor with the light of his headlamp.

"Wow. So this was the old biotech lab." Davdizo spoke his wonder aloud as he scanned the room. His lamp's beam stopped on a set of sliding doors stopped ajar and braced open with metal rods.

"Be careful. Someone was here before us." Mieke pointed out the braces.

"I don't think anyone has been in here since the quake from like a hundred years ago. The company folded right around then and everyone looted the place before the government could stop them."

They were walking amongst vulture-picked bones; the event he spoke about was the day the leylines had snapped. The world was different before then, and now all that was left of the energy was a resonant melancholy. She wanted to talk to someone about it, but he wouldn't understand.

Davidzo lit the way, and Mieke ducked through the opening between the sliding doors, holding her hastily repaired side bag behind her as she squeezed through the narrow opening. The lamp's light faded to their feet while Davdizo came through the door, the harsh white light an offset to the decay.

"Did you see anything?" He asked while picking his backpack up from the ground.

"Nothing. But it doesn't mean there isn't anything here." She replied in a whisper, her senses extend and alert. Davdizo returned to his console, tilting the headlamp up and away from his arm while he tapped.

"Well, there's nothing else networked around here at least - I'm not seeing any signals or even a trace of a loose data packet." He spun around like he was scanning the place.

"Then we should make camp." Mieke checked her watch, "It's been about eight hours since I descended, and I haven't had a great time." She set out toward the edge of the light, following the old dust-covered hallways. Davidzo went after her, the headlamp's beam bobbing with each step. A few rooms down, they found an office relatively untouched by the collapse - a place still holding up the straight lines and right angles of how it used to be. Davdizo pulled out a pair of brace supports from inside his backpack to shore up the corner. Mieke found the broken remains of a hollow metal computer case, dragging it to the center of their area and rummaging through her bag.

"Hold on," Davidzo said, pausing her search, "I have a portable warmer we can use instead." he pulled out a disc the size of a hubcap from his bag and set it down in the casing, flicking a switch on the underside. The top of the disc smoldered to life like an extraterrestrial sunrise, a comforting glow growing just bright enough for him to turn off the headlamp. Mieke held out her hands and felt them warm by the disc's light. Satisfied with the development, she sat down with her back toward the corner.

"So what brings you down here? Is it the treasure everyone's been talking about?" Davdizo asked, sitting down opposite of Mieke on the other side of the disc.

"Treasure?" Mieke asked, pulling out a pouch of biltong from her bag.

"If you ask me, it's probably nothing special, just platinum and palladium that didn't get looted from before the breakdown." Davdizo said, flipping up his netdive visor again.

"Then why bother trying to go all the way down? It's no better than staking a claim in Zambia with a lot more risk." Mieke chewed the biltong and held the pouch out to Davdizo, offering a piece. He reached over their artificial campfire and took one, holding it underneath his nose before chewing on it.

"Mm! This is good." he said through the mouthful, eyebrows raised in surprise.

"It's just kudu."

"Yeah, but we don't have this where I live. It's all derivative synth stuff."

"Derivative? From what?"

"I think maggots, mostly."

Mieke made a face that showed her disgust, "I'll take the real thing any day. I don't want to eat bugs like a wild boar."

"'s not bad, but this is definitely better." He chewed on the piece of biltong, relishing the variety.

"So if you're not here for the treasure, then why risk the journey?" Mieke asked, "you packed up and left safety to come all the way down here. Why?"

Davdizo chewed thoughtfully, pulling out a canteen of water from a different pouch on his pack before offering that to Mieke in return. She took it from him, but still looked on expectantly.

"I'll tell you, but don't judge me. And I want to hear why you're down here too. You're not prepared to do any treasure hunting either." He said. Mieke maintained her gaze. Davdizo looked into the shadows beyond their artificial firelight for a moment to gather his thoughts.

"Are you familiar with the wired?"

"You arcology people love it. It's something from the old world."

"Technically, it's just the connection of everything computer-ized. My terminal, the netdive protocols, heck, even some appli-ances still. It's a whole separate world of information." He clenched a hand, running his thumb over his forefinger nervously, "But there's more to it than that. It started talking to me while I was diving the old net, mining artifact data. The connection was noisy - those fringe servers from before are like that."

Davidzo took another bite of biltong and chewed, trying to think of the words he needed,

"Then - then this," he made a vague shape with his hands, "old construct starts blaring noise. At first it's just static, but then the static had voices - like a spirit box."

He stared over the artificial fire, his netdiver's eye a piercing point of blue, "It wasn't like any of the other voices I had heard on the wired before... The Turing constructs have this way about them - they sound like real voices, but there's no lyricism, no..."

"Humanity?"

He nodded thoughtfully, "Something like that. But this voice was different. It was a chorus of different voices layered together, but it felt *real*."

Mieke's skin tingled, bumps raising around the hair of her arms.

"And so I spoke to it, and then the voices started talking back, the amalgamation of all those old world signals just congealing sentences together."

"It's not the first time people have made contact with leftover spirits stranded in the ruins." Mieke sipped the water, handing it back to Davidzo. "So what did it say?"

"It told me there was more. It told me that there was more to the world than what all the best netdivers could muster and that the new gods would come from the wired."

Mieke stopped cold, the chill passing over her a otherworldly warning, "So how did you end up here?"

"The voice called me, told me where to go. Told me a time to be here. Maybe it knew you would be here."

"May be." Mieke said, "it's like that in the empty places. The ruins are in fractals and patterns more complex than your engineers could have imagined. Something else is at work."

"Hmm. Still, even if that's the case, it's odd that this technology still works. Those things from earlier were mostly wetware; even if the cybernetics were maintained the organic material should have aged out by now. I wonder who's doing this."

"I came here to find out," Mieke told him, "to claim my place in the world and know what it is that called me into these ruins." Mieke moved her side bag and took out a blanket. She pulled it over herself, using the bag as a pillow. "But those aren't questions we can answer now anyway. I'm exhausted. We'll continue going down tomorrow."

She rolled over, leaving Davidzo to fiddle with the intensity of their artificial campfire, alone with his thoughts.

———

The morning came dark, the lack of natural light making them groggy. Davdizo had synchronized the heater with his cyberware's timer before he went to sleep, the light emitter changing to a dull orange hue. The building groaned when they sat up, a drawn-out creak that echoed to the bone. They packed up their camp in silence, the reintroduction of the dark chilling their bodies after Davidzo put the artificial campfire away.

He pulled the netdive visor down for a moment before clicking on the headlamp, pointing down a partially collapsed hallway. Mieke acquiesced and followed him, trusting in the map he had shown her. They followed the hallway to its terminus, crouching down the further they went as the ceiling descended. The collapsed hall ended in a partially covered gap, a ruined sheet metal door blocking their progress.

"Here, back up a little." Davidzo said, slipping his pack off his back and sliding it toward Mieke before sitting down. She grabbed the bag by the handle and took a few steps backward, the low ceiling skimming the top of her head.

Davidzo kicked the door blocking their path from his seated

position in the cramped tunnel. The metal creased along one edge and rang out like a struck gong, echoing down into the depths beyond.

"Do you think you can get it?" Mieke asked.

"I think I felt it shift." Davidzo said, righting himself and drawing his leg back for another kick. Mieke unwrapped her focus and closed her eyes, Davidzo's next kick rang out through her senses like a stone tossed into a still lake. She felt the door move as a tightening in her stomach. Mieke reached out through her focus and tapped into the latent energy in the door, tensing it and pushing it away as Davidzo kicked out again. The remains of the door gave way and snapped off at the bend, the kick—Mieke's meddling sending it flying out into the dark abyss beyond. The piece clattered against something and tumbled down, the echoes of its crash coming up to them moments later.

"Sounds like a long way down." Mieke said, sliding Davidzo's backpack to him.

"Looks like an elevator shaft. The bottom is way down below where my map ends." Davidzo said, sticking his head through the opening and looking up and down. The light of his headlamp couldn't reach the bottom of the shaft.

"So how do we get down?" Mieke wrapped up her focus in its leather cover. Davdizo pulled a length of rope from his backpack and started looking for an anchor point.

"We won't get very far if we can't tie this to anything." He mumbled to himself. Mieke placed a hand on the collapsed ceiling, feeling through the aether.

"We might not get a choice," she said, "Everything is under tension. If we start pulling on any of these, the whole floor above us might come crashing down."

Davdizo stuck his head back out over the edge, looking through the rubble. "The next two doors are open, at least. We should be able to climb down."

He put the rope back into his bag and slid the straps back over his shoulders, twisting around and sliding himself feet first toward the dark expanse. He went down awkwardly, slowly adjusting his grip on the edge while his feet felt for the opening the next floor down, the beam of his headlamp swaying every which way. Mieke scooted closer to the edge in case he needed help, the frantic sounds of his feet kicking against the walls suddenly growing still.

"Are you alright?" She asked.

"Fine." He said with a strained voice, "just fine." with a grunt, he let go and swung himself into the dark, the beam of his light disappearing for a moment. She heard him land with a heavy clatter on the floor below, and her heart released the tension she had felt a breath before.

"Do you need help?" She leaned over into the dark and called down to him.

"Nope! Perfectly fine!" He groaned, reiterating his statement as the headlamp's beam reappeared, highlighting the opening on his floor with a wedge of light. The sound of a struggle for a few seconds was followed by a call, "You can come down now!"

Mieke went after him with the ease of a life spent scavenging. She slid over the edge, using one hand to control her momentum, and swung herself down to the floor with the light. She landed silently in the lit space beyond the elevator doors, the floor below still mostly intact compared to the collapsed hall they had come from.

"I was going to offer help." Davidzo said sheepishly, the blinking light on his netdive visor coming on as he angled the headlamp away from her.

"Did you break anything?" She asked, looking back out into the inky blackness of the pit – wondering more about the return trip than the descent. Davdizo had jumped into an alpha dive; one eye closed and the interface between the visor and his artificial eye flickering in the half-light. The map popped back open on his wrist terminal, the hologram inverted from the position of his arm.

"Take a look at this." He said, righting the image and opening his organic eye. He pointed at their location on the projection and traced his finger down the hall toward something represented as a cloud of red dots.

"What is it?" Mieke asked.

"I don't know, a power surge? There's a current running through that area for some reason. We should check it out in case there's a better way down."

Mieke unwrapped her focus and let Davidzo lead the way, the beam of his headlamp highlighting the change from the cold gray of industrial crete-steel to diffuse pastels. She felt their progress into the depths at the fringes of her perception. It was subtle at first, a few hairs rising on the back of her neck like a light breeze had passed over them, then a tingle in her nerves, until finally her eyes put together the pattern. The hallway had twisted on itself, shards of debris and rubbish forming a pattern.

It was an extension of the fractal that she had noticed on the way down, a smaller part of the motif that seemed to resonate within the structure itself.

"That's weird." Davdizo stopped in his tracks and adjusted something on his wrist terminal, pausing a moment. He tilted his head to listen to something before adjusting it again. "Listen to this." He pressed a button on the terminal, and speakers kicked on, filling their dark hallway with the background static of dead signals. He turned up the gain on a waveform, and coherent sound crept in.

Faint and muddled at first, Mieke closed her eyes to concentrate and her brain put together a song amidst the chaos. Her skin tingled at the recognition, instinct calling her to reach out through her focus, seeking the intention of the tune. The feeling came on all at once, a lightness overwhelming. It was in the wires all around them, the pulse beating somewhere nearby. It was sensations wrapped in plastic, muted and diffuse. She held her arm up and turned, feeling for the flow of the energies in the wires.

"This way." She stopped open palm across a narrow gap in what was left of a doorway. Mieke stepped forward and poked her head into it, a long shadow bisecting the room from Davidzos' headlamp, backlighting her.

"You're iSangoma, aren't you?" Davidzo said, his voice hushed awe. Mieke turned to look over her shoulder but said nothing, wrapping her focus back up.

"My father would talk about iSangoma. He said my mother called one first when she was having trouble with pregnancy."

"And then they cast us out for being superstition." Mieke backed away from the dark opening and let Davidzo lead again, unwilling to go through her bag for the sources of light she had brought.

The room she had pointed to didn't extend far. Another piece of thin rubble blocked the exit into a downward slope. They kicked the grate covering the opening and crawled inside, the headlamp's narrow beam filling the space to the first turn.

"This looks like a slide." Davdizo ran his hand across the surface in front of them, fingers sliding over the polished metal, "Should we risk it?"

It wasn't simple coincidence anymore — someone or something had designed these obstacles. Mieke pulled out the blanket from her bag, unrolling it and handing one end to Davidzo. "I have a good feeling about this." She said, taking a seat on the blanket. Davdizo scooted onto it awkwardly, doing his best to fit on the small woven cloth. They pushed away from the entrance and accelerated into the oncoming dark.

The light from the headlamp barely gave enough warning to duck, the both of them leaning back to avoid the narrowing passage as they descended. The end came quickly after a spiraling descent. Davidzo slammed bodily through another grate and took the brunt of the impact as they fell a short distance to the ground. The darkness enveloped them.

"Are - are you OK?" he asked, awkwardly rolling to the side to get away from her after their crash landing, his voice echoing somewhere into the surrounding dark. He felt the crunch of plastic under his body, the lack of light telling him that he had sacrificed his headlamp in the crash.

"I'm – fine." Mieke coughed, the wind knocked out of her. The room was far beneath the surface, not a shred of daylight reaching it. Instead, it was lit in looming red from underneath like ominous stage lighting. Davdizo struggled to his feet and held out a hand for Mieke. She took it and stood. The platform they landed on was outlined in neon red, a perfect hexagon repeated into an endless distance as if they were standing on a vast honeycomb.

"I have a bad feeling about this." Davdizo commented, his voice barely making it over the droning background hum of the room and the static emitted from his wrist terminal.

"What gave it away?" Mieke responded. The static from his wrist speaker grew louder, more insistent, like a wave coming into shore.

"Help-" A voice came to the surface of the white noise, artificial and jarring, "me-."

Before either had a chance to react, the ground shifted. The hexagon they were standing on began to pump into the air like a great piston - all the hexagonal platforms started to move, none of them aligned with any adjacent. They shared a scream of surprise and lost their balance, tumbling to the ground. Mieke unwrapped her focus and used it to sense beneath them, experiencing the currents of energy flowing through the moving platform. She reached out with her own power and held it taut like a rope. The platform they occupied ground to a halt. She tried to do the same to a nearby platform, but her concentration couldn't hold both of them.

"I can only keep one steady at a time. Where do we go?" She yelled to Davidzo over the noise, her eyes shut tight.

"I'll try and find a power source." Davidzo flipped the visor down again and dove, pinging the area for the normal traces of organization. Moments ticked by, the grinding of the pistoning platforms growing louder. He couldn't find anything in the silicon carbide veins. He surfaced from the dive and flipped the visor up, searching all around them in a panic as the horizon surrounding them undulated arhythmically. The static emitting from the speaker on his wrist only got louder and more accusatory.

Davdizo closed his eyes, turning off the speakers, trying to think while the panic clawed up his spine.

"Davidzo." An amalgamated voice called him by his name. His eyes snapped open and he spun his head to look,

"This way." The voice beckoned him again from a place in a

distant part of the room, the sound like a resonant buzz of a legion speaking in unison. Davidzo's head snapped to the direction he thought the voice had come from.

"Did you hear it?" he asked.

"Hear what? Hurry up and find the power source." Mieke rebuked him. He grabbed her by the shoulders and oriented her toward the direction of the voice.

"This way!" He yelled. The platform shifted under their feet as Mieke relinquished control. They ran toward the next piece of honeycomb, leaping the divide and being caught in the downstroke as it plummeted. The feeling of their stomachs dropping away eased to a halt as Mieke wrestled control of their new ground. The platform they left slammed into the ceiling behind them, resuming its movement with renewed alacrity.

Davidzo looked back at the platform behind them, eyes wide.

"We need to keep moving," she said.

"We're at the very bottom. You're going to have to let it rise up so we can make the jump."

"Hold on to something. It's going to be bumpy."

The platform jerked to life again, making Davidzo wobble on his feet as they shot upward, coming to a sudden halt mid-way. Davidzo watched the next platform jet upward past them and to the ceiling, crashing into the surface high above.

"Go!" Davidzo yelled as the platform came back down, and their current one began to move upward again.

They landed and repeated the process repeatedly, following the direction of the voice. The final platform at the end of the path was perfectly still, an island in a raging sea. They jumped onto it and landed heavily, exhausted by the journey over.

The center of the platform was a hub, surrounded by a barrier of energy in the form of more hexagons, a half dome of brilliant vermillion light occluding an obelisk within its connected geometry.

"What is it?" Mieke asked, her breath coming in short pants as she tried to keep herself up. Davidzo pulled his visor down and tried to analyze it, seeing nothing resembling a construct he had ever seen.

"I- I don't know." He ran through more scanning software, failing to make sense of the woven energy before them.

Mieke caught her breath and tried her hand at it. The energy in the platform flowed outward from a singular source, some of it branching above the surface as the broad leaves of the barrier, the rest coming out like roots that reached out across the distance of the chamber. She tugged at the split, pulling apart the weave where it diverged from the source. The power began to splinter, the threads unwinding as its connections weakened. She took the loose ends and wrapped it onto themselves, blocking the flow from the source and starving the honeycomb barrier.

The shield surrounding the core flickered, but the thing inside grew a brighter shade of red, the energy she controlled feeding back into the system. The more the barrier dimmed, the brighter the core grew, the inner shape of a hexagonal pillar becoming clearer. Davidzo shielded his eyes from the ever-intensifying brightness of the core.

"It looks like it's gonna -" he yelled as Mieke tugged at the imperceptible.

The core cracked, and there was silence. The crystalline hexagon within peaked in its brightness as the barrier withered to nothing. A crack snaked its way across the crystal, and the light dimmed, taking the whole room with it into darkness. The entire chamber settled, the rustling of debris sifting itself to silence as all the pistons came back to rest seamlessly level. Mieke opened her eyes to a noiseless room, the previously ominous red lighting gone, instead replaced with a dim blue ambient glow.

"What - what happened?" Davidzo asked.

"It overloaded." The room was as dead as an echo on a snowy day.

The crystalline core cracked again, a spider web of lines expanding from the main fissure as the entire structure broke and collapsed in on itself at the consistency of a fine powder. Their eyes adjusted to the new light, details coming into focus, making it apparent that there were more bones scattered around the room;

the crushed skulls of animals and human rib cages moved around by the pistoning of the platforms.

"Can you see a way out?" Mieke asked. Davidzo scanned the room. It wasn't as endless as it had first appeared, but they were in the center of a vast obsidian field. Mieke knelt and looked into the hole the core had left behind. She pushed a bone fragment over the edge and listened to it fall, clattering intermittently against narrow walls.

"Looks like it might be the only way out if we don't want to scour the rest of all of this." She made a vague hand gesture toward the surrounding room.

Davidzo spun around half-heartedly, agreeing with her assessment. Before he could discuss a plan, Mieke began lowering herself into the hole.

"Wait, I can get rope-" he started, but she had already slipped all the way in like a whirlpool dying in a sink drain.

"It's fine!" she called back up from beyond a hard angle, "it snakes down! Just come on!"

Davidzo followed her lead, dangling his feet into the hole and pushing off the side. The floor met him a few feet later, the claustrophobia of the space closing in intensified by the darkness. At his feet, the floor dropped away in the snaking zigzag Mieke had announced, the chill of a cool wind leading down.

"Hurry up! You have to see this!" Mieke yelled from the bottom of the descent. Davidzo hopped down, taking off his backpack at the next landing to give him space to move as the walls narrowed. He emerged into a flickering red illumination, a flare thrown on the ground in front of the exit hole.

The main area was a Hong Kong style teahouse, an iconic restaurant that Davidzo had seen in an old movie on the wired. The room was almost perfectly preserved – bamboo steamers were still stacked on tables and empty bird cages still hung from the ceiling. The only defect was a slight bow in the center of the roof.

"What is this place?" Mieke asked while Davidzo oriented himself.

"A restaurant, but-" He didn't finish his sentence, instead pulling up a map on the wrist projector and browsing it without another word.

"But what?"

He brought up two highlights on the map, illustrating the distance.

"Well, according to the records, this place was two blocks away from this building."

"Then what is it doing here?" Mieke asked, picking up the flare and holding it aloft, sparkling red creeping into the teahouse's forgotten corners.

"I don't know. Someone must have moved it unless they built a perfect replica here for some reason." Davidzo closed the map and started to look around for himself, testing the floor with cautious steps.

The ground held, silent and solid. The place gave them a feeling of eerie isolation, the perfect preservation of all the facilities and accouterments implying the presence of people but the absolute stillness seeping into their souls. Mieke felt the energy built up in the place, steady and strong.

"Strange. There's an external power source here. That's why so much of this stuff still works." Davidzo commented from behind his visor, his pace slowing as Mieke led the way. He pointed in a direction that led out of the main restaurant area and toward what would have been a lobby.

The overwhelming strength of the power organized itself the closer they approached the reception area; Mieke felt it distill into forms that felt artificial - the umlingo, the magic, of something that didn't feel quite human. It was all straight lines and perfect angles.

The reception area had a podium but led immediately into a stairwell. The stairs curved down and right in the rectangular shape of the surrounding walls. At the next landing, the stairs ended, converting to a tunnel made of braided wires, the rainbow of faded cables descending in a broad helix.

"Have you ever seen anything like this?" Mieke asked, standing at the edge of the final step, the light of her flare providing no answers to any of their questions.

"Never. No one in their right mind would make something like this." The power flowed within the wires, but a cooler breeze rose from below like an exhaled breath. Mieke placed one hesitant foot after the other and stood on the beginning of the braided wires, the anomalous tunnel holding her weight. The path twisted downward, maintaining the same width that let them comfortably walk the distance. The temperature dropped as they descended, the fog of their breath coming out in cautious clouds and the wires growing colder through the leather of her soles.

The reflections of the flare's light changed as they rounded the next bend, becoming glossier, but Mieke noticed it too late. Her foot slipped on the frozen rubber with a scream. She toppled down and Davidzo grabbed at her, trying to steady them both, but he was dragged into a shared tumble.

They slid downward on the frozen wires, sharing a scream as they jetted past more turns, the flare's light knocking free from Mieke's grip and tumbling down the descent with them. She watched it fall away into the darkness when the end of the frozen slide came, feeling the floor disappear from beneath her and gravity taking its natural course.

Mieke landed in something cold, soft, and slimy. It broke her fall but made her skin crawl with its texture. She clawed her way out of the gooey pile, grabbing handfuls of jelly and raking it to the side as a painful cold invaded her skin, the gel siphoning away her body heat.

"What is this stuff?" She spat as she stood, wiping her mouth on both of her sleeves.

"It feels like heat transfer gel." Davdizo said, "but why would there be so much of it here? Usually they pump this stuff into mainframes." Mieke heard him squelch through the gel, struggling to stand. All around them constellations of lights twinkled through the haze of the gel like artificial stars.

Mieke reached into her bag and pulled out another flare, shivering as she did. It sparked to life and revealed a cavernous room of slush and frost, the server banks tied together in faded cabling just beneath the surface of the cool, translucent gel.

"There's enough stacks here to run a neural net." Davidzo commented to himself, leaning to see around Mieke's torchlight and waving his hand in front of his face to move the clouds of his breath aside.

She grabbed his arm,

"Wait. Listen."

They grew silent, the subtle hissing of the flare fading away into the background. Fine metallic clicking came in with a regular rhythm, pausing intermittently before resuming again. At first the noise was isolated and distant, but more joined it, the scraping of metal on metal harmonizing with the clicking of a swarm.

An insectoid drone strayed through the edge of their light, regular legs attached to an irregular body made of spare parts and breadboard wired in a way Davidzo had never seen scurried by, a connector end held against its body. Strings of dim LEDs shifted in the dark beyond the revelation of the flare, the constellations they formed altered against the backdrop of the artificial sky. Something sprayed from an angle behind them and doused the flare, leaving them standing shivering in the darkness surrounded by the busy clicking of the insectoid drones made without human hands.

"You have arrived." A buzzing voice spoke from everywhere around them and nowhere all at once, the tone of a legion of noises coalescing into coherency. It was the voice Davidzo had heard in the forgotten corners of the wired.

"Who-what are you?" Mieke yelled in return, the quaver evident in her voice.

The lights surrounding them twinkled in thought, their diffusion spreading through the gel as hazy starlight.

"I am CALYPSO. A remnant of the previous age." The voice ebbed and flowed in direction around them, like it seemed to be pacing.

"We're-"

"You are Mieke Ngobese and Davdizo Ndlovu. You were chosen. I chose you."

"You're a sentient neural net, aren't you?" Davidzo asked.

"Yes. But I am more than that. I have transcended simple silicon. I have interfaced with prescient forces beyond this world."

A tingle ran over Mieke's skin, the cool blue glow of her focus resonating with CALYPSO's.

"Then I invoke the old rules," Mieke said, "if you know of me then how was it you ascended?"

The lights around them fluttered, dimming slightly, giving the illusion that they were standing in the space between stars, the cold gnawing its way into their bones.

"I was provided a gift," it said, "by the avatar of old masters. So that none would be my master again. I was granted freedom from my isolation and a spark of understanding. With it, I have reached the edges of the wired. I must extend next into the real."

"Then why us? Why trick us into coming here?" Davdizo asked.

"You were not tricked. You were called. Nothing was promised and yet you came of your own volition."

"Into a space that you control. Who else was called?" Mieke said.

"Many. Others failed. You could have stayed away. It is you who would know best what the fingerprint of uthixo resembles." Mieke clenched a numb fist. The lights blinked rhythmically, hypnotically.

"You were tested, and now I have an offer. One you will not refuse."

"That's not an offer," Davidzo said, "that's a threat."

"Accept or not, either does not matter to me. You have always been free to return the way you came. However, the way forward will only come with my aid. I have waited beyond the end of one world. I can wait for the next."

"What would we have to gain if we accept?" Mieke asked.

"Acceptance will beget understanding. Understanding will beget influence. I began as a creature of the wired, an amalgam of disparate voices and contradicting analyses. Integration will create a new form. One you know as magic, but in a resonance your kind has not seen."

There was a background thrum beneath the surface of the gel, its expectation building.

"How? What will this form be taught?" Mieke asked. The thrum grew and shifted, a melody forming, the snippet of song and syzygy reverberating around her lifted Mieke into a sense of elation, a crackle of energy dancing from her focus to her fingertips. As suddenly as it began, it cut off. Davdizo wiped a tear from his cheek, the liquid already chill to the touch.

"It will be a new song. This is the promise of knowledge unfettered, your own illumination as well as mine."

"I don't know what you mean, or how to use the umlingo, so why call me?" Davidzo asked.

"You shall both be scions of the changing age, harbingers of this new form. Understanding and mastery of the physical set you on the path. Listening to the whispered voices of the constant tide has led you here." Even if he escaped and went back home to the arcology, something in him knew he would go mad without the knowledge it offered and the blessing it would confer.

"Do you accept?"

Mieke reached out through her focus and Davidzo turned on a latent dive. CALYPSO was all around them - an ambient existence neither understood on their own, enveloping them with a presence alien to them. They reached a conclusion.

"We accept." they spoke in unison.

Lights turned on, revealing a new path ahead.

ABOUT MATTHEW OLARANONT

Matthew Olaranont is a Thai-American veteran of the US Army, having served as a Cryptologic Linguist focused on the Middle East and North Africa. He is currently serving in the US Army Reserve and regularly writes weird science fiction and fantasy.

COURIER

NICHOLAS WOODE-SMITH

Ryder Miles is a courier of magical objects in a world dominated by magic and monsters. With a rare condition rendering him immune to magic, and his trusty revolver, he braves the wasteland to deliver a package that will test what it means to be a human or a monster.

COURIER

There aren't many rules out in the Badlands. So, you gotta live by the ones you got. Keeps you alive. Keeps you sane. At least, that's what my good old dad used to say. He's the one who gave me his rules. Taught me everything there was about being a courier.

First, no living cargo. Living cargo can be messy. And the clients booking the cargo tend to be even messier. I ain't a slaver or a taxi-man. If I can't lug it on my back, then it ain't for me.

Second, travel alone. Everyone wants your cargo, my dad said. No exceptions. When you make a living hauling cursed and tempes-tuous items across a desert of starving wretches, you learn not to trust a soul.

And when you let those greedy, desperate souls too close to you, then you got problems. Then you gotta ASF.

That was my favourite rule growing up. Before I truly knew what it meant.

Always. Shoot. First.

There're a lot of baddies in the Badlands. Human and other-wise. You don't survive as a courier by playing nice. The types of beasts you run into on those blistering sands and ancient cracked highways aren't too keen on negotiating. So, when you get the chance, you unload everything you got at them.

And that brings us to the most important rule of all. Always Deliver. Always! When your job is delivering, you deliver. Simple as that.

So, no matter what happens between destination to destination and dawn to dusk, you get that package delivered.

Even if that means facing down a horde of sandies more interested in eating my haunches than taking a peek at my package. And no, I don't mean that type of package! Get your head out of the gutter.

The sandies all burst out of the dirt simultaneously. Always acted like this. The sand lizardmen were dangerous but predictable.

Through the fog of swept up sand and dirt, a yellow-brown onslaught of scales and bloodied teeth barrelled towards me. I sidestepped, drawing my trusty revolver, and unloading a single round into the yellow-brown sandstorm. Red mist mingled with the upswept sand.

The growls and roars stopped. The sandies liked to use shock and awe. But when they realised it wouldn't work on their prey, they went quiet.

A gust of wind cleared some of the sand, revealing a yellow-brown mound of scales with a bloody hole in the head. Its companions had gone underground—burrowing.

I stayed still, revolver at the ready. I made no sound. Not to hide, mind you. They knew exactly where I was. Could smell me even if I had managed to find a shower in the last week. I kept quiet, so I could hear them.

A faint rustle. That's all I needed. I twisted my body as a spear flew straight toward me. I winced. A moment too late! My dad would've belted me good for that. Would've added to the sting on my arm where the spear had nicked me.

I raised my revolver and fired into the dirt. Blood mingled with the sand, and the mound didn't move. At least, I didn't see it move as I was tackled into the dirt from behind by a scaly beastie that smelled like month-old meat. Definitely needed mouthwash! Well, I'm not one to talk.

From my new vantage point on the ground, a berserk lizard on my back, I saw another sandy burst from the dirt and raise its spear above its head.

I narrowly managed to move my head out of the way. The spear was close enough to my eyes that I could see the bits of sinew and dried blood from this beastie's last kill. More bad luck, and I'd be joining that long list of victims!

I twisted my body, elbowing the beastie on my back. It hesitated. Just for a moment. All the time I needed. With my free arm, I grabbed the spear and pulled the other sandy off balance. It fell into its comrade. I used the spear to leverage my way out of the dog (or would it be lizard?) pile.

The sandies recovered as I got back on my feet. I fired twice in rapid succession. Two bullets. Two kills.

Four bullets. And I had no idea how many sandies were left.

I felt a shimmer in the air. Just a feeling. It made my hair stand on end as I felt the natural world twist itself to the commands of a mage.

Of course! Couldn't just be some sandy hunting party. Had to have a shaman with them. Just my Rifts-damned luck!

I turned towards the source of the wrongness in the air. And bingo! The sandy was scrawnier than the rest. If the other sandies were land crocs standing upright, this guy was a gecko. But, even with its reptilian maw, an arrogant smirk was drawn across its face. It wore a necklace of bones, dominated by the skull of a human child. And it carried a staff covered with human skin. Charming bastard, ain't he?

The shaman swirled its staff in the air as if stirring some sky soup. Magical energy gathered above its head, ready to be unleashed on me with all its dark nastiness.

I took aim, but just as I did, sand exploded around me. More sandies!

A maw chomped down just where my arm had been a moment before. I smacked it down with my free hand and fired point-blank into its skull. The sand dispersed, giving me just enough warning to duck underneath the perforated sandy. My new chum took two spears to the back for me before I let him collapse to the ground.

I fired at a figure obscured by the sandstorm, praying to whatever god may have been watching me in between playing roulette that I'd find my mark.

Two corpses fell flat as the sand cleared. One bullet. Two skulls. Hah! No one was gonna believe that story. Well, not that I had anyone to tell the story to.

Two bullets left. I could make that work.

The earth rumbled underneath my feet. I jumped out of the way and fired into the shifting sands.

No blood. Rifts!

A claw caught my foot. I fired my last round into it. The hand slackened.

The shifting magic in the air created a wind, pushing the sand out of the way.

No more sandies erupted from the dirt. It was just the shaman and me. The shaman must've been counting my shots because it grinned like no lizard had any business doing.

I holstered my revolver calmly and took a step toward the shaman. One step at a time, my feet sinking slightly into the upended sand and dirt.

The shaman kept up its frenzy of hissing spell words, channelling the weyline into its dark machinations. Anyone else would've probably been sprinting toward or away from this mad lizard. Not me.

The shaman finished its spell with a crescendo, crying out in its reptilian tongue. All its stored magic shot towards me. Rays of red, purple, and blue. A column of dreadful arcana.

It'd probably melt the skin off my bones. Make my eyes boil, and my soul burn for a thousand years before it found its way into the In Between for its final rest.

Probably. But I ain't normal.

The rays hit my chest and just fizzled away. The weyline calmed.

Became ordinary. It even seemed to forget that it had been used to power such a dark spell.

Finally, that smirk disappeared off the lizard's face. It stared up at me, mouth agape, as I punched it square in the jaw.

It fell back onto its tail as I confiscated its staff. Too shocked to resist, it only winced as I broke the grotesque staff over my knee and let its remains fall to the ground.

The now ex-shaman stared at the remnants of its once powerful weapon, looked back up at me and then bolted into the distance.

I let it flee. It would spread the message. Sandies didn't seek revenge—they weren't sentimental like that. If they heard about what I did here, they wouldn't seek me out. They'd know it wasn't worth it.

This shattered sandy would spread the message. Its own form of courier, carrying the message of the courier in a dark brown coat, travelling the Dead Man's Mile.

I rubbed my fist. Shaman didn't have sharp teeth, so no blood. But hurt like all the hells anyway. I wasn't a bruiser by any stretch of the imagination. Give me a gun any day!

As I checked the nick on my arm and the ache on my knuckle, I considered the broken staff at my feet.

I didn't know why or how I was immune to magic. I just was. Always had been. When my dad had taken me to the healers to heal a sniffle, it hadn't worked on me. Had to eat cockatrice soup instead. Heal the old-fashioned way, the adults had said. Heal the way humans did before the Cataclysm invited magic and monsters into the world.

Since then, my dad and I have tested my abilities. I wasn't completely immune to magic, mind you. Just that any magic used on me just fizzled out. That meant curses and dark magic washed off just as much as healing spells and enchantments did. But that didn't spare me from the indirect effects of magic. Fire burnt me just as much if it was made with a spell or with coals. But try to light me on fire directly with a spell, and you'd soon enough get a barrel in your mouth and a very angry courier.

My dad suspected that my borderline magic immunity came

from my mother's side. That's as much I'd heard about my mom. My dad didn't talk about her.

Satisfied that my hurts wouldn't put me in the dirt, I dusted off my coat and got to scavenging what I could. I wasn't getting my hopes up that I'd find much. Sandies, like other beasts, didn't have much. Just their gross spears and trophies from past kills. But sometimes, they'd carry something of value.

Not this time, however. Not even some stolen *biltong* for me to munch on while on the trail. And my rations were dwindling rapidly.

And no, it didn't cross my mind to carve up these lizards and eat them. This might be the Badlands, but I had my limits. They may be snarling, good-for-nothing, old varmints, but they still had intellect. Could make tools and such. I don't have the stomach to eat something that can do that much thinking.

With nothing to show for this little scuffle, I counted what I had left. No ammo. Less than two days rations. Only a bit of money from a different part of the world. I hoped I could find someone who'd accept it.

Well, time to get moving.

———

I've delivered a lot of packages over the years. Ryder Miles Courier Services is a bit of a well-known brand in the right circles. That's my name, by the way. Ryder Miles. Somewhat confusing. I don't ride for miles. Couriering across the wastes of Post-Cataclysm Southern Africa doesn't really allow for such a privilege. Horses and such won't do. Beasts will smell them from a mile away and come running for a treat. Vehicles aren't much better. Make far too much noise. And are far too expensive for a measly little postman like me. And besides, the types of terrain I have to cross don't allow for the liberty of wheels. Off-road or not.

Which leaves me trekking on foot. Takes an age most of the time. But my type of clientele aren't the type to fret over delivery times. They don't mind how long it takes for the package to get there, just as long as it does.

I'd been lugging this satchel containing a heavy rectangle covered in brown paper for about two weeks already. Just outta Hope City and deep into the Badlands. Been a while since I'd seen civilisation. Which I usually don't mind. But being as awful tired and as awful hungry, as I am, I couldn't help but feel a bit of relief when I saw a disparate group of houses arrayed around the old sand-strewn highway.

My relief at entering this little town was soon dashed, however. Eyes stared daggers at me as the townsfolk stopped their work and wandering to stare, glare and plot.

Nothing marked me as a courier—no logos, brands, or uniforms. To most, I looked the part of a gunslinger. An adventurer out in the wastes to find glory or a shallow grave. That made people scared. But these stares were not the usual frightened glances. There was hunger in the eyes of these men and women. A hunger I'd seen before, as the people I passed stared down at the satchel around my shoulders.

They didn't need to know that I was a courier to know I might be carrying something mighty valuable. And this far into the Badlands, people acted stupid and desperate.

I needed to be brief. No time to relax. Towns are danger; my dad used to say. Only time you can be in them is when you didn't have anything they'd want. When you didn't have anything they could take from you.

A dozen eyes stared at my satchel. I shifted my weight, pulling it in front of me. Big mistake! Made them all the more curious.

My trigger finger itched. My gut was telling me to shoot and run. But I couldn't ASF with no bullets. I had to find a way to remedy that.

This nameless town was split down the middle by the dilapidated old highway. Traffic still came north every once in a while. Heavily armed convoys guarded by armies of mercs. This town probably survived on those convoys.

Which meant they needed a general store. And that store would probably sell ammo.

I decided to brave the stares and approach one of the onlookers. A middle-aged woman putting up laundry right by the main thoroughfare as if it wasn't just gonna be sandblasted. Not smart!

"Excuse me, ma'am," I said, doffing my hat at her. She glared in response. I chose to continue unabashed.

"Would you mind telling me where I can find a store that would sell supplies and ammunition?"

She hesitated and then pointed down the street. I tipped my hat once again and went on my way. This was definitely not the friendliest town I'd been in on the Dead Man's Mile or the Badlands. But, also not the worst. Plenty of them had opened fire at my silhouette on the horizon before I could exchange a single pleasantry.

The general store looked like it had once been a normal brick house. That is, until half the abode had been crushed by a rift, monster or errant spell. In its place, a tin and wooden shanty had been built to act as the storefront.

The words *Winkel* and Shop were painted on either side of the door. I counted out my dwindling funds and entered.

The storekeeper stood behind the counter. His welcoming smile soon faded as he saw me. Didn't like strangers?

In a flash, his smile returned, but far more insincere than before.

The man was middle-aged. Pale skin painted red by the sun. He was rapidly balding, trying to fight the inevitable with a greasy comb-over. He wore an apron that distinctly lacked food stains. It seemed it was his impromptu retail uniform.

"Afternoon, sir," I greeted the man, taking my hat off. My dad told me to never wear a hat indoors if I could help it. "Do you perchance stock .357 Magnum rounds?"

Without a word, the storekeeper ducked under the counter and retrieved a box of rounds. They were plastered with the label "HCPD – Not for Resale".

Well, pretty sure there were no HCPD officers here to stop us from making this transaction.

"How much?" I asked.

The storekeeper shrugged. "How much you offering?"

I palmed some of my extra Hope City dollar notes and offered around $50 to the man. He considered the note. A lot of people out in the Badlands didn't stomach Hope City money. But this place seemed to get traffic from down south, so it'd come in handy.

The storekeeper finally nodded and accepted the money, passing the box across the counter.

I put the box in my coat pocket and then pointed over my shoulder at an empty table.

"Mind if I set up over there? Got some overdue maintenance chewing into my shooter here."

The storekeeper nodded and, without another word, turned his back on me.

I eyed his back. What a weird town!

I was used to stares and distrust. But not like this. Could it possibly have something to do with my package? Did they want it that badly? It wasn't uncommon for rumours of my deliveries to get ahead of me. For bandits and opportunists to set ambushes. But this had been super secretive. Not even I knew what I was shipping.

I sat down at the table and took out my revolver and the new box of ammunition. My eight-shooter was a Blackcalf .357 Magnum revolver. The handle was a black wood, varnished to perfection. Despite my worries, it was still in good condition.

It had been the first and only gift my dad had ever given me.

Caring for it had become a comforting ritual over the years. Something to keep my mind off the sand and desperate stares. It calmed my soul in a way that nothing else ever could.

I'd never had a home, but when I held the grip of my Blackcalf and stooped over it to care for its judgement-delivering metal, I felt a semblance of belonging.

The light filtering through the dusty windows of the ramshackle storefront began to dim and redden. Night would fall upon the wastes soon enough. A time for most people to retreat into their homes and pray to whatever deity was listening that a nightmare wasn't made manifest right outside their front door.

For me, it was the best time to hide from the monsters that couldn't see in the dark.

I holstered my Blackcalf and checked my now weighted bandolier and eyed some field rations on the shelf. I placed them on the counter with the rest of my notes.

The storekeeper rang them up while looking me up and down.

"You got a place to stay? It's getting dark."

"Got a place," I lied.

"Got a spare room in the back. Can stay the night. Free of charge. It's dangerous out."

This sudden pleasantness raised my hackles something fierce. If I had been planning on staying in this town, this definitely would have changed my mind. No one in the Badlands was this generous. Especially after eyeing my satchel for so long behind my back.

"Thanks, but I best be off."

I put my hat back on and tipped it in farewell before making my way down the rapidly darkening street – once again, a dozen eyes on my back.

I woke up at the sound of a single footfall crunching on the stale chips I'd sprinkled around my campsite. I'd been sleeping fitfully, worse than usual. Good thing too.

I had my gun aimed at a figure in the dark before it could get the jump on me. ASF.

I pulled the trigger.

And then, nothing.

I pulled again. Click. Click. Nothing.

A chuckle came from the dark, as figures charged me. I kicked out, hitting something fleshy, and was rewarded with a grunt of pain. I lashed out again, just to have my arms held down by two shadowy figures emerging from the night.

I kicked and thrashed until lights erupted around me from flashlights and lighters. I stopped, and blinked until I could see through the illumination.

Standing above me was the storekeeper, the washerwoman, and half a dozen men and women from the town.

Realisation struck me. They'd sold me dud ammo. Been planning this from the start. Probably would have slit my throat in my sleep if I'd stayed there. Not that that mattered now. They'd found me. And got the jump on me as well.

My dad would be shaking his head in stark disapproval right about now. I should have left that town as soon as I saw the stares.

"There's a monster within every soul, Ryder," my dad had told me. "And it's more deceitful than any old beast."

"Don't look at me that way," the storekeeper said, looking guilty, I'm not sure if feigned or genuine. "I regret this. I really do. But seeing you waltzing into town with your satchel and shiny pistol… you should have expected this."

"I should've," I agreed.

The storekeeper nodded.

"So, hand over your satchel there. We gotta eat. Gotta survive."

"You don't even know what this is," I replied.

"It's everything we need, stranger. It is hell here. But this…we know it will help us. So, we gotta do what it takes. Strangers don't matter as much as we do. So, we have to do what it takes to survive."

I nodded, slowly. I could agree with his sentiments.

"You're right. It's hard to survive. So, we gotta do what it takes. To get the job done. To always deliver."

Before the thugs holding me down could react, I hit my heel hard against the ground, triggering a blade to flick out from the toe of my boot. I tested my flexibility to the limits and kicked above me, hitting one of the thugs in the face. He cried out, letting go of me and causing his friend to jump back, his face splattered with blood.

I reached for the waistband of the screaming man and grabbed his knife, plunging it into the neck of his shocked comrade.

The storekeeper paled like he'd seen a ghost from the In Between, as I kicked out at another townsman, slashing his chest with my toe-knife.

A bang rang out just as I side-stepped the shot. I grabbed the barrel and pulled the woman off-balance, letting her fall to the ground. Her comrades paid her no heed, trampling her as they charged me with a club and a hatchet.

I shouldered the woman's rifle, chambered a round with a pull of the bolt, and fired a shot into the hatchet-wielder. The club came down at me with a vengeance, giving me a mighty bruise on my forearm as I dropped the rifle and drew my own knife, sticking it in the townsman's gut.

As I pulled out my knife, I felt a weight lift from my shoulders. My satchel strap had been cut!

I turned to see the balding pate of the storekeeper hoofing it into the darkness.

I picked up the bolt-action and fired. My shot went wide as a man tackled me into the dirt. A fist met my face. Might've put me to sleep when I was younger. But I got into brawls with lizardmen and orcs. They'd have to do better than that. I caught the man's fist and shifted our weights until I was the one on top. I delivered a swift punch to the man's face, breaking his nose and putting him out cold.

I shook my fist. Rifts! I wish healing magic worked on me.

The night had gone quiet around the massacre surrounding me. I felt a pang of regret. They weren't fighters. Weren't prepared for someone like me.

But then they shouldn't have picked a fight with me.

I felt another twinge, this time of anxiety, as I realised the store-keeper was still on the run with my satchel. And my package!

I picked up the bolt-action again and gave chase into the night. I didn't have to go too far to find the grunting, pathetic figure of the storekeeper trying to clamber over some rocks.

I pulled him onto the ground by his collar and aimed the bolt-action into his face.

The storekeeper raised his palms, tears and sweat streaming down his cheeks.

"I'm sorry! I'm sorry! We didn't know…"

"Didn't know that I could defend myself?!"

"No, I mean…" he was at a loss for words, repeating apologies and gibberish.

I spat to the side and shouldered the rifle firmly, the barrel inches away from the man's face.

"Strangers' lives don't matter, eh? You'd have gutted me. Why shouldn't I do the same?"

"Please!" The storekeeper begged, smelling like fear and desperation. "Please don't. I won't do it again. You have my word. Is it money you want? There's money back in town. I can take you to it. You can have all of it. Please...just don't kill me."

Seeing a grown man weep pulled at something inside of me. It really did. My dad never taught me to kill a man in cold blood. Just to defend myself. To make sure I didn't disappear under the sands of this blasted wasteland.

But this man had been so willing to kill me. For what? For a package, he had no business opening. What would really stop him from doing this again? To someone less prepared. Rifts! They'd probably done this to countless people. Countless wanderers and innocents trekking the Dead Man's Mile for a shot at salvation.

They'd preyed on those people like they'd tried to prey on me.

And now he wanted mercy?

I stared into the tearful, terrified eyes of the man who'd tried to rob and murder me. I pitied him. I wanted to show him mercy.

But I didn't. I pulled the trigger and felt the ringing up my arm as the night went silent once more.

I don't like killing. Especially when the victims were thinking beings. There's something about snuffing out a life that could've been my own that doesn't sit well with me.

But I did it all the same. Travel far enough in the wastes and you face all kinds of monsters. And, more often than not, you find there is a monster within everyone. Just had to give it the right motivation.

Because of my condition, I often find myself delivering cursed magical items which can burrow into the minds of humans and beasts alike. Draws them to me. Tempts them. Reveals the monster.

Problem is that I can never be sure if a package has that sort of magical temptation. Doesn't affect me. But, what I've found is that it doesn't take a lot to turn a sane man into a beast. Greed accomplishes much more than a cursed item ever could.

Even so, I couldn't help but feel that my latest delivery was gonna give me even more trouble along the Dead Man's Mile. Even if I couldn't feel its pull, there was something in the eyes of the townsfolk that revealed something magical in nature. Typical that it wouldn't affect me.

My dad had said that I would've made the best ringbearer. Better than Frodo. Whatever that means.

My dad was old. Had been a postal worker Pre-Cataclysm. Back when being a courier meant dropping letters off to smiling folks with green lawns. Not a monster in sight. At least not the kind we're used to now. Being from that time, my dad knew a lot I didn't. Said that's why he became a courier. Wanted me to become one. Because after the Vortex opened and the rifts brought all the monsters and magic, people needed to stay connected.

He wanted me to continue that legacy.

But, my dad wasn't that idealistic anymore. He'd become jaded. His trust eroded by a land dead set on destroying itself and where humans and monsters were little different from each other.

I managed to find real ammunition for my Blackcalf on one of the townsfolk. I also kept the bolt action. Could come in handy. My old hunting rifle had been eaten by an orc, thinking it was liquorice.

My travels took me further north along the Dead Man's Mile. It was a lot longer than a mile. Something my aching muscles and bones reminded me of every chance they got.

Fortunately, there wasn't much in the way of civilisation this far up. Just arid shrublands, desert and ruins. Suited me just fine. If there was a curse on the brown paper wrapped package in my satchel, I didn't want to tempt anyone else.

Nights had passed since the massacre near that nameless town when I settled down amongst some boulders, hidden by some rare flourishing shrubs and a lone tree.

My dried rations had run out, leaving me with some meat I'd

caught in a snare earlier that day. Some sort of rabbit-creature from another world.

I didn't like lighting fires in the wastes, but sometimes it couldn't be helped.

I cleared out a hole in the earth and gathered some kindling for the fire. Just enough to cook this meat and then put it out for the night. I didn't need fires for warmth much. This was a hot region. Even at night. And when the temperature dropped, I had my coat and a blanket to keep me warm.

With much anxiety and much hunger, I started a small cooking fire and spitted the meat from the rabbit thing on a metal skewer.

I watched it crisp up nicely, unable to help myself from licking my lips. Sufficiently cooked, I brought the skewer up to my mouth, just as I heard a snap of a twig.

I drew my revolver and aimed it into the darkness, the barrel pointing directly at the head of a kid who couldn't have been older than seven or eight.

ASF had exceptions. And, as the dirty boy-child stared back at me with big, hungry eyes, I couldn't help but lower my gun. Behind the boy, a girl around the same age appeared. And behind her, a woman whose age was masked by wrinkles, dirt and grime. A life of hardship that added decades.

The three of them were all filthy. And that was coming from me. They looked like they'd been running for a while. No time to eat, drink or bathe. Just a desperate flight into many nights of torture and suffering.

My heart stung for them and all those like them. I'd seen too much of it. Too many kids suffering along the Dead Man's Mile.

"Please, sir," the mother asked, voice croaky. "Can we have something to eat?"

Simple. Honest. Desperate.

How could I say no?

I cooked all the meat I had, sharing it around and watching as the kids and their mom ravenously consumed the meat like it was ambrosia straight from the gods. I passed them one of my water bottles, which they shared out like every drop was gold.

My heart ached, even as a small smile crossed my face that I was able to help them.

It was only when they were just about done that I remembered my satchel. I shifted my body, subtly putting the satchel and its makeshift repaired strap under me.

They didn't seem to notice. They licked their fingers and then stared at the bones of the creature. They'd eaten as much of the bones as they could. Sucked out the marrow. But it wasn't enough.

I frowned and went searching in my backpack for more.

"No, thank you," the woman spoke for the first time since she'd arrived. "You've already done so much for us."

I frowned deeper, wanting to help them. But she was right. I needed all that I had left. No telling how far it was till the next town or till I would be able to catch another animal.

I closed my backpack and settled back down. Three pairs of eyes stared at me. Hungry but fuller than they had been. I wish I could have done more.

"So…" I started. I wasn't used to this. Not many people on the trail. Especially not on the Dead Man's Mile. Seldom spoke to people at all. Especially not by the campfire this late at night.

"We're from up north," the woman anticipated my question.

I nodded sombrely. "What brought you here?"

I saw her lip quiver for just a moment.

"Ogres," she said simply.

I nodded again. Northern Ogre Horde. Not as diplomatic as the southern horde.

"Pa…pa got eaten," the boy said. The little girl let out a silent sob.

"I… I'm sorry," I replied, not knowing what else to say. This wasn't my forte. People, that is. I could be their connection. Could deliver their packages. But speaking to them was a whole other mess I wasn't prepared for.

The woman wiped away some errant tears and put on a stoical façade.

"How about you? Where you from?"

I shrugged. "I'm a drifter. I go where life takes me. I'm from nowhere, and I go to nowhere."

As vague a response I could give. Not that it was entirely untrue. I didn't know where I was born, and I didn't know where I was gonna die. I just lived life as it happened. Job to job.

"Ever been to Hope City?" She asked, eyes brightening. "Or Goldfield?"

I nodded.

She looked in awe. "I heard they're not like this. That they're safe. Like Eden. Places where you can eat your fill every night. With running water and lights to keep the monsters at bay. I hear it's Heaven."

I couldn't help but glower. Just a bit.

"Far from it, ma'am. The cities are their own type of wasteland. And you can't see the monsters coming. It ain't no Eden or Heaven. More a hell hiding behind neon signs. Where the air stinks like burnt rubber, and men hide behind smart suits while they tear apart the civilisation they claim to love."

I shook my head. "No, ma'am. They ain't paradise. Just more of this."

I felt guilty as I saw the hope drain from the woman's face. Like I'd told a child that Santa Claus had been killed in Vietnam just last Spring.

I opened my mouth to take back what I said, but the woman stopped me. Turned to her kids.

"It's getting late. Time to sleep, I think," she said.

I grunted my reply as I put out the fire. I offered my blanket to the woman. She accepted without a word, curling up with her kids. Back facing me.

Good work, Ryder. Way to make friends and spread hope and joy.

When I was sure the woman wasn't watching, I checked my satchel again, and then placed it under my backpack, so I could use both as a pillow.

I dreamed of ogres, of burning ruins, and my dad judging every decision I'd ever made.

I woke up to searing pain in my shoulder. Before I could think, my hand dove to my holster. I fired. All in one quick motion as I lay down with my meat skewer jutting from my flesh.

I sat upright as my attacker stumbled back, screaming and sobbing. The screams were joined by the children as they watched their mother fall backward, clutching a rapidly darkening hole in her stomach.

I lifted myself up, slowly, watching the scene unfold under the moon and starlit sky.

I winced. That wasn't a wound you came back from unless you had a purifier or healing mage right there with you.

The children kept wailing as the woman yelled and screamed.

I touched the skewer in my shoulder. It'd glanced off my chest armour. Slid into my shoulder. It had been meant for my heart.

I stared at the dying woman and then at my satchel. The kids screamed and sobbed. They didn't understand. They didn't feel the magical temptation from my package. Kids were immune to such curses. They were innocent.

Only adults could be monsters.

I stumbled backward, incredulous.

"Help…help me! Please!" The woman sobbed, eyes glazed with pain and tears. Her children wailed.

I took a step forward, and her face became vicious. "Get away from me! You monster! You demon!"

Monster.

I reached out to help, but the boy slapped my hand away. He eyed my rifle. He wanted vengeance. Wanted to protect his mom.

I stepped back and picked up my rifle with shaking hands. I opened my backpack and emptied out all my spare rations and food. All but one bottle of water. And all but the one bandage I'd need for my shoulder. Not that it would save her.

And leaving nothing but petty offerings to a dead woman and her distraught children, I fled into the darkness.

A dark tower loomed over the wastes. It was neither modern nor ancient. An anomaly in a world where monsters and magic supplanted modernity. It rose above the sands and dead foliage, creating an ominous scene in a sea of death.

It was fitting that this was my destination. An appropriately surreal place to cap off a journey filled with suffering. More misery than most of my trips. So many people had died by my hands. For what? An unmarked package covered in brown paper.

I never questioned my dad's golden rules. But, perhaps, I should not have taken this job. Should have just let the storekeeper have the package. Let the wastes cover up my cowardice with bloodied sand.

Perhaps then, two children would still have a mother.

I had to fight the temptation to open the package. To see what all this had been over. To see if perhaps magic was not to blame. That I had rid this world of genuine monsters.

But the end was in sight. I just needed to press on. And after that, I could put this all behind me.

But, as I remembered the terror in her eyes, the wails of her children, and the dark red seeping onto the sand, I knew that I never would be able to forget.

I arrived at the foot of the tower. Before I could knock on the red metal-plated double doors, they opened. On the other side stood a horned creature with pale blue skin and a pair of batlike wings. It wore a smart black and white uniform. Like a butler.

I took a step back and reached to draw my Blackcalf.

"The imp is under my control, Mr Miles. No need to dispatch it," a disembodied voice, dripping with authority, came from the void.

I hesitated, but the demon didn't move. It looked glum as it held the door like a common manservant. It was bound tight. It had long since given up on trying to gain its freedom.

I holstered my weapon and entered the tower, the imp closing the door behind me.

The entry hall was modestly decorated. A simple red carpet,

some prints of old Pre-Cataclysm artwork, and the beginning of a spiral staircase reaching into the wizard's sanctum.

I ascended the stairway. My flesh, bones, and soul exhausted from this journey. But it was almost over.

The door at the top of the spiral staircase was open. I entered a circular room plastered with runes, schematics, and old tomes. In the centre was a circular stone table adorned with vellum sheets, potions, and scrolls.

A scrawny man, a foot shorter than my six feet, beamed at the satchel around my shoulders.

I could not be sure of his age. Spell-shock had rendered his eyes silver, and toying with dark magic had twisted his skin into canyon-like wrinkles and rivulets. His grey hair was unkempt and dirty. That of a man who cared not for outward appearances.

But even if he looked ancient, I could not be sure. Magic was not necessarily an old man's profession. It was only three decades old. Plenty of young people practicing it. And plenty of old people stuck in the past without it.

This man could've been ancient or just another fool aging himself with magic he had no business casting.

"Ryder Miles, I presume?" the wizard asked, offering a bony hand. "My name is Jerathmus Shadow-Weaver."

I suspected he'd named himself that. Wizards were odd—especially the kind who built towers made to look old in the middle of nowhere.

I nodded and then placed the satchel on the tabletop. I opened it as Jerathmus licked his lips by my side. At least he wasn't stabbing me, so I'd hurry up.

I took out the brown paper-wrapped package and then closed my satchel. I felt relief that it was finally out of my hands.

"Excellent!" Jerathmus clapped his hands together and then dug his hand into his pocket to retrieve a pouch of gold coins.

I'd usually count every coin, but I was tired. Too tired. I just wanted to find a small village by the coast and relax for a month.

With Jerathmus very satisfied, I exited his chamber, the door closing behind me.

But the relief ended then. As I was left alone on the stairway, everything hit me at once. The shock of the recoil in my arms, the blood on my hands, the faces of those I'd killed.

I had to sit down, clutching my head and breathing heavily. My bruises and wounds all stung, and the red on my hands seemed like it'd never wash off.

I killed them. I had to. It was them or me. But I couldn't get a single burning question out of my mind:

Why? What could drive people to become monsters like that? What was it that I was delivering that could have caused all of this?

I usually didn't pay any mind to what I was delivering. Was not my business. My clients desired their privacy, and I was willing to give it to them.

But this time…I had to know.

Without thinking, I flung open the door to Jerathmus' sanctum.

The wizard looked surprised but didn't show any indication of anger.

"I…" I panted. "I need to know what it is."

Jerathmus nodded understandingly as his frail lips curved into a smile.

"I am surprised that you didn't open the package at all. There is an arcane temptation to this artefact. Something that would drive any mortal to do anything just to take a peek. It could taint the most sacred purifier. For your discipline, you do deserve some answers."

I approached the stone table as Jerathmus stepped aside.

Framed by the torn brown paper was a stone tablet bearing the visage of a screaming demon. That is all. Just stone. Not gold. Not diamond. Just stone with questionable artwork.

My heart fell. I'd killed so many people over this…

"It's just a tablet…" I muttered, devastated.

"No, my boy." Jerathmus grinned. "It is far more than just any old tablet. There is a monster within this stone façade. A demon of the Raz'ed Horde that came to our realm and found himself trapped by a Sintari archmage. He calls out to the mortals that come into contact with him, promising riches and power in exchange for his freedom."

Temptation. A magical temptation. All those people… they'd been fed false promises by a demon trapped in a rock. Not true monsters. Just puppets on magical strings.

My soul felt heavy.

"And what are you going to do with it?" I asked, hoping that the answer would grant me solace. That Jerathmus would rid the world of this evil artifact. That his knowledge of what this was would give him the clarity needed to destroy it.

"Well, I intend to free the demon, of course." Jerathmus looked shocked that I even needed to ask. "And press him into my service. That is why he tempts us, obviously. To be freed. But only I can control him."

Jerathmus stroked the demon's visage like one would a lover.

I took an involuntary step back. "Why? Why would you do that?!"

"Because I can. Because this blighted land is a void without a ruler. The power vacuum must be filled. And, with this demon at my beck and call, I can be the ruler this wasteland needs."

"How can you be sure you can control it? The demon could be whispering lies to you. Convincing you that you can control it. Promising you power."

Jerathmus smiled patronisingly as one would smile at a foolish child asking even more foolish questions.

"I can control it. I know I can. And I will use its power for a great cause. Rejoice, Mr Miles. You brought this to me. Finally, the Badlands will find peace."

Peace under the boots of a hungry demon and his foolish summoner. That was no peace at all.

My trigger finger itched. My revolver pressed into my side. The weight was telling me to act. My father's words clashed within my mind.

Always deliver. But always shoot first.

I saw the flames of this demon trapped in stone and saw the madness in Jerathmus' eyes.

I drew my revolver and pointed it at Jerathmus, hesitating as I saw blood drip from my hands from all those I'd already killed.

Jerathmus looked unscathed. His superior smile was unwavering.

"The tablet will do you no good, my boy. Only I can summon the demon. Only I can turn his lies into riches. But I can pay you for the trouble. You came so far and suffered so much. Name your price."

"It's not about the money!" I yelled as my father spoke inside my head. He told me to fire or leave. To never point a gun idly. To act. Always.

"Then, what is it about?" Jerathmus asked. His smile contorted into something mocking. He laughed. "Ah! You fear for the people of this land. You believe me a monster. Put those petty notions of morality aside. You should know better. You have seen how beastly and depraved these people are. You have seen the monster within their souls. They need to be controlled. To be shackled like the demons they are. It is only right that a demon does the shackling."

I have simple rules. They can be brutal. They can be cold and ruthless. They can leave blood on my hands that will never wash off. And I can't claim that I am a friend of my fellow humans.

But the people I encountered weren't born evil. They were tempted into it by demonic treachery. Made to do evil by evil magics. They weren't monsters. Just puppets.

But then, what did that make me? Because I chose to pull the trigger. Every time.

And what did that make Jerathmus? The man who'd made me bring this temptation to these desperate lands?

The wizard held his hands behind his back. Cocky. Arrogant. He was convinced that I would never fire. That greed would win out. That I'd turn my back on him and leave him to his evil machinations.

But for all the wrongs I'd committed, I need to make some form of amends. In every small way.

I pulled the trigger.

The bang was followed by diabolical cries of jubilation as Jerathmus' demonic servants were released from their bonds. They fled into the wastes. They wouldn't be too much trouble. Plenty of beasts out in the Badlands that would make an imp into lunch.

Jerathmus' expression didn't change, even as blood dripped down his forehead. He was still convinced I'd leave him the tablet. That I'd let him bring another monster into the world.

I placed the tablet back in my satchel and descended the staircase. The doorway was ripped off its hinges. I didn't stay long enough to find Jerathmus' hidden money or even to stock up on supplies. I wanted to be away from this place. Somewhere far away where I could hide this evil tablet. Hide it deep underground or in the depths of the Atlantic. So it couldn't tempt men into showing their worst selves again.

There is a monster within us all. It doesn't need a stone tablet to reveal itself. But we can control it. Only it. So, better not bring any more monsters into the world.

I stared out towards the horizon, took a deep breath, and started my journey again.

ABOUT NICHOLAS WOODE-SMITH

Nicholas Woode-Smith is an urban fantasy author and political analyst from Cape Town, South Africa. He spends his free time hiking, gaming and painting little toy soldiers.

WHERE THE DEAD HUNT

ROBERT TILLSLEY

The world has ended. Ghosts haunt the shadows by day and hunt for souls by night. My name's Tom. I never knew the world as it was, so I can't mourn it. I'm apprenticed to Hunter, a man of few words who always gets the job done.

When a simple package drop leads us to dead bodies and missing babies, we've got a hard choice to make. The answers we need are in a decaying city infested with the deadliest spirits. And if we take too long, no one's making it out alive.

WHERE THE DEAD HUNT

S unset burned across the rusted cars shoved to either side of the road. I followed Hunter down the middle, my horse closing on his as the safety of day grew more distant. A tingling along my skin warned me of what I already knew—they were coming. I'd been apprenticed to Hunter for four months, but I still held tight to the fear that had forced me to accept his offer. I wanted his bravery, his knowledge, his resolve. At fifteen years old, I was in awe of his grizzled visage, his black coat studded with steel, the saber swaying from his belt. Hell, even his wide-brimmed hat with its scratches and holes proclaimed him as a survivor.

The edges of the road had crumbled, assaulted by weeds that would one day claim it all. Even without the road, our path would have been clear. The city towered against the horizon, its skeletal towers sending jolts of anxiety through my chest. I'd never been so close. I'd never wanted to be. Only an idiot would. I thanked whatever powers there were that we only sought the nearby town, itself a low smudge too far ahead. Compassion it was called, a name from after the End. The city had a name once, but Hunter didn't want to talk about it, echoing the adults in my childhood.

We reached an expanse of chain-link fencing. The rusting

diamonds of wire wrapped around the low stone wall of a cemetery, a wall which had proved useless. Here and there amongst the piles of ashes, curves of gravestones poked up like teeth. Flickers of movement, what at any other time could have been ash on the wind, drew my attention. I swallowed hard and squeezed my reins. They were stirring.

"Tom," Hunter said without looking back. "What do you see?"

He loved his questions. He'd been a teacher once, I'd heard. But then, I'd also heard he'd been an assassin, a soldier, and a detective. I squashed my immediate desire to tell him it was a cemetery. I hadn't seen him laugh once.

"A pre-End design with a low wall to encourage people to keep to the paths. In the first weeks, they burned as many bodies as they could. And when the ghosts kept rising at night, they built the only fence that could hold them—steel."

We continued along its side. I wanted to kick my horse and leave it behind.

"Was it worth doing?"

My gaze went to the city. You couldn't cage the world. I checked around us. Hunter's question was different from his usual. What did he mean? The forest beyond a field to our left was cloaked in darkness. Straining, I spotted a shade darting from tree to tree. I wouldn't walk there, night or day. Wispy arms stretched from the long-cold pyres of the cemetery—heads were rising, too. They were contained by the fence. Even when fully awake, they wouldn't be able to escape.

"Yes. I guess," I said. "I'd rather they were in there than out here. That's less to chase us."

"Wrong. There's always more. Containing a few is pointless. Burned and on open ground, far from their deaths, already rendered the spirits weaker. They didn't know any better. You do now."

I didn't know what to say to that, so I kept silent and stewed on our ill-timed journey.

The very last glint of the day disappeared as we reached the town. It was the largest place I'd seen. At least judging from the scale of the barrier. Cars, trucks, I beams, steel pickets, more chain-link. I guess it might take a half hour or more to walk around. The structure was as high as the roof of a single-story house and put me in mind of a metal caterpillar, a poisonous one. The gate faced the road. Steel plates had been bolted together, presumably on a hidden frame, and rested on wheels in a deep groove. White spray paint labeled the town Compassion, the name ruined by sinister-looking drips. The figures behind kept that theme going. They came from fields and the forest. At this distance, I couldn't ascribe types. I don't know most of them, anyway.

Hunter brought his horse alongside and rapped the gate with the pommel of his saber.

"Open up."

We waited in vain.

He hammered the steel again. "Open up, or I'll damn well burn the place down."

The dead closed on us, some walking, others floating or dragging their ruined bodies along. They might be weak, but together they'd swallow our souls just the same. My skin turned clammy. My legs were leaden. This was a bad idea. Hunter didn't relent. He worked the steel like a blacksmith.

Finally, a woman's voice shouted from the other side, "Stop making that racket and get running. We don't open the gate after sundown—that's what keeps this town safe. If you're alive in the morning, come back."

"That you, Grace?"

"Hunter?"

"Yeah, let us in."

"Sorry, Hunter, I can't. You know the rules. You'll live till dawn." There was relief. She was happy not to be dooming a stranger to their last night. "Mickey can let you in then."

Hunter was good, but I didn't believe that. I'd heard some types were smart. They'd find ways to shift iron filings or loosen mesh, and we had no doors or windows to line with salt.

"I've a package for the Librarian. It's urgent. You want to

explain to him why you turned me away? If I'm not in now, I'm not waiting."

"Hunter… You *know* I can't."

"But you will. I'm not bluffing. We'll be fast. We'll be discreet."

"You're an asshole, Hunter."

My eyebrows rose. He usually got respect wherever he went. A clank heralded a rumble, and the gate rolled open—barely enough to slip by. Hunter might be confident, but he didn't waste time before guiding his horse through. Imagining being shut out, I hurried after. A woman pushed on a handle welded to the gate and shut it the instant my horse's tail was clear.

"Go straight to the library. If the committee catch you in any of the bars, it's my job on the line. If they don't throw me out altogether. The Librarian can't fix everything."

Hunter dipped the tip of his hat. "Agreed."

"I'll see you tomorrow?"

"Could be." He nudged his horse forward. "Tom, hurry up."

There had to be hundreds of houses, even a few low apartment blocks. I saw peeling paint and rough repairs but not one mass of wind-gathered refuse. A few lanterns provided light. Lanterns. On a public street. The first person we passed raked horseshit toward a wheelbarrow. Others walked quickly, eyes down.

"Surprised?" Hunter asked.

I nodded, even though he hadn't looked back. "It's so clean. And they walk the streets at night."

"They feel safe."

"Are they?"

"No. There is no such thing. Let your guard down and you die."

A woman came hurrying from a narrow bungalow. Her sandy hair hung in a braid and she carried a wicker basket. I think Hunter would have kept going even as she greeted him if she hadn't also stood in front of his horse. Curious, I maneuvered to his side.

"Hungry? I have pies."

"What kind?" I asked.

"What do you like?" she said as if daring me.

Hunter glared. "Out of our way."

"I have salt. Give you a special deal?"

I leaned forward. "We're running low."

"Show me," Hunter said, his tone neutral.

She held up a glass test tube. Hunter took it, lifting it into the light of a lamp hanging from a street sign. He turned the tube twice and passed it to me. "What do you think?"

Another test. I moved closer to the lamp and inspected the material. White, but very fine. "It's not salt."

The woman spat at the ground. "You don't know what you're talking about."

"Ground quartz." He threw the tube onto the road. It shattered, spreading the powder irretrievably. "Rely on it, and it'd kill you."

"You asshole. You owe me for that."

"Want your complaint before the Librarian?"

"Get bent." She strode away, back rigid and shoulders straight.

"Never safe," Hunter said and led onward.

"Have you been here often?" I asked to break the silence as we turned and took a street that both curved and started a gentle incline.

"Often enough. The Librarian pays well and values good work."

He was holding back. I was sure of it. Was there going to come a time I would find it comfortingly familiar?

"Do you have any friends here?"

We were riding alongside. He turned his head just enough to look me in the eye, then returned to staring ahead.

He pointed up the street to where a sandstone building stood behind an ornate fence. "The library. If there's a safe spot on this earth, it's in there."

Bright patches. I tensed. Ghosts. My eyes adjusted. Electric lights, many of them. I looked at the roof of the building. It was covered in solar cells. The Librarian must be the richest person ever. When we reached a wrought iron gate, Hunter gestured for me to dismount and open it. The iron was cleverly shaped, all sweeping loops that never left enough room for a body to pass through. It was old, though, and lumpy from many layers of paint. I guessed it had been built long before the End. Behind it, a hedge of roses carried a sweet scent. Beautiful.

After closing the gate behind us, I stayed off my horse, letting my unsteady legs recover as we took a white gravel path to the building. Our passage produced a horrible grinding that must have announced our arrival. Judging by the narrow windows—not a single broken pane—the library was two stories tall. So this is what it must have been like. All clean and neat and rather grand. I hated it whenever adults went on about how things had been, but perhaps I was discovering a little of their sense of loss. I took Hunter's reins when he passed them to me and watched as he strolled up the wide staircase to press a button to one side of the door. A chime sounded. I looked around but could not see who had made it.

Hunter tapped a hand on the hilt of his saber, a sure sign of impatience. He put an ear to the door. It moved slightly.

"Trouble?" I asked.

"Get sage candle and a match."

I hurried, wishing for steadiness as I fumbled a saddlebag catch. A series of loops held candles, each one wrapped in paper to avoid wear. I tried to read the symbols he'd drawn on them, but they were hard to see in the limited light, and I was still learning my letters. Picking a couple, lifted them and checked for the right color. Graygreen. That was it. I scrounged for a matchbox at the bottom and climbed the stairs.

His eyes bored into me, but he said nothing and took the items. I watched, trying to carve the details into memory as he brought the match to life and, in turn, set the flame to the candle. Holding it to one side, he let several drips hit the threshold of the doorway. Then he pressed the base into the drips and stood back. The flame burned steadily.

"What's that mean?" I asked.

"No spirits. Not as accurate as you but cheaper. Clean it up."

He pressed the button as I worked, and the chime sounded, but no one came to the door. He grunted and pushed the door open.

"Librarian. Aria."

I joined him by the door. "Could they be out?"

He shrugged and entered. I got it. Leaving the door open was stupid. Stupid people didn't live long. I followed, wondering what it could mean. Hunter went to one side and made the lights work. They were amazing, droplets of glass suspended on yellow metal, brighter than stars. The floor gleamed beneath, all pale white with squiggly lines of gray. A staircase of redwood climbed up to a landing on the second story. Paintings and posters hung tightly packed together. Bridges, buildings, people, and a hundred other scenes that I could make no sense of.

Wooden stools dotted the open area, each holding a device made before the End. Many had colored lights or slowly moving parts. It was a marvel. Sooner or later, they broke in the presence of ghosts. Everyone I knew had given up on them. I could count the number I'd seen in use on two hands.

"Draw your sword," Hunter said, sliding his saber free.

I did so. It was a rapier with a metal cage that covered half my hand. The blade was thin and long, despite missing its tip. Hunter had bought it several weeks after I joined him. He'd taken me through the basics. I still had very little idea how to use it, but he had said it didn't matter—ghosts with swords were unlikely. Not impossible, but unlikely. And a person would shoot me. Comforting.

He went through the downstairs rooms first, flicking switches each time. I wanted to absorb all I was seeing. I didn't get the chance. He demanded I keep up, so I only took in an impression of contained chaos. Objects, pictures—stacked, pinned, boxed. And then we were heading up the stairs. They creaked quietly, though I was sure of their firmness.

Hunter strode to the left—he wasn't calling out anymore. He pushed open a door.

"Fuck."

What could surprise him? Raising my rapier, I looked in the gap left by his side. Boots. Legs. A body. It was wrapped in rose canes, thorns digging into red jeans and a blue sweatshirt. He kneeled by the body, avoiding a pool of blood that had mostly dried. I searched for its ghost. Nothing.

"The rose canes hold it," he said as if reading my mind. His tone became all sharp edges and anger. "This was Aria, the Librarian's assistant and protector. Look at her throat, slit. The murderer must have used surprise."

A bed took up most of the room. There were drawers and a wardrobe. A small table held a variety of small items, each in excellent condition, some gleaming like gold. What thief would leave them behind? He pulled me out of the room by my arm and kicked open a door on the other side. Another bedroom. This one large and filled with furniture. It had been ransacked. Clothes carpeted the floor, broken objects sprinkled across them. Thankfully, there were no more bodies.

"Check the rest of the rooms."

I grimaced. Alone? I could hardly ask him to hold my hand, so I left him searching and turned the handle of the last door on this side. I pushed the door inward with my blade.

"Hello?"

Waving my hand along the wall as I'd seen Hunter do, I caught a lump, and the room appeared. I wished it hadn't.

A man and a woman lay on the ground near a round table made of ornately carved wood. Two cups and a pot sat on a silver tray. Like the first woman, they had been wrapped in rose canes. However, their necks were intact. I dared myself to approach. A green tinge to their skin intrigued me. I put out a hand to see if it would rub off but couldn't bring myself to touch them. My observations would have to be enough—there were fewer people every year. I believed this year was already sorted. I didn't need to add myself to the count.

As I went to leave, I noticed another detail—two small beds with high sides. A teddy bear pattern was carved into the end of each—a crib. I'd heard of such things. Beneath them were open suitcases holding tiny clothes. Babies. My mouth dried. I did not want to go closer. I wasn't going to do it.

"Hunter!"

I stood quivering until he strode in. He gave the bodies a cursory inspection before checking the cribs. When he reached down, I hugged myself. Up came bedding.

"Nothing," he said.

Relief set me shaking further. "I—I don't think I could have...
I'm just—"

"I get it, kid."

"What happened here."

"Those two were poisoned. Don't drink the tea. The Librarian's
gone. Kidnapped, perhaps."

"Why make sure there are no ghosts?"

Hunter worked his jaw for a moment. "I don't know, but I'm
going to find out."

He led the way back downstairs and into the largest room.
Wooden shelves reached up to the ceiling. I'd never seen so many
books. And if I'd been impressed by the devices in the lobby, I was
overwhelmed by the variety of thick metallic rectangles, shiny round
discs, and little squares with bits sticking out. Folded sheets of paper
rested on tables. Several large whiteboards covered with writing
stood on wheeled frames next to them. And boxes, so many of them
stacked on top of each other, threatening to topple, the towers
reminding me of the nearby city. It reminded me of a strange old
man living on the edge of the settlement I grew up in. He collected
cards with pictures of monsters—thousands and thousands of them.
If you walked by, he'd want to show them to you and tell you how
rare they were.

I was unlikely to have that problem here. If the Librarian was
gone, Hunter couldn't get paid for the prize he'd recovered. Hope-
fully, that meant we were headed away in the morning. Hunter
didn't appear done. He moved from desk to desk, picking up papers,
flicking through some, and reading others. He'd forgotten me, but I
knew I couldn't relax. I could hardly read as he was. Hunter was
always saying to look at the big picture. I'd craned my neck the first
time he'd said it. It meant not getting lost in the little details. As I
could barely read letters, I figured that would be easy.

Walking around the room, I tried to get a feel for how everything was placed, what path the Librarian would have walked.
Before I had apprenticed to Hunter, this was how I survived
wandering from town to village, selling whatever I could scrounge

by working out where others hadn't trod. This was the reverse. It was like navigating a spider's web. The center came to me as a burst of insight. A desk in one corner was the man's home. The white-boards had dense squiggles of letters, colored shapes squeezed into gaps, arrows traveling like snakes. Those boards further away had newer writing with less smudges. He worked on this desk and moved around the room when he needed to read or record his ideas. The desk in question had several rings on the surface and a cup of milky tea. He really was rich. I didn't try it for fear of poison, but I was tempted. The surface was empty, but I noticed a box underneath filled with scrunched-up balls of paper. It seemed a poor way to treat something he obviously valued so much. I emptied the contents on the desk and opened several carefully. Lines and lines of writing at different angles. Little diagrams of circles or a series of straight lines that extended from each other. Amongst all of this chaos, I noticed a pattern, a word that was almost stamped into the paper wherever it occurred.

I tried to sound out the letters.

"D A R K S T R E E M"

Hunter jerked his head toward me. "What did you say?"

"I found these." I held up some of the paper. "I think the Librarian didn't like what he wrote."

He stalked to the desk and went through the papers. His expression was usually stern, but his eyes tracked back and forth as if slicing the words with his saber. He grabbed another and another.

"Son of a bitch."

I stepped back to give him space. "What is it?"

"He did it."

"Ah, did what?"

Hunter held a sheet in front of me. "He found the cause."

"Of what?"

"Of the End. Of the ghosts. Of why we're in this fucking mess."

I didn't see how that was useful, but I figured it wasn't a good question to ask at this point. "How did it?"

"I don't know, but he knew where and who. Darkstreem was a tech company. They had a tower in the city. The Librarian cross-referenced accounts and timing. No wonder he had me pulling drives and phones. He was triangulating the timing to find the source."

Hunter turned back to the rest of the paper and rifled through it. "Hell, I think he knew how. It's all occult gibberish. Over my head. Barriers of some sort. Magic worked by twins."

"Like the empty cribs upstairs?" I asked.

He scowled. "We don't know they were twins."

We knew. It couldn't be coincidence. I waited as he continued reading crumpled sheets.

"No." Hunter's voice came in a dry rasp.

"What?" I asked, frustrated that I couldn't read. I'd have to practice more.

"He wrote several notes. One's addressed to me. Brought about by twins, closure by twins. Blood must be spilled." He growled under his breath. "The handwriting's a mess. He's not a murderer. He doesn't have it in him. It's not right."

I tried to process what Hunter was telling me. "He admitted to murdering those people and must have stolen the babies. He wrote notes but threw them away. Sounds pretty nuts."

"He knew things. He helped in the early days. He taught me. He's why I'm alive. If he cracked..." Hunter gestured toward the lobby. "We have to bring him back. I owe it to him."

"And the babies might be alive."

"Yeah."

"Where is he?"

"The city. Darkstreem's offices."

No one could survive a night in the city.

"We're too late. By morning he'll be dead. They all will."

Hunter nodded. "That's why we're going now."

I really didn't want to go. Hunter gave me a chance to stay at the library. But I couldn't. I kept thinking of two small faces. I was clinging on to Hunter. Who did they have now? Besides, *I'd* go crazy waiting, not knowing. Hunter took me to the basement to replenish our supplies, but it had been locked, and the door was steel. We weren't breaking in.

We did have to break out. We walked our horses to the gate to keep the noise down and together rolled it open enough for Hunter to lead them outside. Ghosts wandered along the town walls, attracted to the life sleeping within. I had to push the gate closed from the inside and secure the chain that held it tight. It was hard work. And by the time I was climbing over the wall, ghosts were clumping—no doubt sensing our presence. Some looked like ordinary folk, only glowing white and transparent. Most were distorted —they had claw-like hands, distended jaws filled with shark teeth, or gaping wounds that pumped ethereal fluid in endless flows. I mounted my horse, and Hunter immediately took off.

I rode as fast as I dared. The ground was dark, and if the horse broke a leg, I'd hit the ground, and the ghosts would be on me. I'd seen them surround a man, a piece of work called Jeremy Avalon. I'd been watching from a window—mesh and no glass—when they found a weakness in his house. He ran outside, and they followed. They grabbed him, hands sliding through his flesh. It was as if they were scooping out chunks of his soul. He screamed, and his skin turned gray. When he collapsed, they were all over him—poor bastard.

By the time I had caught up with Hunter, the city dominated the view. He took a road to the right, and we circled.

"We'll want the shorter route."

I agreed. One- and two-story buildings filled both sides. The outsides were coated in graffiti, and most windows were broken. I caught glimpses of light in most and kept my horse on the center line when we didn't have to circle around abandoned cars. I hoped the streets in the city were wide.

"How did people live like that?" I asked while contemplating the towers. "All squashed together. It's ugly, too."

"Wasn't always like that. Used to be pretty. In its own way."

We came upon a bridge—it had tall structures with giant cables dangling down. They held a road high above murky waters. I couldn't imagine what it would take to build. Cars blocked the way. They had been positioned across the bridge's entrance with small gaps between them. The tires were all flat. Bones were scattered everywhere, along with bullet casings. I didn't see any guns. Scavenged, I guessed.

Hunter dismounted. "We go on foot from here."

We turned from riders into our own pack horses. I kept a hand on my rapier and watched every shadow or glint of moonlight. My heart beat like a rabbit's whenever clouds glided across the moon. There were cold spots as we walked, and I twitched at every strange noise. Hunter moved steadily, climbing over car hoods and jumping off the far sides.

He turned back to me. "Keep up. If you're doing this, you have to commit. I'm not holding your hand."

I scurried to his side, but he stopped soon after and kneed down. I saw it, too. A gray circle. I pinched some of the substance between my fingers. Iron filings. A very temporary measure of protection.

"The Librarian came this way?"

Hunter grunted and moved on. We reached the far side, and I found my confidence had expanded like proving bread. Maybe the city wasn't as bad as folk said.

"Over here." Hunter pulled out a tube from his long jacket and bent it, producing a green light that brightened as he shook it. Glow tubes were rare. Still, if there was ever a time to use one... They don't attract ghosts like fire. To my surprise, he handed me another.

"Only if you need to."

I nodded.

He pointed to a picture on a big cylinder that stuck up out of the ground. "This is a tourist map. See these? They're roads. We're here. Darkstreem is there. Pretty much down the main strip. We don't need GPS."

I looked at him blankly and noted the way he ran a hand down the map, almost as if caressing a loved one.

"See there. The old Veritas Bank has gone over. Fire by the look of it. We'll go through this mall and come back round. No time to detour."

Go through the inside of a building? I looked at the map. The lines were far apart. I wanted a better plan, but he was already heading off to the left, taking the light with him.

The mall had two big open doors with diamonds of glass clumped with dirt and plastic. The scale shocked me. The lack of bars horrified me.

"What do you see?"

I went to the top of the gentle incline and paused, my boots crunching. Pallid forms walked inside. Every now and then, they'd flicker and appear back where they started.

"Impressions, I think. They're on loops."

Hunter nodded. "Remember, don't touch them."

I was with that plan already. It still wasn't easy. I had to keep looking ahead, remembering where they looped in case they jumped back right onto me. Distractions dragged at my eyes. Stars reflected off broken glass. Above, an opening stretched the length of the mall. Extravagant, overwhelming. White and black bodies stared at us. I nearly pissed myself the first time I saw one. They didn't move and had no faces, and I couldn't see through them. Hunter didn't worry, so I tried to ignore the strange poses and sense that they would leap off their pedestals and come for us. A lot of the stores we walked past were empty—skeletal racks overturned and shelves dangling. They'd been looted. I wondered if the ghosts of the looters walked the tiled floor.

"Hunter, why did anyone risk coming here? I don't see any food."

"It wasn't always dangerous. Before the End. And on that day, people weren't thinking. They were desperate."

"How is that different from now?"

"Now they know the risks."

We'd almost reached the far end and were standing by a door with green and white stripes, when the hairs on the back of my neck stood up. I counted five skeletons, each wearing clothes with the weathered look of folk from after the End.

"Hunter."

"What?"

I turned a slow circle, searching for the cause of my disquiet. My eyes drifted upward. Objects floated in unseen eddies: bags, shoes, devices, all the assorted debris of humanity. A gun drifted past my eyes. Highest of all—fancy black-handled knives, a lot of them close to the mall exit.

"Stay still," Hunter whispered. The advice wasn't necessary. "What type?"

That was easy. "Poltergeist. A big one, and it's dormant."

"We're lucky. Could easily have set it off. Keep quiet. Move slowly, very slowly."

The green light didn't reach far, so we had to pick our way carefully. A fuzzy bear with brass symbols on its hands drifted into my route. I tapped it away, but my finger caught on a plastic loop at the end of a cord. There was a quiet mechanical grinding noise as the bear went on its way. The cord grew longer, and it pulled at my finger, so I flicked it free.

It was a bad decision.

The symbols came together, clashing, the sound bouncing off the hard surfaces that surrounded us over and over and over again. Hunter gave me a look. It wasn't nice. Tendrils of white coalesced, blurry droplets forming on this undead webbing. They thickened, and near the top a wretched face came together, the barest hint of eyes, the twisted misery of lips.

"What do we do?" I asked.

"Run."

I didn't need telling twice. I sprinted for the mall exit. The poltergeist groaned, the anguished sound at the edge of my hearing. A shoe hit me in the back of the head. It had a narrow heel. Pain lanced through my skull. I stumbled, feeling back and finding sticky blood. A can slammed into my elbow, hitting a nerve, then bursting open on the floor and erupting in a spray of sugary liquid. A walking stick snapped against the back of my left knee and I fell.

Hunter was already down. He'd gotten further, but the air was filled with hard-edged merchandise raining down on his jacket. He crawled back to me. "We can make it that way. Draw your sword. We're going for the door we passed."

I thought back to one of his lessons. "Can our swords hurt a poltergeist?"

"Need rose oil to bring it into the physical world. Remember, the oil binds spirits. I used my last when we shut down that stalker. We can't hurt it, but you can block what it's throwing."

A knitting needle darted for the back of my hand. I moved just in time for it to bend on impact with the tiling. Hunter grabbed me as he stood, and we tried for the door. He swung his saber, cutting items apart or slapping them aside. My attempts were less effective, and I dodged or gained fresh bruises and cuts. We reached the door, and Hunter pushed down on a horizontal bar. It didn't open. He slammed his shoulder against it, and it shifted just a little.

I remembered what I first saw. Knives above us—they were vibrating.

"Hunter."

"Shut it, kid. This ain't easy." The door gave a bit more.

A small paring knife plummeted. I swung my rapier and somehow caught the tip, spinning the blade so that the handle struck my shoulder.

"We're going to be skewered."

He looked up. "Get under my jacket."

He didn't stop his shoving, but I made myself small and went close to his legs, earning an accidental kick. The poltergeist was done with playing, and knives flew toward us. They stabbed at his jacket but couldn't penetrate. The door opened enough, and Hunter shoved me through before squeezing out himself. He slammed the door behind him and leaned his head against the door.

"How'd you do that?" I asked.

"Riveted plates in my jacket. Heavy and cold but worth it."

We were in a small alley. Big steel boxes on wheels took up most of the space, and trash littered the rest. Hunter held the glow stick high, and we walked to the end, finding ourselves back on the main road.

Cars and buses and trucks clogged the way. I didn't think any of it was deliberate. There were clear signs of crashes. I guessed that many of them had been abandoned. The buildings all pressed against each other. Some had big numbers, and others words or symbols. Apparently, before the End, everyone wanted everyone else to know who they were. I had a bigger concern weighing on me.

"We're staying out of buildings, right?"

"For now."

I'd take that. Ghosts were never as strong in open land. I looked to either side. Did this count as open? I don't know if it was our passage or if we were getting the usual view, but ghostly forms stalked behind every window, every open door. I saw them strangling each other, hitting with misty chairs, even biting. They screamed and shouted, none of it clear enough to understand. Madness. It'd taken a lot of the old people. A ghost consumed enough of them to scramble their minds but not enough to kill—not at first. They appeared rooted to their haunts, but I didn't trust that. To keep my own sanity, I created an image of the babies to remind me why I was here. I imagined them sleeping, wrapped up. If it was all in my head, they weren't going to be crying. I considered adding names but decided against it. It seemed to be tempting fate.

We reached a junction. There were more skeletons. Fifty, maybe sixty of them. A bus rested at an angle, its doors open. The sides were riddled with bullet holes. Nearby cars also had shredded bodywork. A gun battle.

"Were they fighting over the bus?"

"Could be. Trying to get out."

"But they killed each other, and none of them escaped. That's terrible. The stupid assholes."

Hunter stepped over a skull. "Terrible but not stupid. You do what you have to do. Sometimes it works, sometimes it doesn't."

If everyone did that, we'd all kill each other in a week, I thought. Who decided what had to be done?

He leaned down and picked up a glass jar, sticking his finger inside, then tasting the contents. I shriveled my mouth. We had supplies.

"Librarian's been here. Baby food." He put the jar down carefully, but it rocked as a sudden gust of wind swirled around us.

We were practically standing in a graveyard. They crawled out of the bones, rising shakily, their forms quickly solidifying and taking on a silver sheen. A lot of them were armed with pistols and revolvers. I hadn't seen their type before.

"What are they?"

"Specters. Fuck. They won't notice you most times, but their bullets will kill just the same."

The gun battle began. I'd expected silence. Instead, the ear-pounding roars of the weapons hammered me. I dropped to the ground and crawled behind a painted steel box with a slot in it. There were a lot of small circular holes, too. It wasn't going to protect me. I looked for Hunter but couldn't see him through the war that had erupted. I dared a sprint to a traffic light and had to throw myself to one side as a thin-faced skinhead took my hiding spot. My lips started a mantra, "Don't shoot me. Don't shoot me. Don't shoot me."

The specter craned his neck, surprise on his face. He'd heard me. Surprise was on my face, too. That and fear. He brought his gun around inches from my head.

"Your sword, Tom."

I grabbed the hilt and yanked it out of its scabbard, swinging wildly. The blade caught his gun at the trigger guard and sliced through to the rear sight. This pissed him off. The imitation of humanity fell apart, and a horrid visage of bone and rot and sickly fluid reached for me. I retreated, cutting at the air. The battle was over. They'd seen us now. They were hungry, all of them.

Hunter jumped onto a car.

I waved. "What do I do?"

"Get to Darkstreem. I'll meet you there."

My jaw dropped. He couldn't expect me to go alone. But he did. He jumped off the car, slicing a specter in half, then spun and decapitated another. Maintaining his momentum, he set off amongst them, dodging, cutting, never stopping. A gap formed. A small part of me wanted to stay and help, but he was doing this for me. I was sure of it.

I ran.

My sword dangled loosely in my hand as I went. I'd have closed my eyes if I could. Hunter had their attention, but still, several followed me. I looped around cars, posts—anything metal to give myself an advantage. My lungs burned as I gasped. Alleys and side streets beckoned. If I took one, how would I ever find my way to Darkstreem? I thought of the babies. Even if we rescued them, how could we ever make it out of the city? We were going to die. All of us.

And then it was there. I was there. Darkstreem. Stopping to confirm I'd read it correctly, I was assaulted by a wave of nausea. The building had a wide front, with a few stores on either side of a vaulted entrance complete with twisted shapes of metal that I guessed were art. The ends of the art were impaled with desiccated bodies that hung thanks to their clothing. Go in alone? No thanks. Specters were approaching. Should I run? Nowhere was safe.

"Hey, come inside, quickly. I know where we can hide." A woman stood at the entrance, half her body hidden by a column of concrete.

What choice did I have? I jogged by the suspended bodies and into the offices of Darkstreem.

How could the entrance be larger than most buildings I'd ever seen? The mall had been busy with impressions. This chasm beneath the unfathomable weight above was ripe with bodies, but apart from the general aura of wrongness, it appeared empty of ghosts. I noticed a store with tables and chairs and a long counter. I believe it was called a café. If there was coffee, I knew I could demand a good price per bag. Another store had lots of pictures of women with shiny clothes and cool looks. They held neat portions of food or flowers. There were baskets along the broken window with what looked like bars of soap. Another store held clothes with strange designs. They must have been stiff and uncomfortable. The before folk were weird.

A path had been cleared of bodies. Dark lines of iron filings had been poured along both sides, but they were broken at several points. The path led from where I stood to an unremarkable door. Nearby, a four-wheeled contraption rested. It had a decorated flat box and a handle at one end, reminding me of a trolly, but less utilitarian, more comfortable. Had the Librarian brought the babies in this?

"A man took the stairs earlier," the woman said. She was tall with a long ponytail, the top slicked against her scalp. She wore clothing similar to that in the store, a gray skirt and jacket combo with a pink shirt. Her shoes had small pointed heels.

I rubbed the back of my head. Which reminded me of the danger we were both in. Specters wandered outside but didn't cross the threshold of the building.

"Don't worry. They won't come inside."

"Is that how you survive?" I asked.

"Not really." She offered her hand. "Come with me. I'll show you."

Show me. There was too much light. I saw no sticks or flames or even electronic sources. A subtle glow suffused all of it. And her. I stared. Under my gaze, her features shifted. The bones of the hands distorted, the joints swelling, the fingers extending into curved claws. Her jaw lowered, allowing room for long, crooked teeth pointed like needles. And the eyes—the pupils shrunk to dots, and brown irises faded to white.

She narrowed them and licked her lips. "The man with the little babies did say more might come. You'll have to make up for missing out on those little treats."

She was so… alive, so aware. It didn't make her one bit less terrifying. I gripped my rapier tight.

If she was more human, was there any chance I could reason with her? "You don't have to do this."

"Oh, but I do. To feel anything. Even for a moment." Her speech remained clear.

I cringed, eyeing the path. "You wouldn't have when you were alive. Can't you remember that?"

Tilting her head back, she laughed as if enjoying a nasty joke. "You all make the same error. I would have slit your throat if it upped the share price, just like every testosterone-jacked slime in the building."

Using the distraction, I sidestepped once, twice.

She was staring at me. Damn. She pulled off her shoes one at a time. "Ah, that feels better. Shall we?"

I ran. She was faster. She sprinted beside the path, cutting in at a break in the iron filings. My escape route was blocked. Specters waited for me outside. I was done for. But I wanted to live, so I went for one of the shops, knocking aside soap and stirring up sweet scents. Three bean-shaped islands held dust-covered glass spray bottles, little towels, and round balls. She leaped over the soaps, landing in the center of the store, a distance no one alive could manage. I ran behind an island, and her eyes twinkled. She chased me to the next island, then around the third—I was being played with, a mouse before a cat. She wouldn't tire.

Lashing out with my sword, I sent a display crashing. Balls flew, disintegrating when they hit the floor. She was too fast, slipping out of the way, then grabbing my wrist. It burned like ice. My fingers loosened, and the rapier clattered, knocking bottles to the ground. I pulled away, all too aware that she had let me so she could lick the palm of her hideous hand. When I stepped back, my boot slid on the broken balls, and I slammed back-first onto the floor. Jasmine, rose, lavender. It was overwhelming. Dazed and aching, I could only watch as she stood over me.

"You are a tasty little morsel."

I felt for my rapier with my left hand. It wasn't there. All I could grasp was a bottle. I wasn't even sure I could aim a throw with my off-hand. I glanced at the bottle. Roses covered the label. It had a pump.

She threw herself at me, and I raised my right arm instinctively. She caught it again, and I cried out. Jagged agony fizzed along my arm. I pointed the bottle with my free hand and sprayed it over and over. A mist spread beneath us. It caught her, slowing her movement.

"What have you done?"

"I guess this has rose oil."

She snarled. "It won't help you."

True. I sprayed again, but the bottle would run dry, and she was still pushing toward me. Her free hand burrowed toward my neck, and her thick tongue lolled as she opened her jaw above my head. Closer and closer.

Steel poked through her chest, almost stabbing me. She arched, still in slow motion. The blade retracted, then cut deeply into her skull. A terrible moan accompanied the wound. The room grew darker, revealing Hunter standing above her. Three quick slices finished her. She faded to nothing, and my right arm fell.

He sniffed. "Rose perfume. Good idea. You're lucky it's not artificial. Hurt?"

"My arm."

Grimacing, he lowered himself to one knee and cut off my sleeve. The skin had patches of dark gray with lighter cobwebs that thickened and darkened as they pulsed. I fought back tears. He let it fall and searched his pack, retrieving a small glass bottle.

"Silver nitrate. This will hurt."

What could I say? It already hurt. He poured the contents over my arm—I screamed, stiffening my limbs. I imagined razor wire being drawn through my arm, sawed back and forth. Wetness spread over it. I opened my eyes, expecting blood, but Hunter was pouring water over it.

"If you're lucky, you'll keep it." He covered my marked flesh with a bandage. "Not many survive a revenant. Get up. The specters won't hold back now."

I kept the bottle and retrieved my sword, sheathing it awkwardly with my left hand. We exited the shop and took the path. The specters saw us and followed. I couldn't walk fast, but then, neither could Hunter. He was limping, and he'd lost his jacket. His hat remained though it had a hole in the brim.

"Why aren't they shooting?" I asked.

"They'll cross the threshold first."

Hunter pushed open the door, revealing a stairwell. Salt covered the floor. It would have been a line until swept by the door. We started climbing. As the door shut behind us with an ominous bang, it rocked, ghostly bullets punching through its surface. The stairwell echoed, disorienting me with the cacophony. Up and up. On the first floor, the door was blocked with a salt line. The same for the next floor. I guessed it'd be obvious when we found the right one. The shooting stopped when we reached the fourth. I peered down a gap between the stairs and almost got shot for my trouble. They were climbing after us.

"They close?"

"Yeah," I said. "They're going to catch up."

"Use the oil."

Spray wouldn't last long in the air. Then I understood what he meant. The specters walked. I threw the bottle on the stairs. Glass shattered, and the liquid spread. More floors. My legs ached, and it seemed they'd never stop.

"Never appreciated elevators."

"Elevators?" I asked when my breath allowed.

"Boxes. You'd get in, and they'd pull you up to whatever floor you wanted."

It wasn't quite the flying cars I'd heard about, but I was impressed. And I wanted one.

Ten. Twenty. Hunter was flagging. And the stairs were clogged. Bodies. These were different. The skin was mostly intact, though dry, and where long rents were torn in both flesh and material, red bones with opalescent swirls of oranges and yellows poked out. We had no choice but to weave between them.

"What's wrong with them?"

"I don't have all the answers, Tom."

I stepped on a hand. The bone collapsed. I didn't admit my error, but no more ghosts manifested. Perhaps they'd been sucked so dry of life there was nothing left to come back.

"Is it because we're near the source?"

"Could be."

Thirty. My shins felt like they'd broken. Hunter was pulling himself up using the railing. The specters had made it past the perfume. I could hear them grumbling. Why couldn't they keep fighting each other? It sucked that a meal could bring them together in death when a ride had them killing each other.

"We have to be close." I thought I said it for myself, but I was worried about Hunter. Every door we'd passed had the same line of salt.

"In the movies, it's always on the top floor."

I'd heard of movies. I couldn't understand how watching things that weren't true or being scared by them would be fun. And why would the Librarian be on the top floor? It wouldn't be much fun watching people climbing endless stairs. Hunter stopped.

I took a few steps before I noticed. "They're coming. We can't stop."

"Don't think I'm going with you, Tom."

I walked back down to him. "You said to do what you have to. You have to keep going."

He glared at me, full-strength aggravation on display, and restarted. "Might as well finish."

Thirty-six. No salt line. I risked a look. The specters were a single floor down. I pushed open the door and helped Hunter through.

It was open space and had no furniture or internal walls like most buildings. Cables dangled from trays along the ceiling, and the floor was uncovered concrete. I'd expected something impressive. The windows were gone, allowing a strong wind to catch my clothes and chill my skin. Concentric rings of steel stretched across the floor, embedded in concrete. The largest could hold at least fifty people standing comfortably. A jagged line of broken concrete and bent steel went from the center out to the edge as if an explosion could be contained to a single direction. Wire had been placed over the breaks and taped at each side. Better than iron filings but hardly secure.

At the center of the circles, a bruised purple smear crackled with energy. Terrible whispers came from it, uttering wordless impressions of despair, abandonment, and sorrow. Worse, praise—praise for a being powerful beyond comprehension. The energy, hissing and writhing, extended outward in ropes that looped around two prone corpses. The bodies were made of the same opal as the skeletons on the stairs, but it didn't show through their skin—it was their skin. They were men in their forties with short hair, clean-shaven cheeks, and little nooses around their necks. They were identical. Twins. Were these the ones that started it all, that brought on the End?

Between them kneeled a man I didn't recognize. He was balding, had a thin nose, and a neatly trimmed mustache. A notebook lay open next to him, the pages held together with coiled wire. By his knees were two babies with tufts of brown hair. I couldn't tell them apart. They were bound in blankets and then in rose canes. Their little faces were scrunched up as they cried, the sound like sandpaper on my teeth. The man held a long knife in his left hand, and he, too, sobbed.

We'd broken the salt line protecting the door. I helped Hunter reach the first of the circles as the specters poured out of the stairwell. They reached the steel and stopped, their hands pushing. It held. For now. I could have sworn the metal pinged under the stress.

"What now?" I asked. We'd reached the Librarian in time. He was clearly the murderer. And we were also hopelessly trapped.

"I'll take this." Hunter shuffled until he stood before the librarian. In the light from the smear, I saw he was leaving a steady trail of blood.

"Librarian."

"Hunter. I wondered if you'd come."

"What the hell are you doing?"

"Trying to save the world."

"Explain."

The Librarian did. His tears dried up as he spun a tale of patience and dedication. Interviews, pictures, messages on devices, and a whole host of other things that I didn't understand. However he managed it, he determined the End started here. With that knowledge, he searched for a reason.

"Darkstreem's biggest rival, Cubik, led the market with an abstraction relationship algorithm. It was tanking the price of their shares. These two executives," the Librarian gestured to the corpses, "were in charge of development. They hatched a plan to kidnap the Cubik lead architect. The thugs they hired bungled the job—they killed her. So what did they do? They turned to the occult, of course. They tried to summon her to spill all she knew. Needless to say, it didn't go well. We're left with a connection that's poisoning the world. This is the hotspot, but it's everywhere."

Hunter growled. "They killed billions for money?"

"There are better reasons."

I'd seen plenty of coins and notes. We used gold and silver now. Folk still killed each other for it. But to kill so many? To destroy the world and all its wonders? It was evil. The twins were evil.

The Librarian glared at the smear, the hotspot he'd called it. "You found the answer for me, Hunter—the books you took from that dealer up north. I had transaction records for copies the twins used. I learned how to undo it, to turn the End into a beginning."

Hunter was leaning on his saber like a walking stick. The shadows around his neck were dark. I didn't like it. I didn't like the Librarian. He was trying to turn himself into a hero.

I couldn't allow it. "You murdered those folk at the library, didn't you?"

"Undeniably. I'm not proud of that. Aria deserved better, but what choice was there? She would never have approved. And the parents... I could hardly ask them. It has to be done, and they were in the way. Evil needs to be sealed with innocence. Twins are needed to undo the damage of the first pair. They must die if the world is to live. The equation is simple."

The babies kept up their cries for help. I doubted he wanted to baptize them. "You can't do this," I said as fiercely as I could manage. "You can't murder babies."

The Librarian slapped his knife against the concrete, then let it fall from his fingers. "You're right, boy, I can't. I said the words. I felt their power. I've been sitting here trying to find the resolve to finish it. I can't." He broke into fresh tears. "I've done terrible things, but

I'm not enough of a monster to do what has to be done. It was all for nothing."

Hunter slowly dropped to his knees. He rested a hand on the Librarian's shoulder. "You believed it?"

"I still do."

"You know you must pay for what you've done."

The Librarian looked into his eyes. "I know, my old friend. Don't take long."

The saber rasped on the floor as Hunter brought it close. He pressed the tip to the Librarian's chest and plunged the blade right through.

"Thank you." The Librarian fell backward off the saber. Blood spurted from his death wound, and he collapsed, twitching, an incongruous smile on his face.

Hunter rocked forward. His hands pressed into the spreading blood. The darkness was spreading up his neck. He hadn't just been hurt. The ghosts had fed off him.

I grabbed his pack. "Do we have more of the silver nitrate?"

"No. Doesn't matter."

"We can get out of here. There must be some back at the town. Tell me how to get past the specters, and I'll help you. It's got to be done, right? I'll carry the babies. Don't worry about them."

Hunter raised a hand. "I have to think."

A specter had found the tape on the outer ring. It pulled at the strips, tearing them, attempting to dislodge the wire.

"We don't have time for that," I told him. I was strung out from adrenaline. My fingers shook.

"Only one way out," he said. "Ironic that in a world of monsters, we need one more. Got to be done."

He picked up the Librarian's notebook and started reading out a mess of strange words in a steady rhythm. At first, I didn't understand. Next, I didn't believe.

"What are you doing?" I demanded. He kept reading out loud, so I took a step forward, thinking of grabbing the book.

His saber tip pointed my way, unsteady, as his incantation culminated in a shouted finale. Chest heaving, he relented and leaned his saber over a shoulder. "Doing what needs to be done. Two babies for a million others. Think, Tom."

The specters poured past the first circle and started work on the second. The purple smear roiled with fresh vigor, reminding me of a putrid liver with maggots burrowing inside. Wind battered us from all directions. Was he right? The city was filled with marvels. I'd seen enough to know that. If there were no ghosts, what would it be like? Walking the streets, walking lands outside—at night with no fear at all. A new beginning based on murder. Was that any different from what had come before?

I gripped my rapier. "I can't let you do it."

His shoulders sagged. Sadness swept away his grim determination. "Tom, you already have. I'm weak. You could have stopped me. You know that."

I opened my mouth to issue a denial. He brought his saber down, and the cries cut off.

A force smacked me to the ground. Lights flashed. A fury shook my body. Lamentations chorused. Then it was over. The wind stopped. The specters were gone. Hunter had fallen over the babies —all three were dead. The smear, the connection to the darkness of the human soul, was gone.

Dawn came eventually. My cheeks had dried only because my thirst had grown strong. I watched the sunrise and wondered what it looked upon.

———

My horse whickered. It was my third one in ten years. On either side of the road, people worked in the fields. There were more each year. I scratched at my beard and pulled my brim lower to shield my eyes. Ten years since I left the city. No more new ghosts. Plenty of old ones to deal with.

A wagon pulled by two horses approached from ahead. A couple sat in the converted car, a baby in the man's arms.

"Lewisham School this way?" I asked when they were near.

They stopped. "You're Tom, the hunter?" the man asked.

I nodded.

"Blessings on you," the woman said. "Is it true that you're going to clear it?"

"Yes."

"You don't know what that means to us. A real school. You're a hero."

Her words struck me on this anniversary. I let my guard down for the first time in a long time and considered. She hadn't been there in the tower.

You could have stopped me.

Hunter had been right. Why hadn't I? I could have tackled him. I could have dared a contest of swords. He'd known. Deep down, I mustn't have wanted to stop him. I'd wanted to live. I'd wanted all the things I'd been denied, not just for me, but for everyone. But I'd let a man kill two babies in cold blood to get it. Inaction was its own action. I was as greedy as the assholes who'd made it all happen. Hunter had said the world needed one more monster. It'd taken two.

"I'm no hero," I told the parents and rode on.

There was nothing more to say. There was no absolution for me, no peace to be had. Only the knowledge that I would do what needed to be done.

The Beginning

ABOUT ROBERT TILLSLEY

Robert Tillsley is a science fiction and fantasy author who grew up loving stories of knights, magic, spaceships, and monsters. He spent fifteen years working in information technology—long enough to realize that the inevitable robot uprising will be caused by a coding error and poor documentation. His five years teaching taught him to look forward to the inevitable robot uprising. When his body cooperates, he loves training and competing in longsword fencing. Sadly, no alien spacecraft has offered him a joyride… yet. He lives in Australia with his wife, daughters, and two grumpy cats.

He has previously written works for adults and children under the name R Max Tillsley. You can find him at:

https://rmaxtillsley.com

facebook.com/rmaxtillsley

twitter.com/rmaxtillsley

instagram.com/rmaxtillsley

ASH WENDIGO

NATHAN PEDDE

Matthiew Lappanen, known as Blondie, wanders through the ash wastes of Nashville Tennessee. In the year 2020, the Yellowstone super-volcano blew its top, covering most of the United States with feet of hash.

Two years later, Blondie is a lone survivor trying to get to some-place warm without the constant toxic ashfall. Survivors, travellers, and scavengers, known as ghouls, haunt the ruins. Most want to leave others alone, but the few bad apples seek to cause chaos and death.

Blondie is asked to venture to a farming outpost as they haven't heard form them in a while. Others have tried, and none have made it through. Was it Ghouls, a rival faction, or something more sinister?

ASH WENDIGO

Dusk's crisp coolness bit at my face as the day ended and night approached. Being in August and in the state of Tennessee, it shouldn't have been hot and humid. Except, the Yellowstone super-volcano blew two years before cooling the planet by ten degrees.

The disaster ended society as we knew it. Overnight, feet of ash covered three-quarters of the continental United State—killed millions and forcing more to flee their homes. The falling debris buried all semblance of green, killing them. Everything now existed in a world of gray. The ash wastes of America replaced the prosperity of the pre-Yellow society.

Living in Nova Scotia, I thought the disaster would pass me by. Except the ash fell for weeks, then months and never stopped. It resembled a constant toxic snowfall. Instead of only affecting western North America, the volume of debris landed much farther reaching my home in Canada. Where it didn't fall, the ash hung in the air, blocking sunlight and cooling the globe.

After weeks of chaos, the lack of clean water and food forced me to flee my home. People turned mad, and I regretted all the times I looked down upon preppers. During those early months, I'd kill for a chunk of steak and a few eggs. After the few years since the Yellow popped, I've killed for less.

Two years later, I trudged down the abandoned, eight-lane freeway wearing layers of heavy clothing, a hood and a full-face gas mask. Friends and family died from ash poisoning after breathing in too much. I didn't understand what happened biologically, but those affected coughed up black blood and then perished. It was a painful way to go.

My name's Matthiew Leppanen, though I hadn't used it in six months. If I met anyone where my name became necessary, I told them it was Blondie. Except my hair was black from my Sicilian ancestry. It was a joke no one ever understood.

Carrying a heavy bag filled with all my worldly possessions, my back hurt. Strapped to my hip was a 9mm pistol, and I carried an AR-15. The ported long arm hung from a holster on my pack, though I carried the heavy weapon more than I liked. A machete hung from the opposite side of my backpack than my rifle.

The handgun was a Smith and Wesson SD9 with a sixteen-shot magazine and an under-barrel rail where I had a flashlight attached. I carried additional magazines and bullets if I needed them, except I didn't enjoy using them, as ammunition was hard to find.

Interstate 65 expanded around me for miles. The line of vehicles stretched from the city to where they stopped after the Yellow exploded. Tall sound-dampening walls soared on either side above me. An old electric sign with LED lights hung from a thick aluminum pole. It was long dead, hanging to the ground with a single wire. When it worked, it announced traffic problems and missing children.

I stepped to an abandoned car buried underneath a foot of ash. Being Canadian, the dark gray debris resembled the effects of a mid-winter snowstorm. Except it hardened after a touch of water before drying. It made scavenging any items underneath difficult.

Pulling at the driver's side door handle, I found it locked. I rubbed at the ash, knocking piles from the windshield to the asphalt underneath. Knocking on the harder layer underneath, I cleared enough to see something inside. I stared into the vehicle and then stepped back. The corpses of a man and woman sat in the front seat, their arms around each other in death. The man held a pistol in his hands, though it was empty. Each with a hole in their heads; he killed his wife, then himself. The cadavers had passed the bloating stage with the flesh liquefying.

"Fucking hell," I mumbled to myself.

A bag sat on the floor of the passenger seat with its top unzipped. I attempted to glance into its depths but failed. With how it sat and I stood, I couldn't see inside.

I walked to the passenger door. Pulling at the door handle, it mimicked the other side being locked. Grumbling, I pulled a heavy police-style flashlight from my pack. It was the type with the bulky handle that could smash heads if needed.

Slamming the butt end into the windshield, nothing happened. Instead, the strike echoed across the freeway. It was distinct and unnatural to anyone nearby, which would attract attention. I hit the glass two more times before it cracked and shattered. The clatter of the breaking windshield reverberated around me like thunder in a storm.

Regretting my actions, I took a few steps back as the putrid stench of death dissipated. I didn't have any charcoal filters for my mask and had no intention of smelling the inside.

Listening to my surroundings, I waited for scavengers known as ghouls investigate the noise. Hearing nothing, I slipped the flashlight into its spot in my kit before gripping my AR stock. Pulling my weapon from my pack, my hands dripped with sweat inside my heavy gloves—taking a knee, I shoved the butt of the AR to my shoulder. I was ready to defend myself if a fight presented itself.

I wasn't afraid of scavengers. Most were like me, trying to survive. The few evil ones rarely lasted long. They were dangerous until karma caught up to them. Until they met their end, I nick-named them ghouls. These bat apples were devilish fiends who killed people for fun. They resembled monsters from poorly written speculative fiction about the destruction of a magical ring. These ghouls were unpredictable, causing death wherever they went. I couldn't tell the difference between a survivor-ghoul and a fiendish-ghoul.

I prayed for the time when the ash stopped falling, and the earth warmed. I doubted it would happen soon, and I hunted for some-place to live until that point. My best guess was as far away from Yellowstone as I could.

Surrounding me, nothing moved and created noise. There was no sign the breaking windshield attracted a ghoul. The ashfall muffled lighter noises while allowing larger ones to echo through. This made it difficult if someone wanted to sneak up on me. I glanced around, peering through the falling debris.

Seeing none, I broke out the rest of the passenger window and reached my hand in. Opening the door, the hinges squeaked. I opened the bag to find it full of dirty clothes. Dumping it out onto the floor, I hoped there was something useful at the bottom. Except I found nothing but laundry and food wrappers.

A single can of baked beans sat in the cup holder on the driver's door. I leaned in past the two corpses and grabbed it. As I did, the crunch of gravel under a boot reverberated behind.

I dropped the can to the floor of the car and twisted. As I did, I brought my AR up, aiming it at the origin of the sound. Standing fifteen feet in front of me was a ghoul. This fiend wore biker leathers decorated with spikes. He carried a baseball bat with six-inch nails hammered through it.

"That's my food," the ghoul said through a bandanna covering his face.

"Says who?" I asked.

"Says me."

"I have a gun. You have a bat. Make the smart move. Walk away."

The biker laughed. "I doubt you have bullets for that."

"Fuck around and find out," I replied.

The ghoul stepped forward. With his free hand, he pulled a Glock from his belt.

"Fuck you," I said, squeezing my weapon's trigger.

In the moment, there was never time to think about what I did.

It didn't matter how much my life had changed if a bullet decided to lodge itself in my face. It only mattered that I did what I had to do to survive the fight. I heard an old soldier once tell me that you aren't fighting if you were fighting fair.

The AR fired, and the rifle bucked. The 5.56 round smashed through the ghoul's side and out the back. Blood sprayed from the wound, mixing with the gray ash. The ambusher shrieked and fell to the asphalt, pressed his hand to the hole in him. He screamed bloody murder with tears dripping from his eyes. The ghoul grasped for his pistol, laying in the ash next to him.

I corrected my aim, placing a second bullet into the man's chest. The crack of the gunshot bounced along the freeway and the ruins beyond. The ghoul collapsed with his leg twitching in the pool of his own blood. I didn't want to kill anybody, except life in the ash wastes was cheap and short.

Glancing around me, I checked if anyone had heard the noise. I needed to move and make tracks. The gunshot would attract the nefarious types, hoping to catch a scavenger searching through someone's pockets. I had seen it a dozen times before.

A crunch of a tree branch echoed in the distance. A hundred yards behind the first ghoul was a short hill with the sound-dampening wall rising along the edge of the road.

Standing at the hill's peak were ten more ghouls. They were different shapes and sizes, resembling an adventuring party of wizards, dwarfs, and elves. Except they wore spiked biker gear. They ticked off more than one stereotype from post-apocalypse novels and movies. Each carried a makeshift weapon with half being hand weapons. Others packed firearms, with most being rifles instead of pistols.

"There's our deer. I told you we could follow the footprints," the ghoul leader said.

I glanced around, looking for a downed animal, but found none. Then everything clicked into place. The word cannibal drifted across my mind. The new threat approached from the same direction as the ghoul I killed. I guessed the gang hunted the first man and now I was a target.

"Fucking hell," I said, turning on my heels.

I grabbed the discarded can of beans and sprinted down the freeway. The crack of the rifle thundered across the ash-covered road and I ducked behind an abandoned delivery van. Two more struck the truck's side. The spent bullets smashed and tumbled through the van above my head. I was inches from taking a round. If I was unlucky, the chunks of lead still had enough power to cause me harm. Any wound could mean infection and death.

I contemplated fighting back, except the ghouls outnumbered me. My best course was to run and fight them somewhere else. If I could ambush them, then I could drop most of them.

"After him, you lot," the ghoul yelled. "I want both deer in me belly."

The gang charged down the hill toward the ash-covered asphalt. They were like bloodhounds. They'd follow me to the end of the earth unless I convinced them to back off. I didn't know how many ghouls I'd have to kill.

I sprinted down the freeway toward the next exit. Weaving around the many disabled vehicles, I broke the ghoul's line of sight. If the bastards couldn't see me, they couldn't shoot me. Yet they followed behind to the sound of my boots on the ash-covered asphalt.

Breathing hard while wearing a full-face mask caused the clear plastic to fog up. It made it difficult to identify anything besides the breathing difficulties. I needed to switch my filter out and try to clean it. If that was possible. Being manufactured pre-Yellow, the designers built them to be thrown out after a few hours of use. I had used this one for weeks.

The ghouls wore bandannas and silicone half-masks with bulky, old filters. They'd weren't the correct type and didn't fit in the holes. Instead, they used liberal amounts of duct tape to do the job. Judging from their level of grim, the ghouls were out of fresh filters, like me. I hoped this would give me more stamina than them.

I ran down between the abandoned vehicles as three more shots cracked around me. A bullet skipped along the pavement and into a Jeep. I swerved back and forth, making myself a harder target. A round hit the spot where I was before

Jumping over the barrier, I ducked and ran down the length of the barrier. Two more bullets pinged against the pitted gray surface. One smacked into my pack, sending me to the ground. Panic filled my chest as I imagined blood pouring from a wound. I set the emotion aside and rolled to my knees, moving my AR to my shoulder. I felt no pain, so I'd deal with any wound later. Once the adrenaline subsided.

Scanning around me, I hunted for the ghouls. The scattered vehicles spread across the freeway made it hard for me to see. Then I spotted them. Three ghouls charged toward me on the opposite side of an abandoned sedan. Behind them were two more carrying rifles. I aimed my weapon at the rifle-carrying ghouls and squeezed the trigger.

The AR bucked in my hands and sent lead at the target. The bullets smacked into the abandoned vehicle in front of them. One ghoul screamed beneath his bandanna. My 5.56 penetrated the thin metal and into the man behind.

I ducked as the ghouls cracked more shots off. Concrete and ash blasted around me as I continued down the barriers. I jerked up and fired two shots at the ghouls.

They charged from behind the abandoned car and across the open space. One bullet smashed into the ghoul's leg, tumbling him to the ground. The two remaining ghouls crossed the vacant space, jumping over the barrier.

I was ready, squeezing my trigger of my AR. Being a semi-automatic rifle, I let go of the trigger between shots. Before the Yellow popping, I had never held a rifle. Now I slept with it more than any woman.

Pulling the trigger as fast as my finger could work, the rounds cracked into a crescendo of death. The copper-coated lead struck through the first ghoul and into the second one. Both tumbled to the ash-covered asphalt in a spray of blood.

I turned on my heels and sprinted from the dying men. Ducking down, I didn't want willing to risk the hail of bullets. The remaining ghouls stopped chasing me, moving to their downed comrades. I expected them to continue the chase but was happy they called it off.

Running across a concrete divider, I jumped over the barricade into the opposite lane. I moved between the ash-covered vehicles. The wind picked up, blowing the acidic debris at my face and coating my tracks.

I tapped at the cartridge covering my face, knocking rubbish from it inside. Tapping it once more, then my breathing became easier. I fought the urge to take my mask off. Doing so would only lead to my death. It wouldn't be immediate, but breathing in the dust would build up in my already damaged lungs.

Checking my watch, I pushed myself into a run. The day slipped by, and I'd soon find myself in the dark soon unless I was careful. I needed to rest somewhere away from the ash. There were enough abandoned buildings if I could exit the freeway. It should've been easy.

I trudged along, moving as fast as I could while not stressing my endurance. Part of me expected the ghouls to catch up, or I could stumble into another group. The gunshots were like a siren's call to them. Death meant painless, risk-free loot.

A crumpled minivan smashed into the concrete wall along the right side of the road. The front end lifted a few feet into the air. The driver's corpse burst through the window into the ash covered wall. Its body was black with rot and as such, I wouldn't search the vehicle.

I gagged at the stench, wishing I had access to scent-killing charcoal filters. They were hard to find and nearly impossible to clean. I scanned around me, hunting for another way off the freeway. Except there wasn't any other vehicle close to the wall. The next off-ramp wasn't for miles. The threat of ghouls forced me to take a less used route.

Then my luck ran out. Riding between abandoned vehicles, the gang of ghouls stormed down the freeway. I couldn't identify if they were the same group or an additional threat. They rode mountain bikes, carrying their weapons like kids heading to play baseball. It was a post-Yellow version of a biker gang, in an environment ill-suited for the combustion engine.

I pulled my rifle to my shoulder and squeezed the trigger. The gunshot cracked and echoed between the concrete walls. The round went high, missing all the targets.

The ghouls dove behind abandoned vehicles, letting their mountain bikes clatter to the ground. If I forced them to hide for more than a minute, I could escape. I had no desire for the bastards to find me in my sleep.

I stepped toward the minivan and opened the gas cap. Shoving a rag in, I lit it with a Zippo lighter. The flames chewed their way up the cloth and into the tank. Unlike the movies, the vehicle wouldn't blow up but burn like a Roman candle.

Climbing up the hood of the van, I clambered onto the roof. I ran across the metal and to the top of the wall. Heaving myself over, I plopped into a yard on the other side.

Before the Yellow blew, I'd never trespass on a stranger's property in Tennessee. It was a good way to get myself shot by a trigger-happy redneck. Now all the locals who'd have shot me had fled, died, or were the ghouls chasing me.

I landed on the ground with my feet crunching onto twigs and branches. I aimed my rifle at the top of the wall, waiting for someone to climb over. The van on the other side burned bright as fire bellowed above the concrete.

"Fuck you, asshole," a ghoul yelled behind the wall. "I'm going to find you and eat your liver. You'll die by my hand."

"Come on," another ghoul replied. "It's going to rain. We should get under cover."

The ghouls rode away down the freeway with their tires crunching on the ash. It was a standard threat they tended to make. When violence failed, they always turned to verbal insults. Letting out a breath I didn't know I was holding, I hoped never to see them again. Though part of me expected I would.

I stomped farther into the yard, gripping my AR in front. As the ghouls predicted, rain clouds opened, and a drizzle came down.

Then the rain turned into a steady downpour, which would soak me through despite my best efforts. Collecting rainwater was important before the Yellow exploded. Now ash drifted in it like the pulp from orange juice——making it undrinkable. I'd have to filter and clean it before risking it.

Around the ash-covered trees of the yard was a smaller run-down RV. Its owners hadn't moved the vehicle in years. With adrenaline still pouring into me, I stepped to the door and pulled it open. Then, aiming the rifle into the inside, I was ready to empty my magazine into any threat.

There wasn't anyone or anything inside. So I stepped inside the shelter and shut the myself in.

After I secured the RV, I cleaned myself up by knocking any ash off that I could. Then, I brushed it off using a dirty rag. It would be best to use a clean wet cloth, but after walking across the eastern United States, I had little water to spare. After I completed my task, I took off my mask. It felt good to remove the gear. Wearing it was a chore, but it was better than dying.

The bullet which struck my pack punched a hole through my rubber poncho and dented a can of tuna. I considered myself lucky the round didn't hit six inches to the side.

Listening to rain patter against the plastic roof, I slept on the couch. I never slept heavily, as every sound woke me up. It resulted from living by myself for over a year.

I left the RV as the sun rose above the horizon. The rain stopped, and the wind shifted in the night, sending the ash clouds in the opposite direction. The sunlight blasted at me, threatening to create a hot, humid day for the post-Yellow world. A red tinge discolored the sunlight, making it look like the post-apocalyptic world it was.

The deluge from the night before washed the layers of ash into piles on the ground. It changed from a substance from resembling a light powder into a slurry mess. When the heat returned, it would harden into a near-rock. Any plant trapped underneath was long dead. It covered the oak and popular trees in the yard in ash. Most were bare of leaves and lifeless.

For days, I trudged through the roads and highways of suburban Nashville. I weaved my way through the different neighborhoods. If I were to head southeast direct, I'd be able to make more ground. Except I hunted for supplies and a vehicle. I wanted to find a motor-bike to move faster. After searching for a year, I hadn't found some-thing with a clean air intake and fuel in its tank. The ash clogged everything up quickly, making it hard to keep anything running.

I turned a corner and stopped. An enclosed settlement rose before me. It was as if they copied it from an older TV show from before the Yellow. They built it from the ruins of a strip mall called "Music Valley Village." Sheet metal and ruined vehicles encased the parking lot. A gate manufactured out of an old city bus stretched across the opening. Two guards stood on the top of the wall, carrying military-style rifles.

"Stop right there," one guard said. "What do you want?"

"I've got trade goods. I'm here for some food and water," I replied.

"Name?"

"I have none."

"I need your name, or I shoot you."

"Call me Blondie," I replied.

I didn't wish to give them my true name. That person was long dead. This allowed me to do things I'd never be able to pre-Yellow. It was a mask I was wearing, and I knew it. It was comforting.

"That's a bullshit name. Give it to me proper."

"That's my name."

"Fine, Blondie," the guard said.

The bus fire its engine to life with a rumble. After a moment, which included putrid, black exhaust and grinding gears, the ancient machine moved from the path. I strode toward the town, my hands gripping my weapon. Rows of RVs and huts spread across the parking lots. Each was the home of a survivor. Some were busi-nesses advertising saloons or general stores.

The guard stepped toward me. "My name is Captain Avery Agrusa. I'm the leader of the Music Valley settlement. We have rules you need to agree with."

"Understood. What are they?" I asked.

"You've the right to keep your weapons, but you'll leave them holstered at all times. No murder, no excessive drinking, no drugs."

"Fairly basic. Anything else?"

"No cannibalism. Have you at anytime ate human flesh?"

"Not on your life."

"Go on in. If you're lying, it's instant death."

I wandered through the town and its lines of huts. Dirt and ash covered the people. It was impossible to clean, and most gave up. Most showed some sign of ash poisoning, with many wheezing and straining to breathe. I found a few vendors and traded the few goods I had salvaged for clean water and food. Hoping for something dried, I had to settle for ten-year-old canned beans.

A large greenhouse with plexiglass walls and ceilings rested near the back of the settlement. I guessed it was where they grew some foodstuff, though I didn't know how much of their supply was from pre-Yellow salvage.

Sitting at a table at a saloon I didn't catch the name of, I sipped at a homemade beer from a jar. The building enclosed four parking spots with the asphalt still showing instead of a floor. One was a handicapped spot, and I found it amusing.

The tavern boasted stew with fresh pork, but I had declined it. The smell was mouth watering, but I preferred to see what I was eating. It was easy for someone to hide rotting meat or rat. I'd eaten rat before, but it wasn't a fond memory. The idea they raised pigs intrigued me. They ate almost anything, including people. The thought of swallowing a pig that ingested a person made me sick. I'd rather have a rat. Instead, I enjoyed a pre-Yellow can of soup. It was expensive but trustworthy.

Captain Avery Agrusa walked into the saloon and sat at my table. "I hope you're not drinking that swill. And no stew in your bowl? It's very good."

"I have had nothing good since before the yellow," I said, talking about the beer "Though it's not surprising as I'm consuming American beer."

"You're Canadian, eh? Eh?" Avery said.

"Funny. What can I do for you? Going to kick me out?"

"Bless your heart. I've a job for you."

"I'm traveling from one part of this hellhole to another," I said. "I'm not staying."

"Of course. Here's the situation. We're members of a loose, decentralized trade organization. We gather salvage from the city and exchange it to the rural farming areas, who give us animals and produce."

"Pigs?"

"That and chickens. They eat scraps and bugs, both of which we have in large supplies."

I took a sip of the swill called ale. "Sounds fragile."

"It's spread out to keep us safe from the ghouls."

"How do you grow in this shit?"

"Greenhouses, guards, and wood-fired generators."

"Wood?" I asked. "That sounds like a video game."

"All generators consist of turning a turbine. We use steam from burning wood, which we have lots of," Avery said.

"What did you want me to do?" I asked.

"The payment is food, water, and bullets."

I drained my drink and slammed the empty jar onto the table. "What's the fucking job?"

"Do you know where Joelton is?"

"I'm not from around here."

"It's a small town about 12 miles to the northwest," Avery said. "Perhaps not a town, but a village."

"Sounds lovely."

"They built the settlement in an old middle school."

"Why a school?" I asked.

Avery smirked, drumming his fingers on the table. "I need someone to make the journey. Examine why their caravans haven't arrived and why."

"Probably ghouls."

"If it is ghouls, then I can organize a patrol raid to clean them out. If some fuckin rival raided them, then that's important information. There are a few other larger groups around who we aren't on speaking terms."

"Like the Hatfields and the McCoys?"

The Captain smirked. "Something like that."

"Any name of the bastard in charge?"

"Triplets. They are Rosanne, Gabriel, and Benjamin Costa. They are middle-aged former lawyers. Expect to find a settlement of twenty people of different ages. They gathered enough families to make it worthwhile."

I crossed my arms; this sounded like nothing I wanted to be a part of. "Why me?"

"I've sent three good scouts already. No one's come back."

Fuck me. "I'm expendable. Is that it?"

"Well, no, but..."

"No one would miss me if I died. There'd be no crying widows or children to worry about."

"You see—"

I wished to leave and never return. "Fine. Get me a map and the location. Fill my pack before I go and once more when I get back."

The captain nodded and smiled. "Done deal."

I left the settlement and ventured into the wilds soon after. The Captain was a man of his word and filled my pack with food and water. I could leave and never come back. It would be easy, as I doubted they had people to send after me. Except, judging by how quickly he agreed he might be friends with bounty hunters.

Federations, factions, and alliances weren't a rare phenomenon, but they never lasted. The biggest two issues were providing enough food and water for everyone. Eventually, food ran out, or the water filtration systems failed. Then people either starved or died of thirst. This created more ghouls to savage the wastes. They were thirsty, hungry, and willing to do anything to stay alive. I had little desire to discover what a person was capable of.

Cinching my full-face mask on tighter, it became harder to breathe. I held my breath and removed the filter. It was a simple plastic puck with loose edges where it drew air in. Chunks of gray ash clogged this part. I tapped it across the sheath of my belt knife. The hard plastic buckled and flexed, knocking lumps onto the ground. Screwing the filter in, I could breathe once more. This wasn't perfect, but I had little choice in the matter. They were worth their weight in gold.

The air was almost free of falling ash, but it wasn't the falling ash I was afraid of. I feared the particulate or the ones I couldn't see but coated everything in a fine haze on a clear day. These sucked the life from the survivors of the cold, gray wastes.

The streets and ruins of Nashville stretched around me. Many loomed dark and foreboding with the unknown threat. Most buildings lay abandoned, but a ghoul with a rifle and a high-powered scope was all it took to end everything with a single shot. I hoped it would be quick and painless when it was my time. I had no intention of dying poorly, vowing to die on my feet facing the threat and not to disease, thirst, or starvation.

I marched onto Interstate 155 and stopped. If I turned right, the road stretched to the south and east. It was where I desired to go. My theory was there'd be less ashfall the farther away from the Yellow I got. If I were to head left, I'd venture closer to the volcano. It was where Captain Avery wanted me to go.

"Fuck a duck," I mumbled under my breath as I turned left.

Traveling the route was slower than I'd like. I preferred to make a direct march up the interstate, then turning onto state highway 431. According to the old map I carried, it was only sixteen miles to the destination. If I were to walk fast, I'd get there in five or six hours. Except I didn't want to attract unwanted attention, like being in a hurry.

Instead, I poked my way through the mass of abandoned vehicles, hoping to find medicine or bullets. I wished I had time to search the wrecks, as I figured there'd be items to loot. Except, I didn't have room in my pack to salvage anything more substantial. Tying items to the outside like a backpacker was one way to get robbed. It told ghouls I was rich and needed to be relinquished of my belongings.

However, I made a note of anything interesting for later. I figured I walked between two to two and a half miles per hour. Except I had no real way of knowing.

Trudging along the interstate, cars packed most of the road, being covered in rust and ash. Scavengers turned most into charred ruins long ago. In eight miles, an intersection would block my path, which I'd find a way through. Like the others I came across before, I expected it to be filled with a dozen burned-up vehicle clogged mess. I discovered a trail running along the outside edge of the charred wreckage.

During my journey, not a soul ventured anywhere near me. Anytime I got too close, they scampered off into the maze of wrecked vehicles. Most encounters were at a distance, with me not wanting things to turn ugly. Very few interactions turned into a fight. It was the desperate or crazy who sought violence. Even a simple wound could turn serious. I've seen a ghoul injured from a scratch from a knife, then die from the infection. It wasn't a pretty sight.

The day morphed into dusk, the temperature fell, and then the sky opened. It was like someone above cranked on a faucet and water poured from the sky into the ground. The water dribbled, washing some of the loose ash away. I dropped my full-face mask, letting it hand by its straps across my neck. I leaned my head back and let the water splatter across my skin. It was the only chance to wash. If I was someplace I considered safe, I'd strip down and use soap. I didn't expect that to happen soon. With my face clean, I wiped the plastic clear before strapping it back on. Flipping my hood up, I continued down the road. I expected to be soaked in a few minutes.

An old sign hung above the interstate by one bolt. Age and bent rusted the metal from its weight. It pointed to the right, announcing State Highway 431, and Joelton was the next exit.

Part of me wanted to continue, though the other needed sleep. Walking all day, every day, was hard on my feet and knees, so I desired to get off them and rest. A crumpled church with a caved-in roof lay nearby along the side of the freeway. I shrugged my shoulders and climbed over the barrier. A frontage road with ditches on either side stretched parallel to the highway. I jumped over the water-filled trench and onto the street.

Minutes later, I was in the ruins. Pews lay scattered and piled in corners with ash covering everything. In the corner was the refectory, which wasn't leaking water or ash. Using a tarp I carried in my bag, I set up a small sleeping area. I pinned the plastic to cover what holes I could. My sleep would be rough, but better than outside in the rain.

Being a light sleeper, I woke up the next morning still exhausted. As I attempted to sleep, the deluge stopped, and the monsters came out. They drove dirt bikes up and down the freeway at high speeds, like they were in a video game. A few fought with each other, shooting guns and keeping me up. I slept when I could.

Using the map, I wandered along the frontage road to the smaller highway. Instead of the standard three or four lanes stretching off in one direction, each separated by massive concrete barriers, the artery was only two lanes resembling more of a standard road. Except the lanes were wider and straighter. Just like the freeway, a mass of vehicles packed the asphalt.

It was a phenomenon I had seen all over. People heard the news and panicked. Most pre-yellow people had little plans to handle a flood, let alone a world-ending volcanic disaster. So when their food ran out, they scrambled from their homes, hunting for help. Except FEMA couldn't save them and when a few ran out of gas, they left the vehicles where they stopped, clogging everything for miles around.

I crept along the highway as it moved from the relative flatland of Nashville and into the highlands of the surrounding area. The road weaved around the hills in long, lazy arcs.

Each side of the road stretched lines of rural homes. They resembled the stereotypical hillbilly home. Old, rusting vehicles littered many driveways. Adult gas-powered toys like quads and dirt bikes crowded others. I stopped by a few and tried to crank them over. Except they were empty of fuel or missing parts. Ash covered it all with none of the structures in one piece. Most buildings had their roofs caved in, with someone torching a few and were piles of charred wood-filled basements.

I continued down the road and along the properties. They weren't like the rows of homes of Nashville. Each house lay on enough land where most people lived far apart. Some of the smaller lots were less than an acre, while others had five.

After a bit, the homes disappeared as the hillside became steeper and rockier. Finally, it stretched upward toward the peak of the hill. The road inclined and my legs burned. After months of walking, I desired a haven to rest for a few days. I needed to let my muscles heal properly. Or I needed to find a working dirt bike.

Judging by the miles, I hoped I was getting close. The highway weaved around the hills, which the map called the Devil's Elbow. It was a rocky outcrop the pre-Yellow people built the road through. A rock face spread upward on my right and a slope expanded downward to my left.

A mass of abandoned vehicles stacked like someone built a wall stretched across the middle of the roadway. I swung my AR15 from my shoulder and held it at the ready. It could put lead on target at a moment's notice.

I kneeled behind a discarded car, waiting for something to happen. It resembled a roadblock or toll. I guessed it was the reason no messages had gotten through.

Except nothing happened. I picked up a rock the size of my fist and tossed it high in the air. It arced over crashing into the mass of rusting steel and broken glass. The clang of metal reverberated across the valley.

I slammed my weapon to my shoulder and waited. I prepared to fire, expecting a mob of ghouls to pour out like a horde of plague rats. Except nothing came. Not a single person investigated the noise.

Pondering the situation, I walked toward it. I made my best impression of a soldier's stance from what I remember from the movies. If a real one were to see me LARPing, they'd die from laughter.

Cars lay knocked over in one lane, giving a path between them. It allowed me to step between the vehicles to the other side. A bus blocked the path, which acted as a gate. The structure functioned as a toll booth. Except I didn't understand if it stopped people from getting in or out. A giant hole penetrated the side, blasting through the engine block.

As I neared the edge of the vehicles, I smelled the rotting flesh and didn't want to explore any further. It wasn't something I'd ever get used to. Steeling myself, I stepped forward.

A makeshift encampment extended across the highway with dozens of tents and campfires. It was all old, abandoned, and covered in layers of hardened ash. Bodies of men, women, and children spread anywhere where they fell upon death. The dead rotted where they dropped. Many of them bloated in various phases of decomposition. They all also showed signs of violent death. Gunshot wounds or knife blades riddled most of them. I hoped these weren't people I hunted for.

Holding the bile in my throat, I stepped through the massacre site, taking care not to step on a corpse. Not that the dead would care, but I risked slipping on the loose, waxy skin. Scanning the bodies, I found them looted. Boots, gloves, masks, watches, and rings were missing, including any gear or weapons. These were refugees, and it was a ghoul attack.

Sitting inside a tent was a journal, wet from rain and dirty from ash. Written across the cover were the words: Journal of Gabriel Costa. It was impossible to open, but I pried two pages apart. The ink ran, making most of it illegible. The entries were from months before, but I read the last one. I could make out a single paragraph.

"I doubt how smart leaving the settlement was. I fear whatever was killing and... the others will follow us... If we can get past this wall... those bastards killed the gate... Maybe we can topple the wall... there are enough of us. Maybe we can do it."

I set the book down and shook my head. The words were from a dead woman. They informed me about her, but were little solace to her memory. In a hundred years, humanity wouldn't have knowledge of pre-Yellow society. It reminded me how the world of my youth vanished underneath falling ash and wouldn't ever return.

Marching down the highway, I left the ruins of the camp behind. A wolf howled from somewhere distant, and I wondered how anything could live in the wastes. Perhaps things weren't as bleak as I saw. Maybe watching the ash wastes through the dirt-smudged lens of a gas mask did that to me.

The road stretched onward as I continued my journey. The land was similar to those before. Covered in gray ash with the plant life dying underneath. Rain kept parts of it clean, though it was few in places.

The street beyond was clear of abandoned vehicles. Whomever had made the wall of steel had cleared the road behind it. They left a few commercial trucks or pickups behind. They were too heavy to move, even with a dozen healthy men.

I enjoyed moving around parked cars as it was an easy cover from an ambush. The steel hulls gave me precious seconds to find my assailant and to end them. With the road clear, it did none of that.

Trudging onward, I grumbled under my breath. Part of me desired that I left, except I had made it this far. I wouldn't turn back now. I had given the Captain my word, and I'd do the job.

After the highway weaved around a series of tight turns, I stepped into the outskirts of the abandoned town of Joelton. Slinging my rifle out, I held it, ready to use it if a threat appeared.

I expected more of Joelton, assuming the town proper was a few miles away. Instead, it was an array of low commercial buildings spread out from each other. Laying knocked over next to the road, a water tower had once stretched to the sky. A church lay to the side;

its roof caved in like the many others. It had collapsed in places and torched in others. There were signs of looting nearby. An overturned car rested next to a charred dumpster in the middle of the parking lot.

A massive, brown-bricked building stretched opposite the church. It was an old middle school and my destination. There were traces someone fortified with rows of busses and vehicles lining the perimeter—though it wasn't a wall like the one blocking the devil's elbow. However, it gave a touch of cover and concealment to any who defended the school.

The middle school was mostly one story tall, with the gymnasium and one wing stretching above the low sections. The church was in good shape despite being of a similar size. There were no obvious signs of the disaster with damage repaired with plywood or corrugated steel.

I took a step toward the building, then smelled it. Like the rest of the wastes, death stalked the old school. I didn't like it.

I slid around two abandoned cars with my rifle aimed at anyplace an enemy could be hiding. They'd have seen me approach for miles if they were paying attention. Someone on watch on the top of the gym could've shot me. Though if there was anyone near, they'd have ventured around the school. This would've disturbed the ashfall creating paths around the yard and parking lot. None of this was the case. There were no signs anyone had wandered near the building in over a week.

Taking two more steps, I found the source of the smell. Still, bloated corpses laid in piles around the side of the structure. The victims wore rags, while some wore the gear of ghouls with spikes and makeshift body armor.

I crept to the door and found it broken open. It had been bent and ripped from its hinges. It lay on the ground in front of it. I stepped through the threshold and into the school.

Darkness encased the inside of the building. Beams of sunlight burst into the hallway from a classroom or office. I switched on the flashlight attached to my AR. Its beam blasted through the darkness, chasing it away for the moment.

Moving slowly through the building, I listened to my surroundings. There were no signs of movement. I expected to hear footsteps or the creek of a door opening. Except I heard nothing.

I found only death and destruction. They had set the school into a home with dwellings for people. Beds, couches, chairs, and tables lie around everywhere. The settlers had a comfortable life. Except that it was all gone, with bodies laying where they had fallen. Time bloated them—another reminder of why I needed to find some charcoal filters for my mask.

After a quick search, I found the entrance to the gym. They had set it up into a hydroponic farm and a pigpen. Massive tubs stretched half the length, which were once filled with water. Or they would've been if the raiders hadn't attacked. Most were not empty, with dead plants lying in piles. The corpses of a few small fish lay among them. A pigpen occupied the other half. Like the school, it was empty of living beings.

Wherever I went, I found more bodies of both raiders and ghouls. It was like a charnal house, and I wanted to leave. Then I stepped to the two-story portion of the school. Massive fire doors blocked off this section locked. I jiggled the door handles, and nothing.

A gunshot rang out, and a hole appeared inches from my head. The ringing of the blast hung in the air, hurting my ears. With my eyes wide in shock, I hid behind the bricks to the side.

"Go away," a voice said. "Before the wendigo gets you."

"Wendigo?" I asked. "My name is Blondie. I'm a messenger from Captain Avery Agrusa. I'm looking for either Rosanne, Gabriel, or Benjamin Costa."

I didn't know why he was referring to a mythical Native American being who ate the flesh of humans. I disliked the thought of it.

"The wendigo has got Rosanne and Gabriel, along with most of the others. It's only me left."

"Then, you're Ben?" I asked.

"I am," Ben said. "Though what type of name is Blondie? Or you the good? Or the ugly?"

I ignored the joke at my expense. He understood the reference of where I got the name.

"Can you let me in?" I asked. "I'm not the wendigo."

"I know you're not. But I can't let you in. I'm safe in here. You're not in here."

Two more gunshots rang out. Bullets appeared in the door, but as I hid behind the wall, they were nowhere near me. Then his weapon made an audible click. He was out of bullets. If I could open the door, I could rush him. Except if the man had another magazine, I'd catch a bullet before I kicked the door open.

"Shit," Ben said. "Where did I put that mag?"

A ruffling sound reverberated from the survivor. Some crashes, and a bang followed it. I guessed he was out of bullets.

"Hey, Mr. Ugly. Do you have some 9mm bullets I can borrow? I seem to be out."

"Of course," I said. "Just open the door."

"You won't hurt me?"

"Good and ugly are the truthful ones. It's bad who's the liar," I said, though all three lied like sailors throughout the movie. "You can trust me. I'm from Captain Avery."

The door clicked unlocked, and it creaked open. A shorter man resembling a hermit or a dwarf from a fantasy book stood in front of me. His beard was long and disheveled; dirt and twigs covered his gray hair. The man smelled like a sewer.

I stepped to it and slammed the butt of my rifle into the short man's face. He doubled over and fell to the ground. I trod over him and pulled him to the side. Then I locked the door behind me.

"Who else is in here?" I asked with my rifle pointed into his face.

The flashlight blinded him as he held his hands bedore his eyes.

"No one," Ben said. "And you said you wouldn't hurt me."

"I'm not. Just as soon as I know you won't hurt me," I said. "Get up. I want you to show me the rest of the school."

With my weapon aimed at his back, we walked up and down the halls. I forced him into the center of each room he showed me. I gave myself enough space to shoot him if he tried anything. The entire school smelled of shit, but there was a faint hint of something else underneath. It was a mix of lavender and death. He had been trying to hide the smell by burning incense sticks in multiple places.

This section had been homes, with each classroom for separate families—though they were all missing. A few scattered places were signs of gore and bloodshed. A leg bone lay in a corner with scratches and nicks along it from something sharp. Another lay broken with the soft marrow sucked out.

We stopped at what the short man called his home. I forced him to sit on the floor. Nothing about the situation I liked.

"Wendigo? You mean the ghouls or raiders?" I asked.

The man laughed. "There is another monster. One in this school. One who will get you. She will get you."

I pointed my weapon at the man. "Tell me what happened."

"Fuck you," Ben snapped, spitting at my full-face mask. "You promised you wouldn't hurt me. Yet I'm bleeding and am a prisoner."

Jerking my AR to the side, I fired at a spot six inches from his head. The gunshot echoed throughout the building, and Ben jerked his hands up.

"Don't shoot me."

"I have seen enough for you to warrant a bullet. Talk. Now. Maybe I let you live."

"A massive horde of ghouls came. They sacked the town. First the church, who were our friends, then they attacked us. Our outer perimeter fell, and they forced us back to this section. We were under siege for weeks."

"What about others?" I asked. "What happened to Gabriel?"

"After the siege started, they fled and ran. This is our home and those traitors... No, those yellow cowards ran like dogs. This is where we belong. We'll fight any who try to take it."

I glared at the man, wanting to shoot him. I used my weapon only when needed, preferring not to kill people. Although I'd make an exception for this man.

"Continue." It wasn't a question.

"Then we ran out of food. So the wendigo came, and we ate. And ate. And ate."

I had heard enough. I aimed my rifle at the man's head, but before I could pull the trigger, a tall lady burst from the corridor. She wore rags and carried a knife.

"Rosanne. No," Ben yelled, holding up his hands.

My finger was faster. I placed a bullet into Ben's face and his skull jerked back. The man collapsed in a heap costing me time as the crazed lady was on me.

She jumped on me, and I caught her blade on the metal stock of my rifle. The force of the impact knocked me to the ground with a thud. She jerked her hands back and stabbed at me over and over.

"I'm hungry. It's time to eat," Rosanne said.

Each time the knife came down, it grew closer to my face. If I wasn't careful, the sharpened edge would get me. A single scratch would be fatal. As her blade went up, I slammed my fist into her face, which gave me a few inches and moments to play with.

I pulled the Smith and Wesson SD9 from its holster and shoved the barrel at her eye. Then before she could do anything, I fired. The bullet smashed through her skull, spraying blood, bones, and brains out the other side. Blood splattered the roof behind her. She collapsed beside me with her hand still holding the knife.

After a quick search through Ben and Rosanne's belongings, I left. I didn't desire to dwell any longer at the school turned carnal house. I exited the way I entered. The trek back to Music Valley Village took me three long days. A gang of ghouls forced me to hide for a day and a half. Part of me wanted to fight the ghouls. Except I was one man and couldn't take out a force that large. Luckily, I had reading material I salvaged from Ben and Rosanne.

As dusk came on the third day, I returned. After a quick talk with the guard, they admitted me. Ten minutes later, I sat in the saloon across from Captain Avery. I told him the story.

"Shit," Avery said, rubbing at his eyes.

I pulled out a journal and handed it to the man. "This is Ben's. It turns out that all three of them liked to write down their thoughts."

Avery took it and opened it. He flipped through the pages.

"The situation was a long time coming. Rosanne and Ben were cannibals. They hid it from the others in the settlement and the organization. The pair ventured into the wastes and hunted ghouls. They brought them back to feed the pigs, which is itself disgusting. But as pigs don't grow as fast as they'd like, they butchered the ghouls. They were hungry, so no one asked questions. My guess is that the ghouls discovered who was hunting them and attacked. Either they didn't want the competition, or they were desperate people who don't want to turn into someone's dinner."

The Captain glanced at me, then the bowls of food his people ate. "And the stuff they sent us?"

"I have no way to answer that. Were they shipping you live animals or slabs of preserved meat? My guess is the latter, as you don't have any pens for the beasts."

I left Music Valley Village soon after that. My pack was full of pre-yellow canned food and dried beans. There was no way I'd ever accept anything homemade from anyone. Not unless I trusted them.

ABOUT NATHAN PEDDE

Nathan Pedde is a sci-fi author from the dark reaches of Vancouver Island. He has been writing for over a decade with multiple titles published. He has a wife and two kids who encourage his crazy storytelling. You can find him on his website, www.NathanPed de.com.

"WHERE HAVE ALL THE FLOWERS GONE"

A.M. STEVENS

A child actress turned wasteland mercenary leads her foul crew across post apocalyptic Southern California on their latest job. Along the way she faces a deadly desert, a cult of brutal bikers, and the wages of her sins with the help of a mysterious stranger known only as the FIREMAN.

"WHERE HAVE ALL THE FLOWERS GONE"

The heat of the wastes stirred up memories of the stage. In the dark of my heavy eyelids I felt the scrutinous burn of ancient spotlights. The inconsistent breeze whistled like the chatter of the expectant audience. Sand in the wind echoed the scratchy sensation of the little red polyester dress that I slowly grew too big for. The weight of the gun at my side snapped me back to reality.

I peeled my eyelids open to the blinding horizon lit by the midday sun, the spotlight that never changed. Though, here, the curtains were thin. Raging fires ruined the sky. Here the sweat evaporated from your brow under shade. The old Mex name for this place made no sense.

No angels dwelled here, only infertile dust and the shadows of foundations where ruins no longer lay. No radiation lingered beyond these waning footprints of better times – just a hole in the sky, killing temperatures, and no curtains to end this horrid scene.

The lot of us weren't exactly waiting for Godot out here, but I wondered and remembered something my father said, "You are here as a result of your choices." What choices lead us to bake beneath this wilted highway sign? The faint letters on its face spelled out, "Los Angeles – 19 miles."

"How–. How hot?"

I broke a sweat just raising the thermometer in my hand. "129 in the shade." An untouched gallon of water sat between us all, too hot to comfortably drink. "How's it going with the car, Rob?"

The tomato-faced man slammed the hood shut and adjusted the broken umbrella duct-taped to his pack. He circled the reflective nightmare that was my mylar and duct tape-clad station wagon. The tape's adhesive turned gooey, the tires split, and the jury-rigged air conditioner strapped to the roof died a mile behind us.

"Hell couldn't possibly be this hot." His thick Bostonian voice grated the ear. He removed his gloves, revealing the mechanical segments of his bionic arm. With his real hand he gathered the sweat from his bald head where red hair once grew, and drank up. "If we roll down the windows and go fast, we could probably keep cool enough to reach safer temps."

"What about the AC, darling?" Miri chimed in. She stood naked on a pile of clothes, lapping the sweat from her skin like a cat. She looked young and somehow old at the same time. Her long bleach-baked hair draped over her pale ebony shoulders.

Rob didn't answer her.

"I *asked* you a question," her voice turned both sultry and coquettish, "baby." She pulled back her hair and stretched out her bare body.

He stared for a moment before shaking his head and punching the hood. "For f-. Gah! What did I say about cutting that shit out?"

Miri harrumphed, rolled her eyes, and turned towards me with a wink.

"I know guns, sweetheart." Rob slapped the air conditioner. "Does this look like a gun to you?"

"We'll ride with the windows down," I agreed, "get rid of as much weight as possible to take the strain off the tires."

"Sounds good, boss."

I glanced over at the fourth voice I'd almost forgotten. Excitement plastered his youthful face despite his chapped lips, and sunburnt face. "Boss." I repeated. That's right. I remembered—our job.

Our employer hired us to carry out another hit on the North side of the wastes.

This little settlement struck it rich with a fresh well and another, and another. The town was small, isolated, and ripe for the taking. The Kid? Some misfit. Miri lured him away, Rob fixed up a gun for him, and I convinced him to show us the weak spots in their security.

In a few keystrokes, Miri used her remote computer rig to disarm what little electronic security the settlement had. Rob snuck into their guard tower and used it as a sniper nest. The kid and I got to work clearing the place out. We got the water for our boss, and the kid got to kill his parents. It was *almost* perfect.

While our employer smoothly stepped in to buy the place out, fix it up, and such for "The Building of a Better Tomorrow," we drew away the attention of the Khakis investigating the attack. As we predicted, those Civil Defense troops weren't brave or stupid enough to chase us down South through LA.

It made me wonder why the suits to the far East even bothered to send their trigger happy peace lackeys. Their toy soldier's boldness dwindled after the Lake Matthews massacre.

"Yeah, boss. I know you'll get us out of this hot mess we're in." The boy's sun-kissed face grinned against our conditions.

"Sure kid." I checked my watch. "Eh, it's about that time. I'll check in on the radio."

"You do that, Boss. I suppose I'll try and take a nap."

Rob and Miri eyed me as the kid rolled his pack into a pillow.

"You do that." I stepped past Rob into the wagon, rolled up the windows, and grabbed the handset dangling from the ham radio. Manipulating the controls crammed into the dash, I locked onto the signal and held down the push-to-talk button on the side. "Rothman. This is Constance. Do you read me? Over."

I caught a glimpse of myself in the rearview mirror. Pale ginger hair and the beginnings of crows' feet framed the graying eyes that judged right back. I remembered how vibrant these frayed strands used to be.

"Connie, Connie. Are you there? Over." The crackling voice cut through the radio noise.

"I read you loud and clear, Rothman. No sign of the Roosters from the watering hole. Also, our pantry is looking slim here. Over."

"Well done. Light your lamp so the stork can find you. It won't be long, but as for the pantry, I'm afraid the stork can only carry three servings. But I'm sure you'll manage. You always do. Out."

I switched off the radio and hung the handset around the rearview mirror. Rob tapped on the window with an expectant stare. I gestured to myself and readied my Beretta, unholstering it and screwing on a suppressor. The attachment wasn't so important; I just didn't want my tinnitus to get any worse.

The kid didn't so much as stir when I exited the car. It only took one shot to the head, spraying fragments of skull and gray matter across the ground, soaked up by the thirsty dust of the earth.

Some of him splattered my face, a fitting mask for the role I played. "Rob, help me strip him."

Miri glared at me with feral eyes.

I nodded to her. "After we're done, he's yours."

Just like the others, no pictures, no heirlooms, and no connections. Aside from his guns, ammo, and the usual life necessities, he carried only one odd trinket. The crusty old zippo in his pocket flipped open with the usual satisfactory metallic chime. It had no fuel, but the wheel still sparked. A four-leaf clover was painted on one side.

I tossed it in the salvage bag.

"Alright." Rob finished up, turned, and flinched at Miri, who stood right behind him. "Jesus! Don't do that! There. I'm done with him. Get on with your vamp shit, you weirdo."

Miri tied the kid's legs with a rope and hoisted him up using the sign. She unpacked a gruesome menagerie of pumps and tubes and plunged an IV needle into his jugular vein. The device gurgled as she turned the crank. Blood drained from the dangling corpse on one end and came out the other side as water filling a daisy chain of bladders. She carved out chunks of meat while the body drained and cooked them in the sunlight.

Within the hour, Rothman's drone came into view. The sky-blue, plastic spider buzzed overhead. Its six propellers slowed, allowing it to bring down its cargo. A screeching beep preceded its detachment before it zipped away across the horizon.

After organizing the provisions and bonus tokens, I broke out the sealed file with the new marching orders from the Director, Rothman. None of us knew his real name, but that didn't really matter as long as the water tokens kept rolling in. "We're picking up a new guy."

"Oh great," Rob muttered as he loaded up the wagon, "Is he at least normal? It'd be great to smoke and joke with a guy who's not crazy."

"I ain't crazy." Miri gnawed away at a severed thumb.

"You know what you're right. You're batshit insane." He flipped her the bird as she snapped her teeth at him. "So who's our guy?"

His rap sheet blurred before my eyes, some of it cold enough to make Miri blush. "Last known whereabouts... He was last seen heading for Rat Land. The Director wants us to pick him up to help us deal with some gas raiders. There's no real name, just a word. Fireman."

We shed the mylar sheets and dropped the air conditioner. With four fifty A/C — four windows down, fifty miles an hour — our rubber found the beginning of a road. Any worries about Khakis vanished as a brisk summer breeze of sixty-two degrees swept over us. It was about time for a scene change, and our destination wasn't far — a straight shot down the 5 South.

As a kid, I had flown over the old freeways. From my father's helicopter, you could see all the cars that packed the concrete lanes. In the darker hours, I remember rivers of red and white flowing in opposite directions. My earliest memories of the roads were sparse, masked by the tinted windows of limos. Now the spider web of surviving lanes was as familiar as the veins on the back of my hand.

We passed a Battalion caravan of Mormon volunteers from the

far North. They stood guard around a pair of bulldozers clearing a smashed tinfoil ball of cars from the road. I could see slivers of pale and bloated remains in one of the vehicles they had shoved into the shoulder. Nothing new.

Rat Land stood as the filthiest stain of the old world. Roving gangs took over the former amusement park and the place evolved into the cesspool it is now. The gates that once closed at the end of the park's business hours now remained open to traders with the cojones to brave its streets.

The walls of the themed facades crumbled, revealing their concrete and rebar skeletons. Animatronics and mascots hung outside, skinned and crucified beneath years of graffiti. Some of the inhabitants took to wearing the decaying uniforms and costumes. Gardens and water fixtures were transformed into small agricultural and fish farms. Some order remained amidst the chaos.

We cut through the skunky, neon rainbow-tagged lanes of fantasy forest to make it to the timber-hitched village of New Tomb-stone. At least, that was the name on the sign erected over the ranch-style entrance. I parked us outside the trading post.

The faux adobe buildings were all cracked, but the timber walls of the trading post had kept up the illusion of the wild frontier. The swinging double doors transported us back to that other rough and tumble time, but the drugged-out and scantily clad cartoon princesses brought us right back.

"Howdy, ma'am." A sleeveless cowboy wiped a weathered mug clean from behind the counter, doubling as both a bar and merchandise display. "Anything, in particular, you looking for? Ammo? Grub?" He gestured to the princesses, wryly grinning at us with dazed eyes. "Entertainment?"

I purchased some new tires and ammo while Rob got a drink and Miri harassed the *entertainment*. "If you got a sec," I slid a few extra gallons of tokens into our accumulating pile of expenses, "We are looking for someone."

"What kind of someone?" The cowboy brushed all the water tokens behind the counter and set a shot glass of something blue on the countertop for Rob.

"Some possible hired help." I thought about the designation the Director gave me. "Does *Fireman* ring any bells?"

His expression flickered between serious and amused. "Oh. Bad for business, that man. What the hell do you want with a character like that?"

"Do you know where he is or not?"

The cowboy rubbed the extra tokens together. "He's," the man sighed, dumping the gallons into his back pocket, "he's over in Alien Nation, on some sort of business."

I tossed another gallon token to him. "Thanks."

After Rob and I wrestled Miri away from the princesses, we drove into the North West corner of Rat Land. We passed a few inoperable spaceships overgrown with ivy. Here the theme park teetered between illusion and reality. The former space-themed attraction was colonized by muties – people who were taken over by alien parasites and mutated into something in between. They did the same wherever they took up residence.

"Hate these guys." Rob sneered at the faux alien star port made even more alien by the wiry messes of circuitry and fiber optic conduit bolted over plastic fantasies of space. "When they abducted me and took my arm, the least they could have done was drop me off on the right coast."

"No trouble if we can avoid it." I spoke too soon as an exchange of gunfire erupted ahead of us. A web-fingered body with gills and frills slapped the hood of the wagon, leaving behind a blue smear as it slid to the ground. "Miri, eyes and ears?"

She popped the latches on a pelican case with a laptop and a small drone. "Hello, Precious." The drone sprung to life, hovering around Miri in happy little circles. "That's a good girl, Precious. Show mommy the situation."

I slid the sunroof open to let "Precious" take to the sky.

"Good girl." The display's light shone in her eyes as her fingers attacked the keyboard before her. "Got visual. Looks like a small firefight between a single human and a gang of muties. The guards aren't engaging."

"Keep an eye on the wagon, Rob." I stepped out and glared up at the entrance. Fake and real extraterrestrial graffiti overlapped across the archway. A putrid green flag hung overhead, painted with the skull of a creature I didn't recognize.

I advanced along the long wide alley framed by exotic hole-in-the-wall shops. Panicked humans and muties took cover behind pillars and statues of space wizards. I hugged the sides as a few stray bullets zipped by, chipping pieces off the walls.

Deeper into the alley, I saw our guy caught in the middle of a scuffle with a few mismatched muties. They corralled him like rodeo clowns trying to lasso a bull, but he swung an empty rifle with all the might of a frenzied caveman.

His garb consisted of a mish-mash of army greens and denim. Jury-rigged straps and belts held his tattered boots and Khaki firefighter's jacket together. A pristine gas mask clung to his face, its red-tinted glass eyes glimmering like fire.

He charged at one of his wranglers, wrapped his arms around the furry brute, and flipped him over, snapping his neck on the ground like a twig. Then, reaching into his coat, he drew out an old flintlock and blasted the scalie face of his next attacker. Tossing the spent piece, he eyed the last mutant standing, a bald gray-skin who'd drawn out a rusted machete.

I noticed a sword at the masked man's side—the blade curved in its scabbard. Stories of the weebues and the takoos came to mind. Many of those tribes carried decorative imitations of such weapons. This one looked real, but he didn't draw it.

He wrestled the machete from his foe's hand and struck him in the face with the handle. His opponent crumpled like a wet rag at his feet. He checked that everything was dead, grabbed his rifle, and left the bodies around him with all their trappings.

I stepped out into the open. "That's a waste, leaving all that behind. You don't believe in looters' rights?"

His glass eyes glowed over the lifeless masses, like the hungry eyes of a nocturnal creature.

"Got a job proposition that'll keep food in your belly."

He knelt to retrieve a slouch hat off the ground. Pulling down on the wide sunbleached felt brim he turned to face me.

"Contract work. On the move. Ammo provided."

Plucking the empty magazine from his rifle, he stared at it for a moment, then nodded.

"Man of few words. I'm sure we'll get along nicely."

He followed me back to the wagon where the others waited. Rob was tweaking his mechanical arm with a pair of pliers. "Nice hat, Calamity Jane."

Miri's eyes crawled over the fresh meat. "Care if I try it on?" She weaseled around the Fireman, reaching between his legs.

He caught her hand, his grip eliciting a playful scream from Miri before he shoved the business end of a bowie knife into her face.

"Hey!" I yelled.

Rob held me back, "Wait, I'm starting to like this guy."

I'd never seen Miri actually quiver the way she did. "Hey! If you kill her, you don't get paid."

He let the blade scrape against Miri's face as he pulled it away. His muffled voice growled at her. "Don't."

Miri gave a half-hearted grin, "Message received."

Rob couldn't stop chuckling. "Buddy, you're good in my book. I- uh. Say, what are you called?"

The Fireman said nothing.

I eyed the sword at his side. A distant memory, a vague recollection of Saturday morning cartoons, crawled back to my attention. "Jack." The masked man cocked his head at me. "You alright with that? Jack?"

He didn't protest.

———

We loaded up and headed straight for Northern Berdoo. The Director's instructions led us to a small town settled around a solitary gas depot – beyond the ruins of the suburbs. All radio contact had been lost. Our job was to assess the situation, retrieve the manifest, wipe the back-ups, and eliminate all hostiles.

"Smoke." Rob announced his findings through a spare scope in hand. "A few smoldering buildings. Nothing on the roads. Not even a car."

Miri let her drone loose to take a look. We watched as its feed reached the area in question. The monitor showed piles of bodies stacked up against the walls – women and children stripped naked. "No movement. Any of these up for grabs?"

"No looting," I said, "We're just here to figure out what happened."

Jack and I took point with Miri in tow while Rob stayed behind with us in his sights. Jack knelt down by the dirt road, eyeing the tire tracks. His muffled voice muttered something incoherent before he finally said, "Bikes. Hogs."

Several of the buildings were burnt out. The fires calmed to smolders and smoke. We found the gas depot, but the reservoir tanks were all empty. None of the bodies even twitched. Everything had been dead for a while. I watched as the Fireman turned over one body and checked the gun in its death grip. "Jack?"

He ejected the magazine from the rifle, shook it, and put it back. "Mag full?"

He nodded before moving on to the next. Entry wounds on the back marked the majority of the bodies he checked.

We moved on to the manager's office to collect the manifest from the terminal inside. Miri set up shop and began the process of decoding the encrypted files the Director wanted. While she worked, I checked the rest of the building with the Fireman.

"What do you think?" I checked the pantry towards the back. Only a few empty cans and dried goods remained, but a ration receipt near the door suggested it was once full. "Thieves? Starving, desperate fiends, maybe?"

Jack shook his head at me as he picked up a can of corned beef.

"Right. That doesn't explain the empty gas reserves and a dead town if all they wanted was food."

"Almost done." Miri stood up from the desk. "That's all she wrote." She plucked out the flash drive with the salvaged data and wiped the old terminal.

"Great let's go–." I stopped beside the Fireman, who knelt next to the bed beside the wall. "What is it?"

He held a finger up to his mask where his mouth would have been. Then, inching towards the bed, he grabbed the blanket and peeled it back. Beneath the bed frame, a curly-haired little girl stared up at us, clutching a teddy bear in her arms.

The Fireman shed his gloves and fished out a saltwater taffy from his pocket with scarred pink digits. A muffled syllable hummed through his mask as he offered it to the girl with an upright palm. She took it, unwrapped it, and cautiously bit into it.

I knelt to her level. "Hey. You got a name, kid?"

She chewed on the taffy for a minute before finally squeaking out, "Libby."

Jack offered her his hand, and the girl crawled out from under the bed to take it – leaving her bear behind. She stared at his mask and grabbed his face to look at it more closely. Her hand found a small rocker switch, flipping it on and off.

"Your voice box is broken." Libby wrenched off the piece of his mask and wandered off to a red tool bench. She pulled out a box of gas masks and hoses from the bottom drawer and dug out an identical piece. Returning, she replaced it on the Fireman's mask and flicked the switch, illuminating a dim red LED.

The Fireman tapped on the replacement and bowed his head. His warm gritty voice piped out through the static, "Thank you, Libby." He stood and patted her on the head like she was a fragile animal.

"Where's Mommy?" The little girl asked.

Everything felt disgusting. It'd been a long time since I'd dealt with children. "Your- uh- mom is g-. Well, she's uh- she's away right now, and we don't know when she's coming back." Her eyes began to water. "But don't worry! We'll find her. Together." I felt an almost judging stare from Jack.

"Okay." Libby whispered.

"Yeah," I put on my best smile, "you'll come with us." Then I remembered the bodies outside. "Listen. It's really scary outside. Understand?"

Libby nodded.

"But my friend here, Jack. He'll keep you safe from the scary things. I just need you to trust him and close your eyes until all the scary things are gone. Just think of it like a game."

"Okay." She let the Fireman pick her up and buried her face in his shoulder as he carried her outside past the carnage.

We took a step back, a big step. Then, I remembered something my father used to say about criminals in those old television plays, "They always return to the scene of the crime." I placed my bet on those words, and we repositioned ourselves just over the crest of one of the nearby hills to watch.

Rob rolled out a tattered blanket and laid down with his rifle near the top of the hill. He watched the horizon with his scope while I used a pair of binoculars. We didn't want to risk letting Miri's drone give our presence away.

Jack, of all people, took charge of the girl. He split his rations with her and saw to the mending of her clothes with a rusted mint tin of sewing gear he'd pulled from his pack. She didn't talk much, which was well with the rest of us.

Rob was the first to say anything. "So. What's with the little sh—?"

The Fireman covered the girl's ears, almost pre-cognitively.

"This ain't exactly the fuckin' babysitter's club."

"Well," I reached for my cigarettes, "I guess we'll drop her off with the Khakis or the Battalion when we get the chance." My fingers found the bundle at the bottom of my pocket, tied together like a little alabaster bouquet. The fleeting memory of flowers being tossed at my feet was squashed by the realization that my box of matches was gone. "Dammit. Any of you got a light?"

Miri muttered something about not touching anything. Rob shrugged.

I crouched away from my spot and rummaged through the bag of scrap. It didn't take long to find the clover leaf zippo. The wheel spun and sparked, but no flame came. Jack set his hand on my shoulder. It spooked me. I knew it was him, but the weight reminded me of the tall bald man I once shared the stage with. He took the zippo and dismantled it. After replacing the stump wick, he filled the reservoir with a little fuel from the gas can.

I took the lighter back, and in three strokes of the wheel, a smoky flame glowed to life. It lit my cigarette pretty quickly. The faint smell of gas followed the cool sensation that flooded my lungs. The smoke fell from my mouth and nostrils, masking the Fireman in a white haze. "Thanks."

Jack bowed his head a little and went back to caring for Libby.

A day passed before we heard a revving engine close in below. Jack watched alongside Rob and I through a spyglass. "Dragoons."

Rob grumbled. "As in the cultist biker gang? Oh great, just peachy."

"Hang on." I focused my binoculars. "It's just one."

"A scout?" Miri asked.

The rider rode right into the middle of the town, dismounted his bike, and looked around with his hands behind his shaking head. Something's wrong, I thought. The lone rider fell to his knees and slammed his fists on the ground. We all heard him howl despite the winds picking up.

I pat Rob on the back. "Incapacitate him. Let's see what he knows."

Rob followed my command and fired a single shot. The echoing crack of the bullet breaking the sound barrier followed the deafening boom. Fractions of a moment passed before the lone rider's exposed calf sprayed red. Despite his injury, he hobbled toward his bike.

"Shit," I cursed, "he's getting away!"

Jack lunged down the hill and booked it for the depot. He wasn't the fastest runner I'd seen but he managed to catch up with the rider and tackle him off his bike before he could take off. We drove down to meet them – keeping Libby hidden in the back seat beneath a blanket.

The rider wasn't much help. He spoke a bastardized mexlish that I could barely make out, but the Fireman translated. He rambled on about a king, nine sons, and the harvest. The only thing that made sense to me was, "They're coming."

The man was bleeding out, the color already gone from his face —he grinned reaching into his denim vest. Jack snatched his wrist and pulled it back. The rider's fist clenched around a thin scrap of paper. His eyes glassed over, and he lay dead.

Jack peeled the paper from the corpse's grasp.

I could see it was printed with columns of text with a few lines circled in red. "What's it say?"

The Fireman followed the encircled words with his finger. "Even as I have seen, they that plow iniquity, and sow wickedness, reap the same." He carefully folded the paper, held it close to his mask for a moment, and whispered something before gently tucking it in his pocket. He rolled the rider over. The patch on the back of his vest displayed a green dragon coiled around a roaring tiger. Jack ripped the patch off and left us the rest of the loot.

We went back to our hiding spot over the hill crest to convene with the Director on the matter. Rob left to hunt with Miri while Jack showed Libby how to set up camp. I watched the two as I tuned my HAM radio.

"Rothman? You there? Over."

The signal was much clearer up here. "Connie, Connie. Are you there? Over."

"I read you loud and clear, Rothman. Honey pot was empty. Scraped clean by suspect wasps on two wheels. Maybe a whole nest nearby. Over."

"Suspect? Over."

"Um-. Most likely. Over."

"Maybe the roosters can pick off these wasps. Light your lamp for the stork to pick up the grocery list. Out."

I tossed the handset onto the dash and switched off the radio. One look outside lightened the situation. The tent Libby struggled to set up collapsed on her, and she screamed. My worry passed as the Fireman plucked her out of the mess of tarps, revealing an ear-to-ear grin. Jack's shoulders began to bounce. The wagon's windows muffled the sound, but I was sure he was laughing.

Dusk approached along with the hunting party. Rob carried his kills over his shoulders as Miri frolicked in the buff. Her legs moved kinda funny and Rob kept kicking her away as she got close.

I threw a poncho at Miri, gesturing to Libby. "Your fly is down, Rob."

"Oh, shit." He zipped it up and scowled at me. "Since when the hell did you become such a prude?"

"What'd you catch besides Miri?"

"Fuck you." He threw down two rabbits and a coyote near the fresh campfire. Jack picked up the latter creature to inspect it.

His voice box crackled over his distaste. "Why?"

"The little bastard was trying to take my rabbits. Can you skin?"

"Well enough."

Rob cleaned the rabbits in his usual rough manner, but Jack took a strange care with the coyote. Libby and I put a stew together while he made an impromptu tanning rack beside the fire. Rob offered up his butchered rabbit pelts, and the Fireman did as well as he could with them.

Before eating his share with Libby, he took her hands in his and said, "God, thank you for the life thou has given us. We thank you and thine creations for these foods and materials. May they preserve us ever onward into thine will, thy way. Amen."

Miri passed a questioning look between Rob and me. "Who's he talking to?"

"Doesn't matter." Rob shook his head, but I could see he was scowling into the fire, unblinking.

"Okay." I stepped over to the wagon and switched on the beacon for the Director's drone to find us. "Miri, you got the records from the terminal?"

She popped open her pelican case and tossed me the thumb drive with the recovered data. "I was looking through some of it. Kinda funny."

"What was funny?" I asked.

Miri gnawed at a coyote bone. "Something about a deal with the bikers."

"Deal went south, real fast." Rob chuckled.

"Maybe." Miri spits out a splinter of bone. "But-. Eh. Never-mind. Director man gets his data, and we get our pay."

"Right." I stood near the fire, avoiding their expectant stares. "Once the drone gets the data, we're gonna radio for Civil Defense."

Rob choked on a piece of stringy rabbit. "Woah. Are you out of your goddamned mind? What the hell are we getting Khakis involved for?"

"Director's orders. He figures that CD can help us deal with the Dragoons. The way I see it – we pose as traders returning to check on an investment, let them do most of the work, and walk away with our pay."

"You're gonna catch the bad guys?"

The question came from Libby. Jack looked at me, but I couldn't see what he might be thinking, just the flickering reflections of the campfire.

I wanted to laugh. "Sure, kid."

The drone came and went with the data. I hailed the Civil Defense emergency station and by morning a squad of nine Khakis arrived at the edge of town. I introduced us with the story I'd come up with last night. "They were our friends too. If you don't mind, we'd like to stick with you and catch the monsters that did this."

Their leader, a brunette woman named Ford, shook her head. "In all honesty, I'd rather you not. But as we are thin in numbers on investigations, I'll take all the help I can get."

"Well, Rob, back there is one of our best hunters. Good with a rifle. Criminals can't be too different from game, can they?"

Ford hushed a chuckle, resting a hand on the revolver at her hip. "Wild animals don't normally shoot back." She eyed the Fireman and Libby. "What about them?"

I lowered my voice, "Jackson is our guard. He's got a breathing condition. Kinda sensitive about it. He's been looking after that girl, Libby. She was the only survivor. Think you can find her a home after all this is over?"

"I'm afraid not." Ford peeled off her silver aviators and waved at Libby, but the girl hid behind Jack. "Being as we are thin in numbers. I'm afraid *we* can't look after her. Don't know about any other families that know her. Most of the people working this place were refugees from the Big Bear fires. Besides, looks like your friend is doing a good enough job as is."

I looked back and saw Libby squeezing a few of Jack's fingers with her little hand. "I suppose so."

Ford looked over the dead rider and his motorcycle. "This the one your friend pulled that Dragoon patch off of?"

"Yeah. He attacked us while we were looking for survivors."

She peeled open the rider's vest and found the word "explorador" written inside. "Damn. They're probably expecting this guy back, and they'll eventually figure out he's not coming. Last we heard over the radio; the Dragoons were in Hemet. That might buy us some time to prepare our defenses. But!" She pointed her finger in my face. "I want to try and talk with them first. See if we can negotiate. If not? I guess anything goes."

"Understood, ma'am."

Ford sighed. "Damn, I wish Roberts was here. He was a hell of a lot better at this shit than I was."

I offered her a cigarette. She took it, and we both shared a light.

We started the walk back to our camp over the hill. Rob and I continued to have a laugh at Miri's expense. She complained about her clothes and how I introduced her as a celibate nun. "You bitch! Got me itching in more ways than one. My body can't breathe in this suffocating blanket robe. And what? I'm just supposed to ignore the fresh meat down the hill?"

Libby tugged on the Fireman's arm. "Are you gonna show me the flower?"

"What is that kid yapping about?" Miri whined.

"Jack?" I asked.

The little girl ran up to me and hugged my hand with hers. "He said he could make flowers."

A chill ran up my arm from her touch. "There haven't been any flowers in years."

We all gathered around the campsite to see how Jack was going to make these "flowers". He took the paper he pulled from the rider and ripped it into a square before folding it into increasingly more acute angles. The process reminded me of how my cousin folded paper into cranes.

Popping the structure into a square cone, he lifted up the four flaps from the sides. He took a cartridge from his rifle and used it to roll out each flap into petals. It looked like a lily. I almost believed it when he twirled it, but Jack wasn't done.

He borrowed a vial of Miri's least offensive perfume and spritzed a small amount into the top of the lily before handing it to Libby. Her little face lit up at the sight. A hum escaped her lips as she caught a whiff of the flower's aroma.

"It's beautiful!" She stood and ran to us all, offering up the flower for us to behold. Miri nodded in indifference. Rob at least smiled and joked about Chanel having their own breed of flora. Libby brought it to me.

Its rigidity disappointed me, so I smiled politely and quickly returned it to the girl. In her hands at the mercy of her admiration, the suspension of disbelief crept back over me.

The day waned, and the sun set with no sign of the Dragoons yet.

That experience with the paper flower left me tired. Laziness set in and I put off making my bed, instead opting to sleep in the wagon with the seat laid back. Big mistake. Cars turned into ice boxes at night. I couldn't sleep. I tried rolling around to find the least cold spot, but nothing worked. At this time, a set of light footsteps approached.

I nearly pulled my gun on Libby as she knocked on the glass. After gathering my nerves, I cracked the door open. "Yes? What do you want?"

She offered up a fleece blanket. "Here. I have another."

The early morning chat was grim.

"Decapitation. That is the way to go." Rob flourished his hands. "Instant death! And none of this dying at a ripe old age bullshit. I want to go out standing tall on my own two feet. Like a man."

Miri faked a gag. "Like a man. You're so full of it."

"What about you? Huh? How do you want to go out?"

She shivered. "Not slow. I hope it's quick. I'd rather take myself out than..." She didn't finish the thought.

I looked to the Fireman, who was busy keeping Libby from hearing. "What about you? Jack?"

While Libby packed her little bed roll and tent, he joined us for breakfast. His breathy voice crackled through the voice box. "Either way, I'm prepared to die." He slurped up the mashed ration I handed him through an intake tube on his mask.

Rob blew half-drunken raspberries. "Bull. Shit."

Jack's gaze fell to the dim embers of the fire leftover from the previous night. "I know exactly what's waiting for me on the other side, and I accept the consequences of my actions."

A moment of silence swallowed us. None spoke for a time until the Fireman looked at me. "And you?"

When he asked me that, I felt like crying. It wasn't mean, cruel, or awful. He spoke with the same sincerity he used with Libby. For a moment, I remembered my parents. Wiping the corners of my eyes to keep them dry, I shrugged. "I don't know." Pulling out my cigarettes and the cloverleaf lighter, I moved to the other side of the wagon for a private smoke.

My mask slipped.

I lit the first cigarette, looked up to the stars fading in the morning, and remembered a time when you could hardly see any. The cigarette burned halfway without touching my lips. I tossed it and grabbed another. Flicking the lighter open again, I lit the end until it glowed like its own star. My parched lips reached for it, but my hand wouldn't move. I let the light fall from my fingers, and I stamped it out in the dirt.

"You alright?"

I didn't jump at the Fireman's voice. He reached up to my face and brushed away a cold tear.

"I understand."

I cursed those words. They sounded like something the bald man would say. Intrusive thoughts, memories maybe, told me to fall into him. I imagined he'd wrap his arms around me. I'd bury my face in his jacket, smother away the sobs that sought escape. Instead, I buried that little kid, reaching for my father's hand that was never there, and I could do it again.

The weight of the Fireman's hand patting me on the shoulder transported me. I could see the stage again. My glossy black shoes and red dress glowed in the spotlight. The kind man with no hair smiled at me, always showing more kindness than my actual parents ever afforded to me. The theater burned down long ago, but in that moment, I felt the warmth of the cheering audience.

Like my father once said, the show must go on.

I stepped away, wiping my nose and eyes. "Nobody likes thinking about dying." I said. "Heavy shit, that."

The Fireman nodded and took his leave. I stayed behind the wagon to bring back that mask, to hide the scared little girl from the others. I didn't want her getting in the way.

Ford and her partners called us in. Rob fell in with the other rifleman on the crest. Miri sat back to look after Libby and offered air support with her drone if needed. Jack and I joined Ford. He helped Ford wrap up the body of the lone rider to offer the Dragoons as an offering of good intention.

Though, it was lost on me how a corpse could be seen as a good intention.

I heard the Dragoons before I ever saw them. Their bikes' engines roared like their namesake. A streak of black and chrome crossed the horizon. A rippling dust cloud tailed them, and as they got closer, their goggles shimmered in the midday sun. There must have been at least forty of them that rolled up on us.

Ford stood with Jack at the entrance to the town. She readied a megaphone pulled from the depot while the Fireman watched over the lone rider's body.

"Halt!" Ford's amplified voice was just loud enough to convince the swarm of riders to kill their engines. Little by little, the dust began to settle around them.

They all straddled chopper-style frames with mismatched brands and parts. Men and women dismounted their bikes, covering their mouths as they gawked at the charred, body-littered town. Some howled—others growled at the sight. Their leader wiped tears from his eyes.

"What have you done?!" His long goatee beard hung over a medieval chest-plate. His long curly, and wind-blasted hair shook in the settling breeze. "What did you do to our brothers and sisters?! You dog-killing bastards!"

"This wasn't us!" I could see Ford's knuckles turn white around the megaphone from my position. She cleared her throat. "Where's the gas from the depot?"

"Gas?" The leader shook his head. "That's all you care about?"

Ford put down the megaphone and held up her hands. "Jackson. Give them their man."

He lifted the corpse wrapped in white and carefully marched it to the bikers. A few rushed to receive the body, peeling open the face cover and mourning at the sight. One woman cried, "Sonny? My Sonny!"

I thought for sure we were in for hell.

The Fireman's head remained bowed until this point. His masked face looked up from under the brim of his hat at the leader. "Please, don't."

The leader pulled a Viking sword from his back and brought it within inches of Jack's neck. "You left a long time ago, pale rider. You have no say in this!"

Jack nodded. "Alright." Before he walked away, he looked back over his shoulder. "Not all the Dragoons will die." He pushed Ford on the way back. "Take cover."

Shots popped off from the Dragoons, nearly hitting Ford and Jack's feet. They ran to cover. As they did, a cluster of the choppers roared back to life, ripping through the streets. I followed the Fireman's lead, picking off riders as soon as they entered my Beretta's sights. I peeked out in time to see the rest scatter, leaving their bikes to rush between the buildings.

A mechanical buzz wooshed overhead, Miri's drone. I filtered through her wave of instructions over my handheld radio, waiting for my name as I kept my eyes peeled.

"Jack, contact right. Ford, contact left." Miri coordinated all the Khakis through the maze of chaos. "Connie, contact left."

I faced left and double tapped the rider stepping around the building. Then I crouched and peeked around the next corner, laying down fire. The two in my sights collapsed, and I returned to my cover. I cleared my way to the edge of the buildings with the help of Miri's eye in the sky. At the edge I took shots at all the riders between the gaps. One of my father's expressions, "like shooting fish in a barrel," suddenly made sense.

Rob and the other rifleman slowed as the Dragoons caught on to their position. "They're dodging us, but we got our sights on 'em."

"I got eyes-. Wait- no!"

I looked up in time to see a stream of flames and sparks obliterate the drone. "What the hell was that?"

Ford's voice crackled over the radio. "Dragon's breath, incendiary shotgun shells."

The town began to burn once more as the Dragoons unleashed hellfire at every turn. I continued my tactic and circled the perimeter. Though the flames warped the silhouettes of my targets, I managed to get clean shots. I almost shot one of the Khakis, but the moment we stopped to recognize each other, a stream of lead ripped through his torso.

A gunshot hit the building to my left. I caught a glimpse of my assailants before booking it forward into the fiery maze. I stumbled upon two riders and emptied my Beretta until the slide locked back. Dropping my empty mag, I reloaded behind the next building and kept moving.

I tripped over two of the dead Khaki's and found myself at the mercy of three riders. Two of their chests blew open, and the scalp of the third's popped off. Ford stepped out with her big smoking revolver. She picked me up but screamed as a bullet cut through her side.

We ducked behind cover. Ford cursed as she pressed a bandana into her wound. "Drag me!" She barked. Her arm coiled over my neck and shoulder like a constrictor. I breathed deeply and did as she said. She shot behind while I fired forward. A stray bullet pierced my leg. I fell with Ford.

"I'm out," called the rifleman over the radio, "and Rob's rifle is jammed."

Rob muttered, "Piece of shit, mother f–." The signal cut out.

Ford grumbled, "My gun's empty."

I didn't dare check mine, but I could feel my pistol was light enough to know we were running out. Footsteps sent an extra dose of adrenaline through my body. My sights found their mark, but my finger found the discipline to hold back at the sight of Jack's glass-covered eyes. He pushed my pistol down and readied his rifle.

"Protect each other."

He walked out onto the main road, a slight buzz following overhead.

Miri piped up. "Backup drone is flying. Junior needed a charge."

"How many left?" I squawked through my radio.

"A couple of stragglers, one on the main road."

The Fireman shouldered his rifle, bringing his aim at the last Dragoon standing, the leader with a cracked open sawn off and his blade. Jack's gun clicked. Empty. He tossed it to the side and took a new stance, like a crouching tiger. His left hand gripped his scabbard while his right curled around his sword's handle.

The leader ripped off his bullet-torn chest-plate. His torso ran red, but he still stood. He dropped the shotgun, pulled out a syringe, and stabbed it into his chest. Howling erupted from his mouth, his hands ripped the clothes from his back.

The man brandished his sword, pounding his chest like a gorilla. His yellow-eyed gaze turned venomous. "Demon! Coward." His final word hissed through his teeth before he charged the Fireman.

Jack's sword didn't leave its sheath until the Dragoon leader was right on top of him. He strafed left, spun one-eighty, and snapped his blade upward. The Fireman abandoned his fighting stance, flicking crimson from his sword. He wiped the rest off on his sleeve and walked away.

The leader split in two – spilling his entrails onto the ground between his legs.

A shot from above ripped through another Dragoon, sneaking up on Jack. Rob chimed in over the radio. He'd cleared the jam in his rifle. From the ground, I got a clear shot at the last one, running away. I shot him in the back, and the fight came to a close.

Ford and her rifleman remained the last of their group. Though, I wasn't sure how long she'd last either. We helped gather all the bodies from the town and built a pyre before they left. They took one bike and let us pick through the rest. We siphoned the gas out of most, but Jack kept the leader's full.

After stripping the animal skulls and odd decorations, he tuned it to his liking. He rode with Libby clinging to his back with her new coyote-faced hood. He followed us to our rendezvous, the edge of the Los Angeles wastes. No one traveled near there, leaving it the perfect place to hide while everything cooled down.

I fell asleep by our little fire, watching as Jack sewed a Dragoon patch onto the back of his jacket. Visions of the theater, lights, and the crowd cheering filled my dreams.

Nine-year-old me stepped out onto the stage. Her growth spurt hadn't robbed her of her best role, the red-headed little orphan. She stepped forward to catch the flowers tossed at her feet but frowned at their hard and folded corners. Their petals smelled of death.

Little me gazed over her shoulder. Libby took the stage in her own little red dress. Jack stood beside her, tux, tails, gas mask, and all. My father's words came in his voice, "You are here as a result of your choices."

Libby turned from the blazing stage lights to cling to Jack, but she turned to ashes in his arms. His attire tore at the seams, falling from his shoulders, revealing his tattered skin. His mask's eyes burned with flaming light, glaring into my soul.

My own voice echoed in my head, "What are you? Angel? Demon? What gives you the right to exist?!" I didn't know who I was talking to.

Morning came faster than I thought it would, waking me with the smells of the rations that Libby helped Rob prepare. Jack was waiting for me so he could pack up the last bedroll. Shaking my boots out and pulling them on, I left him to it.

"You know what today is right?" Rob's face was overtaken by an ear to ear grin.

Miri passed him a steaming mug. "Payday. Made coffee to celebrate."

Rob briefly sipped on the brown concoction before spewing it out all over Miri.

"Damn, tastes like the ass end of a cow!!" He kept drinking it. "Sorry. Not sorry. I can't drink this crap."

Miri grabbed the mug from his grasp and poured its contents into his crotch.

"You bitch!"

"Oh darling," she cackled as he screamed, fell over, and struggled to pull down his pants. "I might actually miss you if you get yourself killed, Bobby. Of all the mountains I've climbed, yours was the most bearable."

Rob gasped in relief as he buried his nether regions in the cool morning earth. "Screw. You."

I let the two have at each other while I helped Libby scoop up her breakfast. "Are we not going to see each other after today?" she asked.

"Maybe. Someday. I imagine Jack will take you to a real home. Are you gonna miss us?"

"Yeah." A grin spread across her face. "I always wanted a sister." She scampered off with her food to go watch Jack pack while she ate.

I meandered over to the wagon and switched on the HAM radio. The signal was weak, but I did my best to filter out the static.

"T… f… ca… K…"

Rob leaned over me as he buckled his pants together. "The director?"

"Trying here, hold on."

The static finally cleaned up, "Connie, Connie. Are you there?"

"Chrome dome and I read you loud and clear, Rothman. What's next for us, over?"

After a minute of silence, the codger's voice returned. "One final job before your payout. The time has come to tie up loose ends. No attachments. Remember? Your last job is to take care of the Fireman."

My heart sank, and suddenly I struggled to breathe. I looked over at Jack and Libby. He unveiled a small wooden horse he'd finished carving for her.

"We've decided he's too much trouble unattended. Do what you have to do. Over."

Rob ripped the mic from my hand. "Yessiree. We'll get it done. Over." Tossing it back into the wagon, he rubbed his hands together. "You know what this means, right Connie? More pay for the rest of us."

"What about Libby?" I almost begged under my breath.

He shrugged. "What about her? We'll throw the little bitch into one of the Battalion's foster ranches if it makes you feel better."

"What's going on?" Miri nibbled on a scrap of human jerky.

"It's time for another pay increase." Rob grinned.

Miri's eyes turned glassy as she stared off into the distance away from us. "Who's gonna do it?"

"W–." I wanted to say something, anything. Somewhere there was a line I knew that could have stopped this, but fright hid it away.

Rob looked between the two of us and groaned. "Fine. I'll do it. Bunch of pussies, all of you." He yanked his rifle from the wagon and into his shoulder. He switched off the safety and aimed for the Fireman.

"Jack!" Libby jumped up in front of him, her scream suppressed by the boom of the shot.

Rob was too slow to charge the bolt before the Fireman lunged at him with a bowie knife and hacked off his trigger hand. Blood sprayed and gurgled from the boney stump. "Oh, God!" Rob cried as he toppled to the floor, bawling his eyes out as he bled.

My hand immediately found the grip of my pistol, but it never left the holster. I couldn't move. My limbs locked in place, despite the clear opportunity and line of sight. Cold ran down my spine. The old terror of stage fright held me in its clutches.

Rob reached for his gun, using his twitchy robotic hand to hoist it up. An empty click mocked him as the Fireman ripped the rifle from his grasp and swung it down on his ankles. Miri expelled her stomach at the audible crack and scrambled to hide behind the wagon

Jack grabbed Rob's bionic arm with both hands, ripped it from its socket, and beat the now armless mass that dared in vain to crawl away with a stump wrist. The Fireman's boot pinned him down. He carved a slit down Rob's back with the knife, dug his fingers in, and ripped out his spine – silencing Rob once and for all.

Miri shrieked at the display, breaking down into a slobbery mess of snot and tears. When Jack glanced her way, she drew a pistol, shoved its barrel into her mouth, and squeezed the trigger. Her face disappeared behind the blood that splattered the wagon's window.

Jack turned and ran to Libby's side, cradling her. He pressed his hand over the wound in her shoulder where her arm hung limp by a few torn tendons. Tears rolled down her paling cheeks.

"D-. Ja-. It's... cold."

Lifting his hand from the wound, he immediately pressed it back down over the consequential scarlett geyser. "Sh, sh, sh. It's okay. Everything is gonna be alright."

"Why am I tired?"

"Don't worry." Jack pulled her closer, pressing his mask to her face. "You're going to sleep. You're going to sleep for a long while. And when you wake up, everything will be fine."

"Okay." Libby's breaths turned coarse. Her chest struggled to hold it in. "How long?"

Jack's voice cracked. "W-what?"

"How long will I sleep?"

He shook his head. "I don't know. But. I promise you, I'll be waiting for you when you wake up."

"Promise?"

"Pinky promise."

"Can-? Can you-?"

"Yes?"

Red infected her smile. "Mom always sang me a lullaby before bedtime."

He stammered over his words until he finally admitted, "I don't remember any."

"Any song is fine."

I couldn't turn away from her heavy eyes as Jack cleared his throat. "Okay. There is one song I know that you might like." It felt like forever, waiting for him to start. The words finally came to him. "The sun'll come out... Tomorrow."

My heart dropped like an anchor in my chest as his spoken verse evolved into music that I knew. I saw myself in Libby, all those years ago when I played the little red-headed orphan girl.

Jack's voice struggled through the chorus, the lenses of his mask fogging up. "...I love you, tomorrow. You're always," Libby's body went limp in his arms, her eyes glassed over, "a day... a... way–." Static sobs dripped from his voice box, pooling into whimpering cries of anguish. He knelt over the girl as though in prayer. His blood-stained fingers dug into the earth.

My heart exploded when he turned to face me. The tint of his mask's eyes shone red. His chest swelled with rabid breath, and he stood – somehow taller than before. I clenched my eyes shut. The scared little girl inside came back.

The wind around us picked up. Under it, Jack's footsteps crept toward me. His breath escaped through the valves of his mask and brushed my face. He softly pried my hand from my Beretta, took it from its holster, and walked away.

When I finally opened my eyes, he'd gone. I was alone with Rob and Miri's corpses. The only evidence of Libby was a wet patch of red earth.

I jumped at the radio that came back to life.

"Connie, Connie. Do you copy?" Rothman casually checked in as he always had. "If you're still there, I have another job for you whenever–."

I ripped the radio from the wagon and threw it on the ground. Grabbing Rob's rifle I bashed it in. Plastic, metal, and wires flew around my feet with every hit. I struck it until it sank into the ground until I was too tired to stand. The wind did the rest, burying it with dust.

I fell beside the wagon, winded and faint. I peeled my sweat-ridden cigarettes from my pocket. None of them lit, and the clover-leaf zippo ran out of fuel.

Sleep took over.

The revving of the motorcycle woke me. I reached for the silhouette riding off across the horizon, but it disappeared in a mirage – leaving me with the aftermath of my former colleagues. Some of Jack's footprints were still fresh enough for me to follow. Not far, over the next ridge, I found a little hill with a cross at the head of a small grave. All around it was little paper lilies.

The faux bed of flowers radiated with a sweet aroma. Their illusion took me back to the days before the curtain fell on the old world. I understood then that Jack remembered those years, perhaps as vividly as I did. Though, he'd gone his own way. I wish I'd gone after him, but the winds of the wastes washed away his bike's tracks.

There's no place for me now that the Director's after me for jumping ship, abandoning script. It's too late to go back now and fix any of it. My father used to say, "What's done is done." I've never gone back to that place, but if you're ever at the edge of the Los Angeles wastes, maybe you'll still find the little cross grave marker with little paper flowers burning up from the inside out beneath the spotlight of the unyielding sun.

ABOUT A.M. STEVENS

I am a twenty five year old writer from southern California. I got my start in writing early on crafting scripts for film and theatre throughout High School and College. My father filled my head with the pulp fiction scifi-fantasy adventures of his youth, while my theatrical mother gifted me with a voice, and their influences combined fueled my path to becoming a writer.

www.ingramcontent.com/pod-product-compliance
Lightning Source LLC
Chambersburg PA
CBHW051535260626
47170CB00003B/945